LORD LANGDON'S KISS

"I cannot wonder at Darcy's interest in you, either," James said, lowering his voice slightly. "You have made conquests of everyone at Charlwood."

Again, Nell struggled with her disbelief. How could a few conversations with his dependents have caused such a complete reversal in his attitude?

Aware that he was watching her intently, she answered, "I am honored that you should think so, my lord, but surely you exaggerate. Perhaps I should be looking at the list now?"

She moved toward the desk, expecting him to step aside. He did not, however, and so she found herself standing very close to him, acutely conscious of his height and breadth as he blocked her way.

"Perhaps I should have said you have made conquests of *everyone* at Charlwood, Miss Ashley, including its master." His voice was low and resonant, and she was transfixed by the sound.

He took a step toward her and put an arm around her waist, pulling her toward him. With his other hand, he lifted her chin and looked intently at her face. She stared back, paralyzed with shock.

"Ah, you do not protest, I see," he said softly. Was it triumph or disappointment she heard in his voice?

She tried to answer, but it was too late. He slid his hand around to the back of her neck, pulled her face toward his, and kissed her. . . .

BOOK YOUR PLACE ON OUR WEBSITE AND MAKE THE READING CONNECTION!

We've created a customized website just for our very special readers, where you can get the inside scoop on everything that's going on with Zebra, Pinnacle and Kensington books.

When you come online, you'll have the exciting opportunity to:

- View covers of upcoming books
- Read sample chapters
- Learn about our future publishing schedule (listed by publication month *and author*)
- Find out when your favorite authors will be visiting a city near you
- Search for and order backlist books from our online catalog
- Check out author bios and background information
- Send e-mail to your favorite authors
- Meet the Kensington staff online
- Join us in weekly chats with authors, readers and other guests
- Get writing guidelines
- AND MUCH MORE!

**Visit our website at
http://www.zebrabooks.com**

LORD LANGDON'S KISS

Elena Greene

Zebra Books
Kensington Publishing Corp.
http://www.zebrabooks.com

ZEBRA BOOKS are published by

Kensington Publishing Corp.
850 Third Avenue
New York, NY 10022

First Printing: April, 2000
10 9 8 7 6 5 4 3 2 1

Printed in the United States of America

To my husband, Richard, who inspires my writing
and does the laundry, too.

One

"Damn James! He has stayed away for five years. Why did he have to hurry back now and ruin everything?"

Nell Ashley winced at her companion's words, but after one look at him she decided that it would be neither sensible nor kind to protest. The Honorable Darcy Mayland's blue eyes sparkled with anger, and a scowl had replaced his usual smile.

"Perhaps he has remembered his obligations *here*," she said, trying to speak mildly although she did not believe her own words.

"You mustn't cherish false hopes," he said, brushing a curling lock of golden hair from his forehead. "My dear brother thought little enough of such things all the while he was having all sorts of great adventures on the Peninsula. If he did, he would have returned two years ago."

He paused. Nell kept a sympathetic silence as they walked through the rose garden, even as she tried to hide her dismay at the unhappy turn their conversation had taken. She had expected something quite different when his stepmother, Lady Langdon, had relaxed her chaperonage so far as to suggest that she and Darcy go for a stroll alone through the grounds at Charlwood, the ancestral home of Darcy and his older brother, the fifth Earl of Langdon.

Her pulse had been jumping ever since Darcy had taken her arm in his and they had stepped out onto the terrace. But then she had foolishly made some random remark about Lord Langdon's homecoming and triggered Darcy's outburst. Now she had to calm herself, for he was clearly in need of an understanding confidante—a role she was well used to playing.

"No, more likely he just thinks there's no glory in staying in the military during peacetime," Darcy continued. "He can't ride roughshod over any more Frenchmen, so he must content himself with his own family." He laughed, but the sound was harsh and discordant in the quiet garden.

"I know how much you wished to follow your brother into the army. Believe me, *I* at least know it was no lack of courage that kept you from doing so."

"No, it was my purse-pinching brother who wouldn't purchase me a commission when it was of all things what I most wanted. But it is ever so—he cares for no one but himself!"

"I am sorry. You have not spoken to him about the cottages then?"

"No, I did not."

She felt his arm tense under hers. She bit her lip, wishing she had never brought up the subject of the earl and his iniquities.

"Please forgive me. I did not mean to press you. No doubt you and your brother had many other things to speak of last night."

"Forgive me instead," he said, giving her arm a little squeeze. *"You* do not deserve to bear the brunt of my bad temper. It's just that all James did last evening was lecture Lady Langdon and myself about our extravagance and wastefulness."

"How could he behave so unfeelingly on the very evening of his return?" she asked. But she didn't expect an answer. Anything was possible from one who had shown such callous disregard for the well-being of his family and dependents.

Nell could only guess at Darcy's feelings on being reunited with Lord Langdon. It had been a mere few weeks since they had received word of victory at the Battle of Toulouse and of Napoleon's abdication. She remembered how relieved Darcy had looked upon seeing that the earl's name was not among those who had fallen in the last battle. It was then that she had known for certain that, beneath his resentment, Darcy still cared for his brother. Her heart ached for him. She had always longed for a younger brother or sister of her own. She would never have treated them as Lord Langdon had treated Darcy.

"I suppose it was hardly the moment to apply to your brother to spend more money on the estate," she continued regretfully. "But I do hope you will still try to speak to him. The hovels some of your laborers are living in are not fit for pigs! And many of the pensioners are suffering needlessly from illnesses that could be prevented, or at least eased, by a few simple comforts. And there really ought to be a village school to—"

She stopped, fearing she had said too much. "I am sorry. You must be tired of hearing me on this subject by now." She was torn between hope that Darcy shared her concern and fear that he, like most of the local gentry, would laugh at her for her obsession with the poor of the parish. But in the past month, since Darcy had returned to Charlwood and they had become reacquainted, he had shown nothing but sympathy for her concerns and a ready kindness toward his family's dependents. Nor did he disappoint her now.

"I could never tire of listening to you. And you are right about the estate. I will talk to James, but I warn you: It may not do any good."

"I will always admire you for having tried and for wishing to do what is right," she said and promptly blushed. He must think she sounded hopelessly moralistic.

But then he rewarded her with one of his dazzling smiles. It was as if Michelangelo's *David* had come to life and beamed down at her.

"To have your good opinion means a great deal to me, dearest Helen. You do not mind if I dispense with 'Miss Ashley,' do you?"

"No, not at all. But please call me Nell." Although they had played together as children in a dimly remembered past, she wouldn't have expected Darcy, an earl's son, to be so eager to abandon formality now. She was glad of it. But even as she smiled at the thought, a slight chill crept over her despite the warm May sunshine. She wondered whether Lord Langdon would view things the same way. For all she knew, he might regard her as a mere countrified nobody totally unworthy of his younger brother.

Darcy must have seen the worry in her face. "What is wrong, dear Nell?" he asked.

She was moved by his perceptiveness, but how could she answer? How could she say that she feared that Lord Langdon would part them when Darcy had not yet declared his feelings for her? "Nothing really," she said after a pause.

"But I am sure there is something wrong—I see it in your face. I hope it is not anything I have said or done. If so, I shall be obliged to shoot myself!" he said theatrically.

She had to laugh, but then she shook her head. "If you must know, I am a trifle concerned that Lord Langdon may not approve of our . . . friendship."

"And what if I were to tell you I don't care a snap of my fingers for what James does or does not approve of? Anyway, I don't want to think about him anymore. Shall we talk of something more pleasant? The rose-garden is coming along well, is it not?"

"Indeed it is," she said, looking about her. Weeks of vigorous pruning and weeding had done much to begin reversing the neglect caused by the sixteen years that the Maylands had not been in residence at Charlwood. A multitude of buds promised a splendid show of blooms in less than a month's time. Better yet, the task had provided some much needed employment to the sons of some of the needier families in the parish.

Just a few days previously, all this would have given her great satisfaction. Now all she could think of was Lord Langdon's likely reaction. Although Darcy and his stepmother had been given leave to engage as many servants as necessary to make Charlwood livable again, none of them really knew whether the earl would consider the restoration of the gardens a reasonable expense.

"Shall we go down to the lake?" asked Darcy, interrupting her uneasy thoughts. "I think the ground is finally dry enough to walk about on the island."

She was sorely tempted. Darcy seemed to have gotten over

his earlier irritation, and this might be their only chance to spend some time alone together before she had to meet Lord Langdon. Perhaps Lady Langdon had had that in mind when she had suggested that they take a turn about the gardens while the earl was engaged with his steward. But she had also invited Nell to share their noonday meal, and it would not do to make a tardy appearance.

Nell looked a little doubtfully at the sun, which seemed ominously high already.

"Is there time, do you think?"

"Of course there is time," Darcy assured her and led her out of the rose garden toward the ornamental lake just visible through the stand of trees that grew just beyond.

A few bluebells still lingered under the trees, giving out a subtle, enchanting fragrance. When they came out by the lake, she saw that the rhododendrons and azaleas along its banks were bursting into bloom, reflecting splashes of brilliant color into the still waters. The end of the sinuous lake was screened by another stand of trees, giving it the impression of a river bend, and an island in the center was adorned with a miniature Greek temple.

Nell was struck afresh by the beauty of the scene. What a shame it was that Darcy had been denied the opportunity to enjoy Charlwood for all the years since his mother's death. But then, she reminded herself, it was not by choice that he was here now. Lord Langdon, while still in France, had sent orders to close the London town house, and his man of business had made certain that Darcy and Lady Langdon removed to Charlwood, with strict orders to remain there on pain of having their funds cut off.

But Nell could not be sorry for circumstances that had brought them together. Perhaps her companionship had consoled Darcy for missing his usual friends and entertainments at the height of the London Season.

"I suppose I *do* have something to be grateful to James for," he said, leading her over the stone bridge that arched over the narrow channel to the island. "If I had not been rusticating here, I would not have met *you,* beautiful Nell."

She couldn't think of a reply. How could he have read her thoughts so easily? And his compliments always left her feeling both elated and confused. She had never thought of herself as beautiful.

True, she was looking much prettier than she ever had. Her soft brown hair, with its hints of chestnut, was now cut in front so that it fell in ringlets about her face rather than pulled severely back into a knot atop her head. And her new primrose muslin gown was certainly more cheerful than the sober-colored, high-necked gowns she was used to wearing. But she knew that neither the hairstyle nor the new dress could disguise the facts that her features lacked a certain classical perfection, that her eyes were a rather ordinary hazel, and that her figure was not at all dainty. She was too tall and built more like a buxom milkmaid than a fashionably slender sylph.

If the local gossips were correct, Darcy was accustomed to flirting with all the prettiest ladies in London. She had initially resisted his advances, thinking he was just amusing himself with the best available substitute. But lately there was a look in his eye and a warmth in his voice that she was sure had little to do with mere flirtation.

Since she wasn't a true beauty, didn't his words prove that he cared for her in ways that extended far beyond the merely superficial? Moreover, Lady Langdon would not have thrown her and Darcy together in such a way if she did not think his intentions were totally honorable.

Nell felt her pulse quicken again at the thought. At nineteen, she still hoped to find a love such as her parents had shared. Yet a little doubt entwined itself about her growing anticipation. Could such perfect happiness really be in store for her?

Darcy stopped as they reached the top of the curving bridge. Turning to face her, he took her hands in his.

"You know I have had an uncommon pleasure in your company, do you not?" he asked.

She nodded, unable to answer because of the sudden lump in her throat.

"I hope I have been able to bring you some happiness as well," he said.

She looked up into his face, touched and thrilled to see that he was looking anxious himself. Her own unease lessened a little. "Of course you have," she said. Daringly, she returned the pressure of his fingers.

"I am glad," he said, looking relieved. "For I hope and trust that this is only the beginning."

She gave him a shaky smile as he led her the rest of the way across the bridge and under the open columns of the folly. There a stone bench had been built to command a view of the surrounding lake. Although the bench seemed warm and dry, he took off his coat and spread it out for her to sit on anyway.

She thanked him awkwardly and sat down. She told herself it was pleasant to have someone looking after her comfort for a change. She just hadn't become accustomed to it yet.

Darcy sat down so close beside her that his knee brushed hers. She should move away. What if someone were to see them? But Lady Langdon would not intrude, and the earl was probably still going over accounts with his steward.

Putting one arm around her, Darcy moved closer. With his other hand, he took her hand in a warm, firm clasp.

She stiffened. She could practically hear the voice of Hannah, the cook and housekeeper at the vicarage, warning her not to permit such a familiarity. But Hannah hated men, so it was no wonder that she mistrusted Darcy, even though his behavior had always been perfectly gentlemanly.

His embrace could only be a prelude to a declaration. It would be tempting fate to resist him now. Indeed, she had no wish to do so. Only a vague sense of unease that threatened to spoil what should have been a perfect moment. She pushed it down and willed herself to think only of Darcy and the happiness they would soon share.

He brought her hand up to his lips and kissed it, sending a little shudder of delight up her arm. A few final doubts floated through her mind, only to drown in the sight of his intensely blue eyes. He leaned toward her, and she knew she was about to be kissed for the first time. Her heart thudding, she closed her eyes in anticipation.

She opened them again as Darcy suddenly cursed and sprang

to his feet. In shock and disappointment, she followed the direction of his gaze and saw a tall gentleman in a scarlet uniform advancing purposefully toward them across the bridge. His uniform, as well as his unmistakable resemblance to his brother, warned her that she was about to meet Lord Langdon.

Two

Lord Langdon's thunderous expression made it clear that he had seen everything. Nell's cheeks flamed while her heart sank like a stone. Too late, she realized how foolish and indecorous her behavior had been. How awful it must appear to Lord Langdon! Could Darcy manage to smooth it over?

"Hello, James," Darcy stammered.

"I trust I am not intruding," his brother answered in a deep baritone voice with a hint of a growl in it. He came to a halt before them.

"N-no, not at all," said Darcy hastily. "This is Miss Ashley. I was just showing her the temple."

"I see," said Lord Langdon, turning to look at her.

Nell got up from the bench, gathering her courage to meet his gaze. She felt an absurd compulsion to stand at attention in the earl's presence. For a few moments, they stood surveying each other. Now that he was closer, she saw that Lord Langdon's facial features were much like Darcy's, but marred by a heavier jaw and a weather-beaten complexion that made him seem more than seven years his brother's senior. His eyes were a deep blue like Darcy's. But where Darcy's eyes were likely to sparkle in amusement, Lord Langdon's seemed to coldly scrutinize every inch of her. She had the uncomfortable sensation of being a soldier on review by a superior officer and of being found lacking.

Her face was burning. She put a hand up to her cheek in a vain attempt to cool it and brushed against the curls that framed her face. Suddenly, she was convinced that her new hairstyle was too frivolous and the neckline of her gown immodestly low.

Seeming to complete his inspection, Lord Langdon bowed stiffly.

"I am charmed to make your acquaintance, Miss Ashley," he said in a tone that clearly indicated otherwise.

She curtsyed silently, trying desperately to think of something to say that would salvage his first impression of her. She looked to Darcy for support.

"Miss Ashley is the daughter of the vicar at Smallbourne," Darcy said. His voice faltered a little, making her wonder if he was ashamed of her.

Lord Langdon looked her over once more. His expression clearly said that she did not look at all like a respectable clergyman' s daughter.

He looked back to Darcy and said coldly, "Lady Langdon informs me that there is a nuncheon awaiting us in the Yellow Parlor." The statement had the air of a command. He turned, and Nell found herself and Darcy following him over the bridge in single file like obedient schoolchildren.

Lord Langdon set off toward the house, at an unhurried, yet ground-covering stride, with Darcy following closely behind. Despite being an energetic walker herself, Nell had to almost run to keep up with the two brothers.

Her mortification was growing by the minute. How dare Lord Langdon look at her as if she were some brazen, designing hussy? How could he judge her so? Although she had behaved improperly in encouraging his brother to kiss her, Lord Langdon was guilty of much more serious sins himself!

And could not Darcy at least slow his pace a little? Perhaps she should just go home to the vicarage rather than stay where she was clearly no longer welcome to eat a meal for which she had not the slightest appetite. But it would be craven to run away at this point. Lord Langdon would certainly think her a coward if she did so.

And if she had any hopes of Darcy, she couldn't afford to make matters any worse. If the earl hadn't interrupted them, Darcy would have declared himself. She was certain of it. It would take more than Lord Langdon's disapproval to keep her away from Charlwood now.

But Nell soon regretted her decision.

Lady Langdon met them in the Yellow Parlor, nervously pacing and twisting her long strand of pearls about between her fingers. The countess tried to be polite and gracious, but Lord Langdon's forbidding expression and curt replies to her polite inquiries as to the success of his morning's work soon quelled her usual vivacity.

Darcy made a valiant attempt to engage his brother in conversation, asking him to describe the Battle of Salamanca, but Lord Langdon's reply silenced him as well.

Nell burned to tell Lord Langdon exactly what she thought of his behavior. However, an unwillingness to embarrass Lady Langdon, on top of her deepening sense of mortification over the scene he had witnessed, prevented her from doing so. Since she was not adept at small talk under the best of circumstances, she was reduced to pecking at her meal and studying the pattern in the faded yellow silk hangings for which the room was named.

Finally, the meal came to an end, with no one having eaten much, except for Lord Langdon, who had calmly consumed a vast quantity of cold ham and beef, disgustingly oblivious to his companions' discomfort. Afterwards he took Darcy off to accompany him and Lytchett, the steward, on a tour of some of the farms comprising the estate.

Nell knew Lord Langdon was deliberately separating them, but she was a little comforted by the look Darcy threw over his shoulder at her as he followed his brother out of the room. She was cheered by the mixture of reassurance and defiance she read there. Clearly he planned to explain things to Lord Langdon, to defend her character against any false inferences the earl might have made. At least, she felt, he would try. She returned Darcy's look, trying to put all of her unspoken feelings into her smile as he left her.

* * *

James, turning his head slightly, caught the exchange of glances between his brother and Miss Ashley. His excellent peripheral vision had saved him on the battlefield more than once, but he had never thought he would need it to spy on his errant brother. His frown deepened, and the rage he had been suppressing ever since he had first caught sight of him kissing Miss Ashley in the folly threatened his self-control. He made a quick decision. Instead of going directly to the study, he went down the passage toward the library.

"I thought we were going to meet Lytchett?" said Darcy, coming up alongside him. The look of innocent surprise on his face was almost convincing.

"Lytchett can wait. We will have a few words first." As they entered the library, he turned and looked down into his brother's face. "Explain yourself, Darcy."

"What have I to explain?" Darcy asked, his chin up and his hands on his hips.

"I think you know," James answered grimly, restraining an impulse to use a fist to knock the impudence out of the young fool. "You must tell me how it is that I came to find you carrying on with Miss Ashley. It would have been bad enough if you stooped to seduce some girl from the village, but when you start with one of the daughters of the local gentry you have crossed the line."

"James, I was only kissing her—or trying to anyway!"

"And would probably have succeeded at that, and more, if it hadn't been for my timely interruption. I will not tolerate my brother making a fool of himself over some country miss with no sense of decorum!" He had not intended to shout, and yet somehow he could not restrain himself.

"I was not making a fool of myself. And Miss Ashley is no mere flirt, I assure you."

"All the worse then if she is a lady of character, which, however, I will take leave to doubt. Have you stopped to consider that your actions could lead to unrealistic expectations on her part?"

"Oh, you think I'm only trifling, do you?" asked Darcy. "What if I told you that my intentions were serious?"

"I would think you were trying to convince me that the hazards of country life are as disastrous as those of London in the hopes of being allowed to go back to town. It won't fadge, brother. I know you can have no intention of offering for Miss Ashley."

"Don't be so sure of that!"

"Your threats don't frighten me," James said, still convinced Darcy was bluffing. "I cannot see what reason you could have to offer for the daughter of a country parson."

"She is pretty and amiable and altogether the sweetest and most innocent girl I have ever met," said Darcy as he began to pace about the long room.

Unbidden, an image of Miss Ashley arose before James's eyes. Her tumbled chestnut-brown curls, her big hazel eyes, the way she had blushed from the top of her forehead down to her—what *was* he thinking? Surely he was no longer vulnerable to such charms. He was not a callow young man prey to the wild impulses called up by a mere pretty face or shapely figure. He was old enough to know that there were women who used these assets to cloud a man's judgment and warp his sense of honor. But Darcy had no such wisdom, it seemed.

James would have to intervene, but he would have to act carefully. If his brother was really infatuated with the girl, it would do no good to antagonize him.

"I think perhaps you are mistaken about the innocence, at least. I will grant you, she is attractive," he said, forcing himself to speak calmly.

"I assure you, Miss Ashley is a lady of the highest character," said Darcy, pausing by a window.

"Since when has that been a factor in your choice of female companionship?"

"How can you possibly have any idea of what I like? I was still at Eton when you left for Portugal."

James paused, feeling a queer mixture of guilt, regret, and annoyance. He did have some knowledge of his brother's tastes, but unfortunately he had had to gain it secondhand. Darcy didn't know that their man of business had given James a volume of detail on the debts he had incurred in London.

But that was not a subject James wanted to bring up now. Better to deal with one problem at a time.

"I am sorry. You are right," James said carefully. "But I am still not convinced that Miss Ashley is in truth as you describe her."

"I told you she is the vicar's daughter."

"Yes, but since there are any number of red-faced parsons about more concerned with the hunt, the table, and the bottle than their congregations, I cannot see that being the daughter of one is any guarantee of virtue."

"He's not like that at all. He's a distinguished classical scholar. He doesn't hunt or gamble. And regarding drink, he's practically abstemious—well, he does like his sherry but—Damn it all, James! He's a most respectable person."

"And her mother?"

"She died four years ago. She was the daughter of Viscount Luddington and a good friend of our mother's. I was too young at the time to remember her, but perhaps you do."

James wrinkled his brow. Now that he came to think of it, he did vaguely recall his mother exchanging visits with Mrs. Ashley at the vicarage.

"Yes, now I remember. I am surprised Luddington permitted his daughter to marry a vicar."

"As a point of fact, he didn't. They had to wait until she was of age, and even then, the family disowned her. But why do you care? You may feel that as the earl you need to marry the bluest blood in England, but is there any reason why I should have to do the same?"

"No. If I see that Miss Ashley is the virtuous lady you describe, you may marry her with my blessing."

"I can see you don't believe a word I have said! But you will soon find that she is known throughout the parish for her generosity and her work among the poor."

James frowned. It was highly unlikely that a lady of good character would encourage a gentleman's attentions so freely. More likely, she was looking to raise her social station by marrying a Mayland. Darcy was by no means a poor match for her; although a younger son, he was the possessor of a modest fortune passed down from their mother. But James had not thought that his brother could so easily be taken in.

"She does seem generous with her favors," he said, unable to contain his annoyance. He regretted his words when he saw the anger fairly blaze from his brother's eyes.

"It is not like that at all!" Darcy exclaimed.

"No? Then tell me. Do you think she is in love with you? Are you in love with her?" He tried again for a milder tone, and yet the questions still came out sounding like an interrogation.

"What business is it of yours? Who I choose to marry is my own affair after all," said Darcy, once again facing the window.

James cursed himself. He had commanded many young soldiers and counseled them through their personal troubles, and yet he could not reach an understanding with his own brother. But he would have to keep trying. He walked over to where Darcy was standing and put a tentative hand on his brother's shoulder.

"My only wish is to protect you from harm," he said stiffly.

Darcy jerked away.

"I do not need your protection. Soon enough, I will be able to do as I please!" he shouted, heading for the doorway.

James watched him go, feeling rage and hurt twisting him inside. "And how will you do that? You have not forgotten the arrangements of our father's will, have you?"

Darcy paused in the doorway and looked back. "How could I forget that my own father did not trust me to manage my own fortune until I am five-and-twenty? But I won't wait four more years to be free."

"If you are expecting me to end the trust now, I can only tell you that until your conduct gives me reason to believe that you will not run aground—"

"Rest assured I am not expecting anything from you!"

With those words, Darcy left the room. James took a few steps after him, then stopped. It was pointless to pursue Darcy while both of them were so heated.

He paced about the room a few times, and his own anger

ebbed quickly, leaving a sense of dull depression. He slumped down into a dusty leather-covered chair, wondering what scheme Darcy had in mind.

Clearly, James had come home not a moment too soon. It might already be too late to reestablish any sort of rapport with his brother. He had felt guilty about leaving his regiment in such a rush, leaving his men in the care of a fellow officer, but the increasingly ominous letters from his man of business in London, combined with an indefinable sense of trouble, had forced him to arrange for the quickest possible transport back to England.

Now he realized that the problems facing him at home were as formidable in their own way as the enemy he had faced across so many battlefields. At least there the challenges had been straightforward. But there was no use wishing he was simply Major Mayland of the Fourth Dragoons. It was time he learned to accept his role as the Earl of Langdon and head of his family, though he did not relish the prospect.

Meanwhile, Lytchett was waiting, and there was work to be done. James got up, feeling more weary than he had after many a long day's hard ride. Squaring his shoulders, he strode out of the room to meet his steward.

Nell had breathed a sigh of relief as she heard Darcy and Lord Langdon go down the hall. She hated strife of any kind, but contention within a family was the worst by far. She felt almost ill with the strain of keeping her temper, the guilty awareness that she herself had behaved unwisely, and the lowering feeling of having widened the gulf between Darcy and his brother.

But however badly her first meeting with the earl had gone, at least it was over. Now all she wanted to do was go home by the lengthiest possible route. A long, brisk walk would surely make her feel better.

But as she rose and prepared to take her leave, Lady Langdon invited her to join her in her drawing room for a little gossip. The elegant little countess was looking unusually harassed and in need of a confidante herself, so Nell agreed.

"What an odious, odious man!" said Lady Langdon as they went down the hall. "My dear Nell, I am *so* sorry to have had you subjected to such an uncouth display! Will you ever forgive me?"

"Of course, ma'am," she answered. "I am sure you could not have foreseen how his lordship would behave." She was glad Lady Langdon was not looking at her; she did not feel ready to explain the blush in her cheeks or the real reason behind the earl's displeasure.

"But I hope you will not let yourself be frightened away from us by my stepson's abominable behavior," said Lady Langdon, turning to Nell, her large, dark eyes wide with concern.

Her words, delivered in the warmest tones, soothed Nell's jangled nerves.

"No. I am not afraid of Lord Langdon. But I do feel for you since you have to live with him. I hope I have not caused more trouble for you."

They entered the drawing room and sat down on one of its needlepoint-covered sofas. Lady Langdon leaned back and visibly relaxed, clearly happy to be back in her own domain.

"I assure you there is enough of *that* without your having anything to do with the matter. If you had only heard the things that horrid man said to me yesterday, lecturing me in the most severe manner about how we all must practice the strictest economy from now on."

"I'm sure he can't expect you to have to huddle up in several shawls rather than build a decent fire or to wear the same shabby gown year after year!" protested Nell. "I have been obliged most of my life to practice such economies, but I don't see why you should ever have to do so!"

Lady Langdon blinked and stared at Nell for a few moments. Then she shook her head and said, "I should hope not indeed! I don't know how I should be able to go on in such a manner. You know I was not brought up as you were. I suppose I could learn if there were a *need* to do so. But when Charles was alive, he paid every bill without complaint. I am certain he would not have done so if the family fortunes were endangered."

Nell nodded. Although she herself had been only three years old when the fourth earl had left Charlwood, she had heard both Darcy and Lady Langdon speak of his kindness and understanding. Nell was certain he had managed their affairs sensibly.

The fourth earl had moved away from Charlwood after the death of his first wife. It had been widely rumored that he was heartbroken at her death and could not bear to continue to live in a place where every sight, every shrub, every flower in the gardens reminded him of the mother of his sons. Nell was glad to think that such a loving man had been able to find happiness again with his young and beautiful second bride.

"But here is James, throwing every little bill in my face!" continued Lady Langdon, recalling Nell's wandering thoughts. "He spent a mere three days in London, not even ordering himself new clothes! But he still found time to closet himself with Willett, our man of business, and go into all the particulars of Darcy's and my expenditures. He even cut up stiff over the bill for one of my hats!"

"A hat! But that is absurd. Why would he bother with such a trifle?"

"He resents me—he has done so ever since his father remarried. He was then just as he is now: polite, but so cold, so reserved! And I could see he was terribly annoyed to see all the gifts and jewels Charles bought for me. I know he never thought me worthy of succeeding his mother. And now he is taking his revenge on me."

Nell watched in concern as Lady Langdon nervously twirled her pearls about between her fingers. Nell herself was content to be alone much of the time herself, but she knew how important friends and society were to Lady Langdon. Perhaps it was difficult for Lord Langdon to accustom himself to having a stepmother who though a few years older than he, looked younger. But it was patently unfair of him to incarcerate her here, where a quiet, rainy morning could throw her into gloom.

"I am so sorry," said Nell. "How childish of him! One would think that after ten years he might have learned to accept you, knowing that you had made his father happy."

"He never gave me the chance! He entered Oxford the year we were married and spent all of his holidays at friends' houses rather than with us. And as soon as he graduated, he entered the army and was stationed in Canterbury. A year later he was off for the Peninsula. What could I have done?"

The question was clearly rhetorical. Nell remained silent as Lady Langdon brooded over her stepson's iniquity. Looking at Lady Langdon's dark, curling hair, her expressive eyes, and her elegantly slim figure, Nell wondered why her friend had not remarried. Surely Lady Langdon would have had offers. That would have been the easiest solution to her difficulties with her stepson. But perhaps, after only two years of widowhood, she was not yet ready to remarry.

The countess shook her head slightly and smiled again, making a visible effort to shake off her depression. "But you and Darcy are such comforts to me. He has always been such a good-natured boy. And I cannot tell you how much your companionship has helped me to support life at Charlwood."

"I am glad to have been a help. But I fear now that my presence may only cause grief for you. Perhaps it would be best if I did not come here anymore," said Nell, squaring her shoulders. It was one thing to hope that Darcy would continue to call upon her and take her out driving. But it was quite another to subject her friend to the earl's ire.

"Please do not even say such a thing," protested Lady Langdon, "when we have become such good friends and you have done so much for the gardens! And I was so looking forward to introducing you to some of my friends! Once the Season is over, people will return to the countryside. I expect I shall manage at least a few dinner parties, if not a ball, for even James has admitted that he thinks it is important to be on good terms with our neighbors."

"For your sake, I certainly hope he will allow it," answered

Nell, smiling a little. She knew the neighbors Lady Langdon spoke of included exalted persons such as the Duke and Duchess of Richmond, and not the local squire or the gentleman farmers.

"My dear, you don't sound happy at the prospect! You do understand that I mean for you to attend any entertainments we will have here, do you not?"

"Yes, ma'am. But there is no need for me to do so. I will be perfectly content if I can just continue to visit you here informally."

"But, Nell, I have been so sorry for the lonely life you have been obliged to lead. I had hoped you would enjoy a few little parties here."

"Indeed, I do not wish to seem ungrateful. But I really am not very good at parties."

"But you have not had much opportunity to learn, have you?"

Nell smiled ruefully. "At my first party, I disgraced myself by arguing with the squire over poaching. I told him I thought it unduly harsh to flog a man and sentence him to hard labor just for stealing a few hares for his hungry family. You may imagine his fury at being lectured so—and by a young girl, no less!"

"Why, yes, I can," said Lady Langdon with a little laugh. "I believe the squire is an avid sportsman, is he not? Dreadful how all men want to do in the country is to shoot everything in sight! But surely that cannot have been enough to ruin you in local society. After all, you were a young girl and had recently lost your mother too. One would think they could have made some allowances."

"I suppose if I had outgrown my outspokenness they would have," Nell replied with a rueful smile. "But it is not just that. There are many who cannot understand why Papa and I live the simple way we do. They think we should employ a man-servant and don't understand why we just keep a horse and gig at the Fox and Hounds rather than setting up a stable and buying a closed carriage."

Nell paused to draw breath. She knew already that these

things did not matter to Lady Langdon, but still it was important to explain why she felt shy of entering society.

"They think a young lady should grow only flowers, not vegetables to share with the poor," Nell continued. "And while it is my duty to visit and assist the unfortunate, it is going too far to take such an intimate interest in their affairs or wish to set up a school for them. I must warn you that some say I am fond of low company and unfit for proper society."

"I do not care what a parcel of rural dowdies think!" exclaimed Lady Langdon. "And you should not heed them either. Such persons are too uncertain of their own position in society to tolerate anyone who is different. In *my* circle one may do and say what one pleases, so long as one does so with an air of utmost confidence. Remember that, Nell, and do not be ashamed to show your concern with the poor of your papa's parish."

"I am not ashamed."

"No, I know you are not. And I know that I have been too careless of such things in the past. It will do none of us any harm to be reminded that, as we enjoy ourselves, we should remember the welfare of those less fortunate. Fashionable persons are not *all* completely heartless, you know," the countess ended in a low voice. It seemed she was trying to reassure herself as much as Nell.

"I could never think you heartless after all your kindness to me and the times you have accompanied me on my visits to your pensioners. I certainly hope more great ladies will follow your lead."

"Why, yes, I think we might even succeed in making benevolence fashionable! But this is all straying away from my point. I only wish to tell you that you need fear no snubs when you are making your appearance in society under my sponsorship. Does that not sound worldly and conceited? Nevertheless, it is true. And now that you are becomingly gowned and are looking so very pretty, you will soon lose count of the compliments you receive. Ah, you are blushing. I know you care for compliments from no one but my scamp of a stepson! Now please look me in the eye and tell me you would not enjoy dancing with him at a ball at Charlwood?"

"I cannot say that," admitted Nell. "I would dearly love to dance, but I have to admit I have never learned how."

"Then Darcy and I shall teach you. Nothing would give either of us more pleasure!"

"Thank you, but I am afraid Lord Langdon is not likely to approve of your doing so. Truly, I do not wish to be a cause of contention among all of you."

"Once he comes to know you better, Nell, I am sure he will come to appreciate your good qualities."

Nell wondered how the countess could be so certain of the actions of a man neither of them knew well at all. She couldn't forget the look she had seen on Lord Langdon's face as Darcy introduced her. Clearly, he thought her unworthy of his brother, and he didn't seem a man to change his opinions easily. And that was only fair since it was highly unlikely that she would ever change her opinion of *him*.

Three

"Pardon me, my lord, but I have been asked to inform you that there are some ladies visiting Lady Langdon who wish to see you."

Looking up from the books and papers littered about his desk, James scowled and restrained an impulse to tell his valet to go to the devil. Half a morning's study of the estate accounts had brought him little closer to a clear assessment of the situation at Charlwood, but that did not make the interruption any less of an annoyance.

"What? We've been here just two days and already half the countryside is paying morning visits! But you must tell me why you have been obliged to convey this request. What about Alton or one of the footmen?"

Farley only grinned. James had to smile back. That stiff-necked butler Alton would certainly disapprove of such familiarity, but James was glad that Farley, who had been his batman throughout most of the Peninsular campaign, had agreed to accompany him back to Charlwood. It was a small comfort to know that there was at least one person there who was neither frightened nor hostile. Darcy hadn't so much as talked to him since yesterday's falling-out.

"I suppose I have not been in the best of moods, old friend," he admitted. "But really, the domestic staff has nothing to fear from me. It is about time they learned that."

"I expect they will soon enough, my lord," said Farley respectfully.

"So do you think I should see these ladies, Farley?" he asked, rubbing the back of his neck, amazed at how stiff it had gotten.

"Perhaps it would do you good to take leave of your work for a half hour, my lord."

"I'd rather saddle up Jack and go for a long gallop, but I suppose it would not do to offend our neighbors. By the way, who *are* these ladies?" he asked. It seemed odd of them to request his presence in such a manner, but he had been out of the way of doing the pretty for so long that perhaps he just wasn't remembering what was expected of him.

"Lady Nettlehurst and Miss Nettlehurst."

James looked up eagerly.

Farley continued. "They are with Lady Langdon in her drawing room. And Miss Ashley, of course."

"I will come at once."

"I thought you would, my lord."

James hurried out of his study and down the long passage-way toward the drawing room. He quickly entered the room, looking for his visitors. Unfortunately, they were seated on a sofa that faced the window with their backs to him. He strode across the delicately patterned Aubusson carpet and suppressed an oath when he almost tripped over a small sewing table he did not recognize. In his mother's day the room had not been cluttered with such frivolities!

As fate would have it, Miss Ashley sat facing the doorway and must have had an excellent view of his near mishap. As he regained his balance, their eyes met, and she smiled at him.

Caught off guard, he came close to responding in kind. There was something indescribably appealing about her wide hazel eyes and the way her generous mouth curved when she smiled. But he had to keep a cool head about him if he was ever to make out her true character. For all he knew, it was all just a ploy to cozen him into accepting her as a suitable bride for his brother. He wasn't going to encourage any such expectations.

He nodded briefly to her and Lady Langdon, then turned to face the other ladies, hoping he had not offended them by acknowledging them last. The older lady greeted him excitedly in a shrill voice he remembered well.

"Dear Lord Langdon, it is such a pleasure to see you again. It seems such an age since you and my poor Adam played as boys! Perhaps you do not remember me, but your Mama and I were bosom bows in those days, you know."

He barely heard her, for his gaze was arrested by the vision sitting next to her. The pale golden curls, the wide blue eyes, and the expression of trusting innocence—all were exactly what he expected from a sister of Adam Nettlehurst. In an instant, he was transported back almost a year to the last bottle of wine he had shared with Adam. They had laughed and joked and speculated on the plans for the upcoming engagement, neither of them realizing that Adam would soon be lying dead on the heights above Vitoria while James escaped unscathed, his own regiment having done nothing that day but maneuver.

And here sat Adam's sister with her hands clasped in her lap, looking like an angel in a pale gray mourning gown trimmed with misty lace. Despite her feminine apparel, and even more feminine features, she was so much like his friend that the ache of his absence throbbed anew.

Finally, James dragged his eyes away and tried to pay attention to Lady Nettlehurst, who was now busily expressing her delight in visiting Charlwood again after so many years. As a boy, he had instinctively distrusted her, contrasting her pushing manners and ostentatious dress to his own mother's kindness and simple good taste. Now he found that time had not improved Lady Nettlehurst.

Would she never cease her infernal chattering and introduce him to her daughter?

"I am sorry to say that my dear husband has been unable to accompany us and pay his respects," she was saying. "He does not enjoy the best of health, I am afraid. But he is most eager to welcome you to Southcott anytime you should choose to call upon him. And you must allow me to present my daughter Clarissa."

He bowed deeply and said, "I am happy to make your acquaintance, Miss Nettlehurst. Or should I say, happy to become reacquainted? For I remember you, although perhaps you do not remember me."

"N-not very well, my lord," she answered in a soft, breathless little voice.

He saw Lady Nettlehurst look warningly at her daughter. Hurriedly, he replied, "I shouldn't have expected it. You must have been all of four years old when we left for Eton."

"But Adam always talked about you and mentioned you in his letters from the Peninsula. You served together, did you not?"

"Yes, although we were unable to obtain commissions in the same regiment, as we had wished. Adam spoke of you often, as well."

"He was the best and kindest brother one could ever wish for."

"He was a fine soldier and the best of good fellows."

He could see the tears starting in her eyes. He was about to express his sympathy, but was interrupted by Lady Nettlehurst.

"Yes, Lord Langdon. I assure you I never saw a brother and sister so attached as my Clarissa and poor, dear Adam! I am sure Clarissa would enjoy hearing about your experiences in the Peninsula, Lord Langdon," she said, moving to a seat near Lady Langdon.

"I will be happy to oblige." As he took the vacant place on the sofa next to Clarissa, however, his eyes once again met Miss Ashley's. This time she did not smile. That should have made it easier to focus his attention back on Clarissa, and yet he had to force himself to look away. He told himself there would be other opportunities to confirm his suspicions regarding Darcy's latest interest.

At the present moment, it was more important to share his memories of Adam with his sister. So he concentrated on responding kindly to Clarissa's shy questioning, and telling her some of the more repeatable stories of the life he and Adam had shared.

* * *

Nell watched in disgust as Lord Langdon seated himself beside Miss Nettlehurst and engaged her in low-voiced conversation. Such a contrast to the manner in which he had repulsed her own tentative attempt at friendliness! It was obvious he still held the lowest opinion of her. Darcy must not have succeeded in explaining matters to his brother. Or had he even tried?

She had come back to Charlwood in a more hopeful frame of mind. A long walk on the Downs, followed by dinner with her father, had done much to restore her spirits. Not that she had told Papa everything, of course. Her conscience pricked her over that, but she still thought it best to be silent over what would only have distressed him.

But the soothing effects of exercise and her father's company had raised her confidence that she might succeed in reestablishing herself in Lord Langdon's eyes. And so, this morning, she had donned her staidest brown dress and come to visit Lady Langdon as she had promised, planning to conduct herself with the utmost modesty and good sense.

When the earl had stumbled on entering the room, she had hoped that an understanding smile might help break the ice between them. How foolishly optimistic she had been! It was clear now that he would be cordial only to those whom he deemed to be his social equals, like the Nettlehursts.

"Miss Ashley, I understand you are the vicar's daughter," said Lady Nettlehurst, interrupting her thoughts.

Nell looked up, surprised at having been addressed by Lady Nettlehurst, who had not condescended to say one word to her since they had been introduced.

"Yes, ma'am," she replied.

"Dearest Vivian here has been telling me how useful you have been to her. When my little Clarissa marries, I really must employ someone like yourself, an active young person to run my errands and keep me company."

"Miss Ashley is not a servant, Lavinia. She is my friend," said Lady Langdon with a gentle reproof in her voice.

"Oh, yes, of course," answered Lady Nettlehurst.

After a brief pause, Lady Nettlehurst directed all of her conversation toward Lady Langdon, keeping to the subject of their mutual acquaintances in various noble families. After Lady Langdon tried, but failed, several times to bring the discussion back to topics in which Nell could have a share, Nell decided it was useless to stay any longer.

It was kind of Lady Langdon to try to include her despite Lady Nettlehurst's snubs, but it must be distressing for her to have to play hostess under such circumstances. And there would be no chance for conversation with Lord Langdon, so she would have to wait for another day to prove to him that she was worthy of his brother. If it was even possible to do so.

Lord Langdon got to his feet briefly as she left, looking annoyed at the interruption. Before she had even left the room, he sat back down, resuming his conversation with Miss Nettlehurst.

Anger at his rudeness gave wings to Nell's feet as she walked down the gravel drive winding through the vast lawn in front of Charlwood. But as she passed through the gates, she paused and looked back at the house, standing there in all its classical serenity, pale stone gleaming against the lush green backdrop of lawns and woods.

With a pang, she wondered if she would ever be welcome there again. Although Lady Langdon was still her friend, she hadn't seen Darcy that morning. That meant little—he often spent the morning out riding, and perhaps he hadn't known that she planned to visit. But couldn't he have realized that, after yesterday's events, she might wish for some reassurance that all was still well between them?

She turned off the lane into the small wood that lay between Charlwood and the village of Smallbourne. It was in these woods that she had first met Darcy. Drifts of bluebells had carpeted the ground with their sapphire blossoms, perfuming the air with their sweet scent; the trees had been veiled in a pale green haze of emerging leaves. Only a few faded bluebells remained, and the trees were nearly in full leaf, but she could still remember that first encounter.

They had both been en route to Matthew Cowden's cottage.

Old Matthew had been a groom at Charlwood before his retirement and had put both of the Mayland boys on their first ponies. Now he suffered heavily from age and rheumatism. Nell had been so touched by Darcy's kindness in visiting his old friend. Such a contrast to his arrogant brother!

Upon reaching the broad gate at the other end of the woods, she climbed over the stile beside it. Then on impulse, she sat down on the stile, half closing her eyes. Willing herself to forget Lord Langdon, she tried to remember the way Darcy had looked at her yesterday and the gentle way he had taken her into his arms. But the vision of his face suddenly wavered in her mind. Darcy's candid blue eyes turned icy. And then it was Lord Langdon's face before her, full of cold contempt.

Hastily, she jumped back down from the stile, trying to push his image from her mind and recall Darcy again. Yet she couldn't do it—the physical resemblance between the two brothers was too strong. She hoped it went no deeper. She'd seen clearly enough yesterday that Lord Langdon did exert some influence over Darcy. Would he use it against her? And was Darcy's affection truly deep enough to withstand the pressure that might be brought against it?

But it was useless to speculate and stupid to imagine the worst. Still, she felt a deep sense of relief when she turned down the small side lane leading to the vicarage. The squat, irregular little flint house had never seemed so welcoming, with its tiny lawn before it and the lush garden behind.

The garden was what she needed now. There was nothing like a nice, vigorous session with a hoe to clear the mind of foolish fears. She sprang up the front steps, between tubs of geraniums, opened the green door and entered the front hall.

But as she passed into the kitchen, she realized she should have gone straight into the garden through the side gate rather than through the house. Silas, their elderly gardener, with whom she shared the task of tending the vicarage garden and their small flock of poultry, was laid up with the lumbago, and Betty, their housemaid, was away visiting her family. But Hannah was right there, standing near the oven, flour all over her apron, a meat pie in her hands. Hannah might be hard of hearing, but her old eyes missed very little.

Nell had no desire to explain her fears to Hannah, who already held stubborn suspicions of Darcy. So she forced a smile onto her face and greeted Hannah cheerfully.

"So you are back, are you, Miss Nell? I think you had better—"

The rest of Hannah's words were drowned in the sound of barking and the scrabbling of doggy paws on brick. Nell tried to warn Hannah of Oddy's approach, but it was too late. The huge rough-coated dog burst through the open garden door and bounded toward his mistress, knocking Hannah off balance so that she dropped the unbaked pie onto the kitchen floor.

Pandemonium ensued as Hannah burst into biblically inspired threats of the fate that befell the wicked. As verbal fire and brimstone rained down on him, Oddy sat on the floor, barking excitedly and reveling in the attention.

Nell stifled a giggle. She really must calm Hannah and Oddy down before her father suffered a nervous breakdown from the commotion. She picked up the pie. Fortunately, the heavy iron pan had fallen right side up, chipping the brick floor but leaving the pie intact.

"Hush, Hannah. See. Dinner is not ruined after all." After placing it into the oven, she knelt down next to the panting dog.

"Yes, yes, Oddy. I'm happy to see you, too," she said, feeling unexpected tears sting the back of her eyes as she put her arms around his shaggy neck. Odysseus could be a nuisance sometimes, but at worrisome times like this, she blessed the day she had found him, a bedraggled mongrel puppy wandering in the woods, and brought him home to the vicarage. Not that they'd realized then how much he would eat or that he'd grow to the size of a small pony.

"You're not going to sit there and reward that dratted animal for such behavior, are you, Miss Nell?" asked Hannah.

"You are quite right, Hannah. I should not." Nell took Oddy's jaw into her hands and looked sternly into his liquid brown eyes. "Oddy, I've told you before. You are *not* to run about in the kitchen while Hannah is cooking. Do you understand?"

Oddy thumped a tail on the floor and grinned at her.

"Shall we go outside to the garden, do you think?" she asked. Perhaps she could make her escape before Hannah could see the trouble in her face and start questioning her about it. Oddy obligingly jumped up and headed to the door, but Hannah was not to be so easily distracted.

"Not so fast, Miss Nell! I was about to say you had better go and see your Papa." Hannah's expression was more than usually severe. Nell wondered what had happened.

"He is not unwell, is he?"

"No, dear. But you had best go on into his study. He has something to tell you, if he can lift his nose out of those heathenish books of his for a few moments. I'll never understand why a man of the cloth must muddle his brain with such nasty rubbish. All about gods wandering around disguised as swans and cows and people marrying their mothers and I don't want to know what else!"

Nell wondered what was bothering Hannah. Over twenty years with the vicar and his family hadn't cured Hannah of her prejudice against the classics, but she usually did not grumble about it quite so forcefully.

"I suppose I had better take some food in to him." Nell gathered bread and cheese on a tray and made her escape from the kitchen.

She walked quietly into her father's shabby, book-lined study. As she had expected, the vicar was hunched over a book. He looked up nervously as she entered. Then his brow cleared and he smiled, a little sadly, she thought.

She dropped a kiss onto his balding head and said, "Papa, it's time you had a bite to eat. You can let Virgil rest for a few moments."

"Ah, thank you, my dear. I hope nothing untoward has occurred today? I thought I heard angry voices."

"Nothing, Papa. It was just Hannah scolding Oddy, as usual. I am so sorry you were disturbed by it." She carefully moved several books to the other side of the table to clear a spot for the tray. Seeing that he still seemed agitated, she poured him a glass from the bottle of fine sherry kept in his study. At moments like this, she was glad she saved a portion of the household money for Papa's one extravagance.

He drank the sherry, but seemed uninterested in the bread and cheese. He took off his spectacles and started to clean them with his pocket handkerchief, fussing over them far longer than was necessary. Clearly, he had something more to say and didn't feel at all comfortable about it.

"What is it, Papa? Hannah said you had something to tell me."

"Yes, my dear. Young Darcy Mayland came to call this morning. He has requested my permission to pay his addresses to you."

For a few moments she was silent from surprise. So Darcy had not given her up! Far from it. This was what she had been hoping for, after all. So why didn't she feel elated, or at least relieved, at the news? Then she realized her father was watching her, an unusually grave expression on his kindly face.

"And did you grant it, Papa?"

"Yes, child. The decision is yours, of course. I would never wish to stand in the way of your happiness. But, my dear, I must confess that I am not at all certain that he is the man I would have chosen for you."

"I mean no disrespect, Papa, but—but what is it about Darcy that you find objectionable?"

"Nothing, nothing, my dear. He seems quite amiable. In fact, I have been glad to see you enjoying yourself so much with your new friends. You have been too much alone since your mother died. It was high time for you to put off your mourning." He sighed and continued. "I am afraid I have been very remiss as a parent. I should have tried harder to arrange for you to enjoy more youthful society than mine."

"Oh, no, Papa. You have been the kindest and best father one could wish for!"

"It is like you to say so, my dear. But that is precisely why I hope that you find a man who is worthy of you. I must say

I would have thought you would have chosen someone more serious minded than young Mr. Mayland."

"Papa, we cannot all be classical scholars."

"Yes, of course. But—forgive me—have you seen any signs that he aspires to be anything but a town beau?"

She couldn't shrug off his questioning as she could Hannah's obviously biased criticisms. The vicar never spoke ill of anyone; she could see it was costing him an effort to come so close to it now.

"Papa, I do agree with you. Darcy does lack a useful occupation. If his brother had only permitted him to join the army when he wished it . . . But I don't think soldiering is the only thing that appeals to him. I have seen how he loves Charlwood, but it frustrates him so to be powerless in its management. I truly think if we married and had a home of our own he would be much happier."

"Perhaps you are right, my dear. He has shown the good judgment to prefer you, my child. You might be the making of him. But I shall miss you sorely."

"Oh, Papa, thank you for understanding," she said, jumping up and kissing him again. She didn't wish to spoil the moment by telling him about the obstacles she was likely to encounter from Darcy's brother.

Her papa must have seen the worry in her face, for he began fidgeting with his glasses again. At length he said, "But, my dear, you still don't look happy. Please tell me what troubles you."

She had always confided in Papa; why was it so difficult now? Perhaps because the whole story would distress him so. Lord Langdon's arrogance. Her own indiscretion!

Yet her father deserved to know of the earl's likely opposition to the match. He was dependent on Lord Langdon's goodwill for his living. Dear heaven! Might the earl stoop so low as to take advantage of that?

Would he threaten to take away Papa's living? Could he do it? It would be so despicable. Papa was so comfortable here, had become attached to his parishioners, as they—wretched as many of them were—had grown attached to him. If she and

Darcy married, they would certainly provide for him, but would Papa be happy away from Smallbourne?

She took a deep breath and forced herself to think rationally. She might never be forced to choose between Papa and Darcy. But since the possibility existed, Papa had a right to know what Lord Langdon might do.

"Papa, I am afraid Lord Langdon will not approve. I suspect he wants Darcy to marry someone of greater wealth and standing in society."

"Are you certain of this, my dear? I would not have thought it so poor a match in worldly terms. Your mother was the daughter of Lord Luddington, after all, and you are to have two thousand pounds from your uncle Joshua when you marry."

"But Mama's family disowned her, and they are all dead now anyway. And I'm certain his lordship will think my dowry too small. Not to mention the fact that it is derived from trade. No doubt Lord Langdon is the sort to sneer at an honest merchant like Uncle Joshua."

"I am sorry to hear it, my dear. I remember the earl as a lad, and I quite expected him to have grown into an admirable young man by now."

"He has grown up very proud and disagreeable. From what Darcy says, I fear we shall see no improvement in his administration of the estate, such as we hoped for. Also, we cannot forget how he ignored the letter we sent to him in Spain on the occasion of his father's death."

"Perhaps he never saw the letter. And remember, child, he has only just returned from the wars. You must allow him some time to become better acquainted with you. I am sure that then he will withdraw any objections. We must also give him some time to become acquainted with the state of affairs here before we judge him too harshly regarding his treatment of his dependents."

It was like her father to be so tolerant. She nodded, knowing it was useless to debate the matter further.

"And you know as well as I do," he continued, "that among our good people here there are a few who already harbor a spirit of rebellion in their hearts. And Lord Langdon owns lands in several other parishes besides ours. No good could come of it if the laborers in all these areas were stirred up to violence. It is our duty to work as best we can toward a peaceful resolution."

"Yes, Papa." She nodded, knowing the wisdom of her father's words. Blood had been shed elsewhere in such circumstances; and the result seemed inevitably to consist of increased oppression.

"I shall call upon his lordship to discuss it when he has had a few days to make himself comfortable. I have every hope that he will be willing to undertake the necessary reforms once he properly understands the circumstances."

She knew Papa had to go. But she hoped Lord Langdon would not snub her father as roughly as he had snubbed her. And who knew? Her father's loving kindness had made a dent in quite a few hard hearts in the neighborhood. But it remained to be seen if Lord Langdon actually possessed that vital organ.

"I certainly hope so, Papa," she answered.

"Trust in God's goodness, my dear. I am sure all will be well."

Later that day, Nell rhythmically wielded her hoe between rows of beans and cabbages. Usually the chore of protecting her little plot from the onslaught of weeds made her feel better, more in control. But her usual solace was failing her now.

She couldn't share her father's optimism regarding Lord Langdon. Worse, she couldn't decide on a proper course of action. It would be dreadful if she drove a wedge between Darcy and his brother. Even more dreadful if Lord Langdon used his power over Papa to turn him out of his position and the vicarage. If Darcy had declared himself just a few days ago, how overjoyed she would have been. Now, she didn't know how to answer him.

The hoeing completed, she went past the vegetable plots, past flower beds filled with irises and late tulips, fragrant pinks and delicate columbines to the little orchard at the back, where several large apple trees grew.

She sat down on the garden seat placed beneath one of them, leaned back, and closed her eyes, the better to sense the light breeze blowing through the small orchard and hear the hum of the multitude of bees that visited her little haven. The haven her mother had made, where Nell had played as a carefree child.

Perhaps she need not despair. Mama and Papa had overcome obstacles to marry. Surely she and Darcy might do so as well. All she asked was the opportunity for a life such as her parents had made—for love, for children, and for a happy home. Was it really so much to wish for?

Four

Fate had not been kind the last few days, Nell thought as she hurried through the mud covering Smallbourne's main road. Why did influenza have to break out in the village just now?

It had all started the same day Darcy had visited Papa. That afternoon a village boy had delivered a note from Betty telling them she was ill and would likely not be able to return to her duties at the vicarage for several days at least. Despite her father's misgivings, Nell had gone to visit and found the whole family afflicted. The sickness had spread rapidly through the village, no doubt aggravated by several days of miserably wet weather. Nell was soon busily occupied helping to care for the more elderly and infirm of the sufferers.

She had decided not to visit with Lady Langdon until the minor epidemic was past. The countess's constitution was not nearly as robust as her own; Nell couldn't risk passing the infection on to her friend, particularly since no one at Charlwood had yet succumbed. But it was a shame she could not be there to support Lady Langdon through the ordeal of adjusting to Lord Langdon's presence in the household.

Even harder to bear was the fact that she had had to turn down several invitations from Darcy to go out driving with him. But who else would care for the aged and impoverished among her father's parishioners if she did not? A sickness such as this one could be fatal to those who were weakened by age or want.

Darcy was rarely out of her thoughts. Knowing he continued to seek her company was a comfort. But she dreaded being apart from him at such a time, when his older brother was probably doing his utmost to poison Darcy against her.

She had seen Lord Langdon several times the past few days, still wearing his scarlet coat, riding through the village on his large chestnut. Each time, as they met, his brow had wrinkled and he had looked penetratingly at her. Yet he always seemed to be in a hurry, giving her the most curt of greetings and then riding on. Clearly, he had no time to waste on an unassuming female in a muddy dress with a humdrum basket over her arm. It was just as well, she decided. At the moment, she was too busy herself to make any further attempts to gain his lordship's friendship or approval.

She turned into the apothecary's shop. Having obtained what she needed, she hurried back out, almost colliding with Darcy, who had just come out of the adjacent shop.

"Nell! It is you! I thought the sun had just come out," he said, with a graceful bow and a melting smile that made the day seem just a trifle less cloudy.

"I am happy to see you too, Darcy," she answered, cheered by his smile and his compliments, but wishing, as always, that she could say something witty and charming in return. But surely he understood how she felt.

"May I ask where you are going in such a rush?"

"To visit the Mullens. My friend Peg is ill, I am afraid, and in need of some help."

"Must you? Wouldn't you rather come out for a drive with me? My horses and the curricle are at the Fox and Hounds."

Nell stared at him, wide-eyed. Didn't he understand that she couldn't go, not just yet? "I am sorry, but I cannot," she answered. "The Mullens need my assistance. Perhaps in a few days—"

"A few more days! But I have been missing you so. One would think you cared more for the Mullens and the rest of them than you do for me!"

"Oh, no! You know that is not true. It is just that, at present, they *need* me more. Please try to understand. This is what I was brought up to do." She looked at him beseechingly. He couldn't be so indifferent to the villagers' plight.

"Oh, very well then," he said impatiently, looking away. But almost immediately, he looked back at her and addressed her in a softer tone.

"Please forgive me," he said, taking her arm in his and walking toward the outskirts of the village. "I am a brute for pressing you so. Of course you must do whatever you can to help those poor souls. It is just that I have been longing to see you these past three days, and you know we cannot have a proper conversation in the middle of the village like this."

She relaxed. So his annoyance had stemmed from a frustrated desire to be private with her and not from any lack of proper feeling! It was touching to have someone care for her so much.

"I understand," she said. "But I trust that it will not be long before this horrid influenza has died down."

At that moment, they passed the smithy and Hinkson, the old blacksmith, looked up from his work briefly and bade them a respectful good day. After returning the greeting, they walked on, Darcy setting a pace slower than Nell would have chosen. She didn't complain, not wanting him to think she didn't enjoy his company.

"By the way, how is Lady Langdon?" she asked. "I trust she continues to be well."

"Oh, yes, except for being blue-deviled at not having any visitors except for the Nettlehursts. And of course James has been as bad tempered as a bear."

"I am so sorry. Has it really been so awful then?"

"It hasn't been pleasant. James and I barely talk. The only diversion lately was dinner at Southcott. And *that* would have been a complete bore except for watching the Nettlehursts try to lure James into their trap."

"Do you mean the Nettlehursts wish him to marry Clarissa?"

"Of course. The Nettle wouldn't miss the chance of marrying her daughter to an earl."

Nell had no difficulty in recognizing Lady Nettlehurst under this label. She could only pity Clarissa, caught between such a mother and such a suitor.

"Poor girl!" she answered. "Has she any choice in the matter?"

"None, of course. All she ever does is say 'Yes, Mama' and 'No, Mama.' Why, she won't so much as dance with a younger son like me, for fear of Mama's reproaches. Such an insipid miss should suit my brother perfectly."

"Does he seem partial to her?" she asked, recalling the interest Lord Langdon had shown in Clarissa the day the Nettlehursts had called at Charlwood.

"I don't know. He hasn't said anything. Now that Adam's dead, maybe she stands to inherit her father's property. If that's so, James will probably want it to add to our estate. I wouldn't be surprised—the land is all he ever thinks about."

They stepped to the side of the road to let a heavily laden cart pass.

"Does that mean he is looking into the state of affairs here at Smallbourne?" Nell asked as they walked on again.

"He's ridden about with Lytchett a few times, and he spends the rest of his time holed up in the study poring over the estate books. He doesn't seem happy with what he's seen, but of course, he won't tell *me* anything. I did overhear him say to Lytchett that he doesn't understand why the estate hasn't been more prosperous, what with prices having been so high during the war."

"Exactly what I would have expected him to say," she answered, feeling gloomy. A few days ago, her papa had paid his planned visit to Lord Langdon. He had come home in an optimistic mood, telling Nell that his lordship had been perfectly courteous and had listened carefully to all he had to say. However, Papa had admitted on questioning that the earl hadn't said much or promised any particular improvements. She had drawn her own conclusions, and now it seemed that she was right. But she held on to one thin shred of hope: that Darcy might still be able to bring his brother round to their way of thinking.

"I take it you have not had an opportunity to speak with him on the subject?" she asked.

"No, I haven't," he said impatiently. "Believe me, I will do so when the time is right."

Her heart sank. She had not meant to irritate him again. What a wretched situation this was for all of them!

"This is intolerable!" exclaimed Darcy, echoing her thoughts. "Nell, I am sorry. I can't help but be frustrated. If you only knew how things were up at Charlwood! And not being able to see you for the past few days—well, it's been almost past bearing. When will you be free again?"

"Soon. I promise."

They had reached the beginning of a little used lane branching off from the main road.

"I am counting the days," said Darcy, taking her hand and kissing it.

Slightly comforted, she turned down the lane and walked the short distance to a broken-down hovel. She knocked on the door and entered to the sounds of a screaming baby.

She came back out about half an hour later, bearing little three-month-old Alice Mullen, wrapped tightly in several tattered blankets and still wailing. Nell had done all she could to make Peg more comfortable. Now all she could do was give her friend some much needed rest by minding the baby for a while.

She walked up and down the lane, humming soothingly to the colicky child. At length, the fresh air and rhythmic movement had their effect. Alice's screams subsided into whimpers, and her rigid little body became limp in Nell's arms. Seeing that Alice had fallen asleep, Nell sat down on a crude bench in front of the cottage to rest her tired feet.

She looked down at Alice cradled in her arms. Thank God the baby had escaped the infection thus far, and the colic was something she would outgrow soon enough. She was sleeping peacefully now, breathing softly and making rhythmic sucking sounds with her tiny bow of a mouth. She had that lovely smell of a baby still at the breast. She was a darling.

Gently, carefully, Nell kissed Alice's forehead. What she wouldn't give to hold a baby of her own! Her own little one to soothe through colic and teething, to cuddle and play with. But why did it seem so unlikely?

Try as she would, somehow she couldn't imagine having a child with Darcy. But then, she was tired and under the weather and probably refining too much on the quarrel they'd just had. And she was allowing Lord Langdon's opposition to frighten her into imagining the worst.

She should stop wallowing in self-pity. There were those whose problems were much more serious than hers. Alice was healthy enough now, but her future was cruelly uncertain.

Nell spent the next hour sitting quietly and pondering the Mullens' problems without coming to any satisfactory solution. Her arms and shoulders began to ache, for she was afraid to shift her position.

She was at the point of wondering whether she could get Alice back into the cottage without arousing her when she heard the sucking sound of a horse's hooves on the muddy lane. She looked up to see Lord Langdon approaching on horseback. He had exchanged his uniform for breeches and a riding jacket, but there was still something decidedly military about his erect posture in the saddle. His thoughts seemed to be far away, however, and not in any pleasant place either if his grim expression was any indication.

She said nothing, hoping he would ride on without noticing her. But as he drew abreast of the cottage, their eyes met, and his frown gave way to a look of astonishment.

"Miss Ashley! What are you doing here?" he asked unceremoniously.

"Hush!" she said as softly as she could, but not caring if she matched him in rudeness. "I am minding this baby for her mother, who is sick."

She hoped he would go away. There were many things she wished to say to Lord Langdon, but it was not the right time. She was far too tired to be diplomatic, and she might say something she would later regret.

However, instead of riding on as she had fully expected, he dismounted. Letting his horse loose, he came over to stand in front of the bench. He towered over her, leaning down so that they could maintain a whispered conversation. She caught the scent of horses and old leather.

"Do you do this sort of thing often, Miss Ashley?" he asked more quietly.

Even lowered, his voice had resonating quality. More than ever she wished he would go away. He might wake the baby, and in any case, his curiosity could only be founded in the desire to prove to himself just what sort of low female his brother had embroiled himself with. No doubt the earl was disgusted to see her consorting with the dregs of the village social order. That was probably why he was staring at her as if she were some freak exhibited at a fair.

"Perhaps you are unaware that it is one of the duties of a clergyman's daughter to minister to the poor and the sick," she whispered with all the dignity she could muster. *"Someone* must care for these people, after all."

Instantly, she regretted her words, for his eyes widened and his body tensed. The last thing she wanted right now was to precipitate an argument.

"Miss Ashley, please do me the favor of explaining that last remark," he asked, raising his voice slightly.

"Softly please!" she hissed as Alice stirred and moaned. She would have to answer his question or he would think she was afraid of him. But first she had to be sure Alice was soundly asleep again. Then she had to get to her feet. She couldn't bear having him looming over her any longer.

When she tried to get up, she found her legs had gone numb from sitting too long on the hard bench. She staggered, clutching the baby tightly against her chest. Then she felt Lord Langdon's hands, large and strong, under her elbows, steadying her while she regained her balance. His firm hold sent a warm, pleasant sensation spreading through her. She felt an absurd compulsion to relax, to lean on him a little longer, but fought it. She was just tired—that was all. And it would be dangerous to show any further sign of weakness.

She straightened up and found that, standing so close, she still had to tilt her head back to look him in the eyes. She wanted to back away, but that would mean speaking more loudly, and she did not want to risk waking Alice with what she had to say.

Common courtesy obliged her to thank him for helping her up. If anything, his face hardened in response to her mild expression of gratitude.

"Please explain your earlier statements, Miss Ashley," he said impatiently.

"I am sorry, my lord, but I cannot in good conscience condone your neglect of these people," she whispered. "Just look at this horrid place in which the Mullens must live and raise a child! And your steward, Lytchett, has just this day threatened to evict them—or were you unaware of that fact?"

"As I understand it, Ned Mullen has taken to drinking and neglected his work. I see no reason to continue to employ every drunken wastrel in the neighborhood."

"Perhaps you are unaware of all the circumstances, my lord," she said, struggling to keep her voice lowered. "Ned was a hardworking, honest plowman before the accident. Can you not take some pity on him in his misfortune or, if not on him, on his family?"

"What accident?" he asked, a frown creasing his face.

"Ned's leg was broken by a kick from a green plow horse. Lytchett did not see fit to fetch a surgeon. Mr. Olden, the apothecary, did his best, but Ned's leg has not healed properly, and he cannot walk very well now even with a stick. His wages were stopped the day it happened, and since then, Peg has tried to support them by doing the odd bit of sewing. It is desperation that drove Ned to drink, my lord, not laziness. Can you not find it in you to at least allow them to continue here until Ned's leg is better or he can find other work?"

She had intended to speak dispassionately and keep to the facts, but at the end of her recital she was annoyed to find that her voice trembled a little. The earl had stood quietly throughout, watching her keenly, his arms crossed in front of him.

"I assure you that if there has been any injustice done, it shall be rectified. Are you satisfied now, Miss Ashley?"

His voice was cool, his manner totally unrepentant. Nell's heart sank; it seemed clear that he intended to do nothing at all for the Mullens—or anyone else for that matter. There would be no timely end to the neglect and misery she'd witnessed in the district in recent years.

"No, I am not," she answered. "I will believe it when I see it, my lord. You have neglected your responsibilities for so long. How can I be sure you will lift a finger for your people?"

His tanned complexion darkened a shade, and his eyes took on the color of the evening sky before a storm. It seemed that she'd finally managed to pierce his arrogance.

But after a short pause, he answered in a completely even, expressionless voice. "Because I have said it, you may trust that I will look into the matter of the Mullens. But Miss Ashley, it seems their case is but one of many you hold against me. Please be so good as to tell me what else I have done to incur your disapproval."

She wondered why he spoke with such exaggerated politeness. Was he testing her? Or perhaps mocking her for being so presumptuous as to criticize him? She didn't know, and she didn't care anymore. She would tell him all that he had asked, and in no softened terms, as her father had probably used. It was time someone did so.

"You have permitted that scoundrel Lytchett to neglect the land so that many of your honest tenants have left. He has replaced them with friends, rascals as greedy as himself, on short leases so they don't care how they farm the land or whether they ever plow a penny back into it.

"It has been years since anyone has bothered to repair these cottages; as you can see for yourself, they are not fit for animals to live in! You have neglected your pensioners, people like poor Matthew Cowden, who taught you to ride your first pony. Now Matthew is living in a drafty cottage, suffering from rheumatism, with nothing to do but try to remember the days when his faithful service was appreciated."

She paused to draw breath and looked down at Alice to make sure she was still asleep. Then she looked up to see what effect her words had on Lord Langdon. For a moment she felt a little fearful, for he looked angry enough to hit her. But it was no time to falter. No matter how much he despised her, she wouldn't let him think she feared him or the power he wielded.

James watched, rocklike, as she continued to cite instances of neglect and hardship among his people. Her accusations pierced his conscience, which was already stinging from the sights he'd seen in the past few days, and yet he tried to pay close attention. He couldn't afford to ignore any information about the state of affairs in Smallbourne, no matter how dubious the source. Still, his concentration faltered as he watched Miss Ashley.

She did look tired. Although her eyes were glowing with excitement, there were faint circles under them. Her chestnut curls seemed a trifle disorderly, but perhaps that was just the style she affected. There *was* something intensely protective about her attitude, the way she clutched the tiny infant. It reminded him of something, but he had no time to determine just what. For now, he had to deal with her accusations and determine why she was making them.

He'd been nearly certain that her charitable pose was just a ruse to convince him of her pious character. But her recital revealed an intimate, detailed knowledge of each of the families living in the parish. And as she spoke of them, her voice was low and passionate as if she truly cared. Was she indeed an honest woman or merely one of the cleverest actresses he'd ever met?

He broke off his speculations when he realized that she had moved off the subject of the villagers and on to the subject of his own family.

"And you have treated *them* with the same callous miserliness," she was saying. "Keeping them on paltry allowances, so that poor Lady Langdon is afraid to even buy a new hat for fear of your recriminations. And you have come near to ruining your brother's life! First refusing to buy him a pair of colors just so you could have all the adventure and glory for yourself. Then tying up his fortune so that he cannot set up his own establishment, as he has been longing to do. And then you cut both of them off from all their friends. Perhaps you have no close friends yourself, so you cannot know what that means. But it was the act of a monstrous tyrant!"

His eyes narrowed. So that was her game! Accusing him of miserliness to convince him to loosen his purse strings for his relations. Of course, she hoped to become one of them soon. He'd almost fallen for it too. But she'd gotten herself too worked up, played her role too thoroughly. She would learn that he was not so easily tricked.

"You take too much upon yourself, Miss Ashley. I do not need you to tell me how to manage my estate, much less my family. If you are wise, you will meddle no further in our affairs. You can have no right to do so."

That should be a sufficiently strong warning. But the look of distress that swept over her face was quickly replaced by a look of determination. So she was not to be so easily discouraged!

"I have all the right of sincere affection for them," she retorted, forgetting to keep her voice lowered. "A sentiment you apparently know nothing about!"

He started to answer, but at that point, the baby cried out.

"See what you have made me do!" said Miss Ashley. Looking down, she made some incoherent soothing noises, but the infant began to scream in earnest.

"This child needs to be fed," she announced. "Please go away now. You are not wanted here. Good day!"

With these words, she carried the baby into the cottage, slamming the door behind her.

Five

As Nell walked home from the Mullens, the nervous excitement that had carried her through her confrontation with the earl faded quickly into an uneasy sense of doubt. What exactly had she said to Lord Langdon? She couldn't even remember for certain—only it seemed that she had flung every possible insult at his head.

Plague take the man! Why had he insulted her, irritated her so that she forgot her resolution to behave in a civilized manner and express her concerns with sense and moderation?

But the fault was really her own. Papa had tried hard enough to teach her self-control and forbearance. She should have known better than to recklessly antagonize a man who held so much power over everyone she held dearest. And to make it worse, a man of such absolute pride and despotism. He would never let such an offense pass without retribution.

If he took his revenge on her alone, she might be able to bear it, but that was unlikely. What about her father? What about Darcy? What about the very people she had been trying to help?

The worst of it was, she couldn't think of anything she could do to mend matters. Perhaps she should apologize. But why should she when she had said nothing but the truth? And it was probably useless anyway. He would do whatever he pleased, riding roughshod over everyone who opposed him. Groveling would only add to his victory.

She tried to think of other plans, but her temples were throbbing and her mind refused to work. Her limbs felt weak and heavy, unwilling to carry her the bare quarter mile that remained to reach the vicarage. Somehow she got home and stumbled up the front steps.

This won't do, she thought. Betty and Silas were both ill, and someone had to feed the chickens, and it was high time she pruned the peaches, if she expected to have a decent crop this year. On the other hand, perhaps a short lie down on her bed before dinner would set her to rights.

If anything, she felt even worse when Hannah came up to rouse her for dinner. Touching her forehead briefly, Hannah forbade her to get up again. When the apothecary came, he confirmed Hannah's diagnosis of the influenza, reassuring the vicar once again that it was nothing more serious.

For the next three days, Nell was confined to her bed, trying not to complain about the hammers thudding in her head and through her entire body. In her less feverish moments, she remembered to thank Hannah for her services and to request news of the outside world.

Comfort arrived each day in the form of flowers from Darcy and little notes from Lady Langdon, sending wishes for a speedy recovery, along with the news that Lord Langdon had taken himself off to London.

It seemed that he had taken no immediate action against her. And yet in her depressed state of mind, she couldn't help wondering what his business was and whether it had anything to do with what she had said to him.

"So what do you think, Edward?" James looked expectantly at his friend, who was smoothly guiding the pair of bays around a curve in the carriage way at Hyde Park.

Colonel Huntley looked down at the horses. Thoughtfully, he pronounced his opinion. "I must say I prefer a high-perch phaeton myself. But the prads do go well together, and they seem sound enough. But, James, I hope you are never planning to *race* them?"

"Of course not. I'm too old for such things. I just want something that I can drive about in when I'm not riding. I find nothing so abominable as being cooped up in a closed carriage."

Edward laughed, a hearty, cheering sound. "You old? Then I'm a senile dotard! Well, buy the bays if you wish, but now that the surgeons have done with torturing me I'm going to find myself something more exciting to drive!"

"That's right. You've come into some money recently haven't you? How *is* your shoulder? Should I have let you drive so much?" James asked, taking the reins back from his friend.

"As good as new, dear boy. I just wish I hadn't had to come back to England before we'd made an end to it, that's all. But how are *you,* old friend?"

"Perfectly well. Why do you ask?"

"Look at yourself! You're only eight and twenty. You've just survived a damned bloody war. You're an earl and owner of one of the grandest estates in the south of England. Now, instead of enjoying yourself, all you can talk about is responsibility and duty. Next I'll hear you are setting up your nursery!"

"You are quite right, Edward. That will be another of my duties. Darcy and I are all that's left of the Maylands. He is too young to marry, I think, but I at least should take steps to assure the succession."

"Well, don't sound so enthusiastic about it, old fellow. Perhaps you've forgotten, but the society of the fair sex *can* be rather enjoyable sometimes. Just look!"

James followed Edward's gaze. Several young ladies in filmy gowns carrying frivolous parasols were strolling down a path near the carriageway. They giggled and looked away as they became aware of the gentlemen's regard.

"See what I mean," Edward continued. "I'm sure there are any number of pretty young things about town who would be more than happy to make your acquaintance."

At that point, they were obliged to stop and exchange greetings with a fashionably dressed matron riding in a barouche with several elegant young ladies beside her. She waved at James and, as the two carriages drew abreast of each other, declared herself to have been a friend of his parents. Her daughters simpered coquettishly as she introduced them, but as soon as it was reasonably polite to do so, James drove on.

"Now why did you do that?" asked Colonel Huntley in an aggrieved tone.

"I'm sorry, Edward. Did you wish to speak with them further? Are you hanging out for a wife yourself?"

"No, of course not. I'm a confirmed old bachelor, as you well know."

James smiled at that. Colonel Huntley was only thirty-eight and clearly not impervious to feminine charms.

Edward continued. "But that's no reason why *you* should snub such lovely creatures. And their mother said she knew your father, didn't she?"

"There are any number of ladies in London who knew my father. And it does *not* follow that I should have any desire to meet their daughters. They would not all be so eager if they knew my circumstances."

Edward flashed him a questioning look.

"I have just taken out a mortgage on Charlwood."

"No, really? I am so sorry, dear boy. I had no idea things had gotten so serious. I could have given you a loan. My aunt Agatha has left me quite well to pass, you know."

James paused, concentrating on guiding the phaeton past several slower-moving carriages. If he had remembered that Hyde Park was so crowded at this hour, he would never have agreed to Edward's suggestion to try out the bays here. However, he could see that Edward was enjoying the outing after his convalescence, so he forbore to complain.

"Thank you," he answered, grateful for his friend's characteristic generosity. "But I don't take advantage of friends. I have really been quite fortunate, however. My father's banker was surprisingly eager to oblige me. The amount and the terms of the loan are more generous than I had any right to expect. I suspect it is because he has a son in the army as well. In any case, I shall do quite well now, if only I can keep my family in line."

"I thought you'd paid off their debts and packed 'em off to

Sussex. Why do you still look so worried? Surely they can't get into much trouble there."

"I had certainly thought not."

Edward looked at him keenly and then laughed again. "What, has your brother taken up with a milkmaid or something?"

"No. Would that it were so simple! He's besotted with Miss Ashley, the vicar's daughter. It's only calf love, but I'm afraid he may do something foolish." He frowned as he thought of what might even now be happening back in Smallbourne. He certainly hoped Miss Ashley really did have the influenza and hadn't made a miraculous recovery when his back was turned.

"Would it be so very bad, his marrying this parson's daughter? It's no brilliant match, I'll agree, but you're not so high in the instep as to care about that surely?"

Edward was looking at him with his usual expression of kindly concern. Perhaps it would do no harm to tell his friend some of his troubles. He could trust Edward not to blab, and there was no tiger behind them to spread the tale of his family's indiscretions.

"I can imagine no greater disaster," he answered. "All he feels for her is a passing lust. You'll admit I've dealt with enough men Darcy's age to know the signs if he were truly in love. I've seen none of them. He would be bored with her before they were married a year! I also fear she is a fortune hunter. My family has introduced her to a style of life far beyond that to which she must be accustomed. Darcy's infatuation must seem a heaven-sent opportunity for her to advance herself. I shudder to imagine their life together. Frittering away their money on every fashionable frivolity, living beyond their means, and—"

"And coming to you every time they need rescuing?" asked Edward with a knowing look.

James nodded. "I'm afraid my father never taught Darcy any sense of responsibility. He allowed my brother to spend a fortune on horses, cards, and opera dancers. He might have at least tried to interest Darcy in the estate. Things might not have come to such a pass. I should have come home two years ago. I know that now."

"Oh, don't blame yourself, James. Are you sure matters are as desperate as all that? Maybe this Miss Ashley isn't as bad as you think. Neither is your brother, I suspect. What young man of—twenty-one, isn't he?—was ever perfectly steady and reliable? Excepting yourself of course." Edward chuckled.

James was obliged to smile, but shook his head. "I should have come back sooner. It isn't just my brother. My stepmother hasn't been precisely a model of economy either. How I ever hoped a daughter of Rotherby's would have the slightest notion of managing her own budget—"

"Rotherby, did you say?" Edward interrupted unexpectedly.

"Yes. Did you know him?"

"We met a few times."

James looked at his friend curiously. There was a strange note in Edward's voice, and an odd, hard expression on his ruddy, good-natured face. Whatever had passed between him and Rotherby must have been pretty unpleasant. But a moment later Edward had recovered something like his usual jovial manner.

"So your stepmother is expensive, is she?" he asked thoughtfully.

"Yes, just like her parents. Every year a new carriage, new furnishings, a new wardrobe. I shudder to think what she cost my father in jewelry alone. Well, she will have to accustom herself to living within her jointure, for there is too much that needs doing on the estate for me to continue to let her hang on my sleeve. Which reminds me, I will be going back tomorrow."

"Yes, you're longing to get back to Sussex, aren't you? Some fresh air will do you good. Can't say that I blame you. I like London well enough at times, but I've been thinking of finding some nice place in the country myself."

"Why don't you come along? You know you don't need to wait for an invitation."

Once again, there was an odd constraint in the colonel's manner. He returned a noncommittal answer, and James let the matter drop.

* * *

Lord Langdon nodded with satisfaction as he urged his new bays up a hill about ten miles from Smallbourne. While not up to the standard of Darcy's chestnuts, they were proving to be as reliable and well matched as the seller had claimed. Going as they did by easy stages, they should have no trouble reaching Charlwood by nightfall. But the fresh air and the sprightly action of his new pair still didn't quite succeed in dispelling his anxiety over what awaited him there.

He had timed his trip to London as well as he could. Since Darcy couldn't very well propose to Miss Ashley while she was laid up, it had seemed like a good opportunity for him to leave Charlwood.

And his errands *had* prospered. It really had been a relief to be able to pay off his family's debts. He'd still have to make sure neither his brother nor his stepmother overspent their allowances again. But the truth was, they would be able to live quite comfortably now, if they kept their expenditures to what was reasonable.

And now he could set his house back in order again, make it what it was in his mother's day. Come to think of it, Edward was right. He really should start thinking about marriage. With a few children running about, Charlwood might not feel like such a damned mausoleum anymore. That would have to wait however. For now, it was more important that he get his estate back in order.

Miss Ashley had been right about that, at least. He'd never imagined that the tidy, prosperous village of his youth would come to so closely resemble some of the war-stricken towns he'd passed through in Spain and Portugal. He'd seen enough starving peasants there to last a lifetime. It had been a kick in the belly to see them on his own estate.

He wouldn't rest until every man, woman, and child on his lands had at least enough to eat and a decent roof over his or her head. And his steward would have to go, even if he couldn't find a replacement immediately. James had talked to his tenants and pored over the books just enough to discover the discrepancies between the rents that were paid and what ended up in the estate coffers. Lytchett was not only incompetent, but he'd also been stealing from the estate off and on during the years since he'd taken over the job from his father. Uneasily, James realized that Lytchett's character was yet another point on which Miss Ashley had been correct.

He had relived that scene outside the Mullens' cottage time and again these past days. Even now, when his head was cooler, he couldn't decide what to make of the young woman. Had she been sincere or was it all just overacting?

Then he remembered how tired she had looked and how she had practically stumbled into his arms when she tried to get up from that bench. An odd, keen pleasure had surged through him as he'd held her for those few moments. But he thrust back the memory. This was no time to let his baser instincts cloud his judgment. She could have just been stiff from sitting there waiting for him to ride by and be impressed by her charity.

The fact remained that she had spoken the truth about the people on his estate. Had she been right about his family as well? Had he indeed treated them unfairly?

He'd never taken the time to get to know his stepmother. His opinion of her had never been high; he still saw no reason to change it. But she was part of his family now, and it was time to accept the fact with a better grace.

And what about Darcy? He really hadn't given his brother a chance to prove he was anything but a complete ne'er-do-well. He would have to try harder. Perhaps he should show Darcy the books, get him more involved with the estate. It might do his brother good to be set to work for a change.

But that still didn't solve the problem of Miss Ashley.

He'd learned a few things while in London that complicated matters further. A chance statement about the Ashleys to his man of business had brought to light their connection with Joshua Ashley, an India merchant with quite a respectable fortune. Further discreet inquiries turned up the fact that she was to receive two thousand pounds from her uncle on the occasion of her marriage. It seemed that she would not be a penniless bride, but that was no comfort, since it only made a speedy marriage all the more likely. But it did raise questions.

Did Darcy think they could live on Miss Ashley's dowry for

four more years? Not at his previous rate of expenditures, they wouldn't. But was *that* what Darcy had had in mind when he'd stated that he expected nothing from his brother? James fervently hoped that he hadn't antagonized Darcy enough that he'd make the attempt. He might have to act quickly to make sure his brother didn't make a mistake he would regret the rest of his life.

But was it a mistake? How could he know whether Miss Ashley actually cared for his brother? It would be useless to confront her. Just as futile to discuss the matter with her father. The vicar was too mild and innocent to recognize underhanded motives in anyone, let alone his own daughter. James had early on rejected the idea of using his influence over the Reverend Ashley to thwart Miss Ashley's suspected schemes. There was no harm in the old gentleman and, James suspected, a great deal of goodness. His parishioners seemed fond of him, at any rate.

This was all getting nowhere. He had to find a way to discover whether Miss Ashley cared for Darcy for his own sake, or whether she, like too many of her sex, wanted Darcy only for his prospective fortune and noble name. James remembered the ladies he'd met in the park yesterday and how eager they had been to meet an unmarried and ostensibly wealthy lord. No doubt some of them looked for love, but he thought, cynically, there were probably at least as many who were perfectly willing to sell themselves to the highest bidder. He couldn't let Darcy fall prey to that sort of trap.

The highest bidder. The words echoed in his mind, forming the beginnings of a plan. No, he couldn't do it. It was devious and underhanded and would require some subtlety. Subtlety was not his forte. But for his brother's sake, he had to learn Miss Ashley's real goal.

The highest bidder. The highest bidder. The thought kept repeating, in the rhythm of his horses cantering up the final stretch. If his plan failed, Darcy might never forgive him. But no one in Sussex knew that things had come to such a state that he had to mortgage Charlwood. It could work.

He came to a decision as he steadied his horses for the

descent on the other side of the hill. He knew now what he had to do.

Nell looked defiantly up at Lord Langdon. This was her first visit back to Charlwood after recovering from the influenza. She had hoped to get through it without having to endure a meeting with him. She had had a pleasant chat with Lady Langdon, although her hopes of seeing Darcy were frustrated. Lady Langdon had said that Darcy had gone out to exercise his horse and hadn't realized that Nell was up from her sickbed yet.

So she had swallowed her disappointment and taken her leave; she had gotten all the way to the marble entrance hall before Lord Langdon intercepted her there. No doubt, with the intention of repeating his warning not to meddle with his family. She felt a sudden chill. It was probably just an aftereffect of the influenza, she told herself, squaring her shoulders and resolutely meeting Lord Langdon's gaze.

"Good morning," he said. His tone was surprisingly cordial, but she noticed that his smile did not reach his eyes. In fact, his expression was no more revealing than those of the marble busts of various ancestors and classical figures that decorated the cold, lofty hall.

"Good morning, my lord." She curtsied and would have gone on her way, but he held her back with a hand on her arm.

"Miss Ashley, I have been thinking about the conversation we had a few days ago. I have drawn up a list of the repairs I believe necessary to my pensioners' cottages, and I would greatly appreciate it if you could look it over and see if there is anything I have missed. Would you join me in my study for a few moments if it is not inconvenient?"

She looked at him in amazement for a few moments. It was impossible. She must be imagining it. He couldn't actually be asking to consult her about his pensioners. After all the harsh accusations she'd hurled at him in front of the Mullens' cottage? But he was watching her expectantly. It must be true.

Should she go with him to be alone with him in his study?

A little misgiving fluttered through her again, and she stifled it. This was no time to be fearful or missish. She would never forgive herself if she gave up such an opportunity to be of real use to her dear old friends. She couldn't disregard the little hope growing inside her. The hope that Lord Langdon had had a change of heart.

She nodded and followed him into his study, noting with relief that he left the door wide open. As she stepped over the threshold, she looked about in curiosity. She had never been in this room before.

She found it rather depressing. The faded green walls were bare, although they showed marks where pictures once hung. She wondered why Lord Langdon hadn't had his father's pictures retrieved from London or bought some new ones of his own.

Although the room was furnished with a broad mahogany desk and several large, comfortable-looking chairs, the earl neither offered her a seat nor took one himself. Instead, he walked over to stand by one of the two tall windows that overlooked the gardens.

Nell realized that he had probably been watching her and Darcy from this very vantage point on the morning of their first meeting. That would explain his perfectly timed interference. She tried to set aside the memory. Perhaps Lord Langdon had actually given her concerns some serious consideration. If that were so, perhaps he had revised his opinion of her, as well.

He turned back to face her, but she found it difficult to read his feelings from his face or his manner. His expression was guarded, yet she sensed that he was tense, even ill at ease, if that was possible for one so commanding.

"Is that the list, my lord?" she asked, gesturing toward a pile of papers set in the middle of the desk.

"Yes, Miss Ashley," he said, interposing himself between her and the desk. He cleared his throat before continuing.

"Before you look at it, I must tell you that I have been speaking to some of my pensioners about you. I have heard the most glowing reports of your kindness to them. I am glad to know that in my family's absence they have had such a good friend."

She looked at him uncertainly. His words were more than kind, and yet there was still something forced about their delivery. Was the man naturally so stiff? Perhaps it was just a sign of the effort it cost him to come so close to admitting a previous error. One so proud would surely not find it easy to do so. If so, it was greatly to his credit that he was making the attempt. The least she could do was to show she appreciated his effort.

She gave him the most sincere smile she could muster. An odd grimace passed so briefly over his face that she wondered if she had imagined it.

"I cannot wonder at Darcy's interest in you either," he said, lowering his voice slightly. "You have made conquests of everyone at Charlwood."

Again, she struggled with her disbelief. How could a few conversations with his dependents have caused such a complete reversal in his attitude?

Aware that he was watching her intently, she answered, "I am honored that you should think so, my lord, but surely you exaggerate. Perhaps I should be looking at the list now?"

She moved toward the desk, expecting him to step aside. He did not, however, and so she found herself standing very close to him, acutely conscious of his height and breadth as he blocked her way.

"Perhaps I should have said, you have made conquests of *everyone* at Charlwood, Miss Ashley, including its master." His voice was low and resonant, and she was transfixed by the sound.

He took a step toward her and put an arm around her waist, pulling her toward him. With his other hand, he lifted her chin and looked intently at her face. She stared back, paralyzed with shock.

"Ah, you do not protest, I see," he said softly. Was it triumph or disappointment she heard in his voice?

She tried to answer, but it was too late. He slid his hand around to the back of her neck, pulled her face toward his, and kissed her.

Six

The kiss began lightly, but almost instantly escalated in force. It was like nothing Nell had ever imagined. Lord Langdon's mouth was hot and hard. It demanded entrance to hers, then explored it with fiery thoroughness. His powerful hand kneaded the back of her neck; his other arm, around her waist, crushed her against him so that she felt his every heartbeat.

For a shocked instant she yielded to his fierce caresses, to the unfamiliar, feverish response his demands triggered from deep inside her. But all her senses, as well as her mind, told her that his desire for her was laced with contempt. It was now abundantly clear how he thought of her.

She twisted her head aside, breaking the kiss, and struggled to free herself. She suffered a moment of panic when she discovered that, even one handed, he could hold her securely.

An instant later, he abruptly released her.

Although her legs trembled, she backed away, watching him warily, desperately trying to catch her breath. He took a step toward her. She backed away farther.

"Do not touch me again!" she warned, holding up a hand against his advance even as she realized it was hopeless to think she could hold him off.

Then he stopped, clutching the back of his chair as if to restrain himself. He was breathing quickly, a thunderous look on his face. Clearly, her resistance had surprised and infuriated him. Did he think her totally lacking in virtue merely because she had innocently welcomed his brother's kiss? She had to make it clear to him that she was not some sort of country trollop ready for his amusement.

"How dare you? Did you think I would welcome your advances, Lord Langdon?"

He stared at her for a moment, the angry expression fading to a frown.

"I thought you might," he admitted. "But I assure you I have no intention of repeating myself."

She stared back. Once again, his face was an impenetrable mask pierced with icy blue eyes. No mere lecher could look so cool so soon after being repulsed. Not if he had really desired her. She was safe now, but why had he behaved so?

Then she remembered Darcy saying that he planned to meet Lord Langdon in his study at about this very hour. With a sinking heart, she realized the true motivation behind Lord Langdon's advances. How foolish she had been in hoping to ever be accepted by Darcy's brother!

When she thought of how easily she had almost fallen into the earl's trap, she couldn't decide if she was more furious with him or herself. Or why her fury made the tears well up in her eyes.

"You thought that you could seduce me with your title and wealth, that you could force me to betray myself before Darcy," she said, surprised to find that her voice didn't shake. "You were mistaken, my lord. I warn you: There is nothing you can do to prevent Darcy from marrying me, if he wishes. You will be the only loser if you persist in this contest!"

"We shall see about that," he said, the anger in his voice belying his stony expression.

She turned and walked quickly out of the room before he could see her tears begin to flow.

James waited, motionless, until he could no longer hear the rustle of Miss Ashley's skirts as she ran down the hall. Only then did he seek relief in furiously pacing the room.

It was no use. Finally he sat down at his father's desk and

tried to concentrate on the papers spread out upon it. They blurred before his eyes. He got back up and went to stand by the window.

He wondered what had delayed Darcy. Now he could only be thankful that his brother had not arrived in time to witness his botched attempt to expose Miss Ashley.

He cursed himself. He should never have tried such a trick; he was always better at a more direct approach. It had seemed that subtlety was necessary in this case. If he hadn't lost control of himself and forgotten his plan, it would have had a chance of success.

He had meant to entice the girl, but all he had succeeded in doing was to frighten her. Yet for one intoxicating moment, she had yielded. He could still see her wide hazel eyes looking up into his, could still feel the lips that parted so easily to admit his kiss, the softness of her breasts pressed up against his chest. Her smell still lingered with him, earthy and floral like a meadow on the Downs.

He hated to admit it, but he had yielded as well. In that moment, he had felt more alive than he had for months, perhaps years. And he could almost swear she had enjoyed his fierce attentions. If he had been gentler, more adroit, would she have pulled away? Could he have prolonged the kiss until Darcy's arrival? Guiltily, he realized that he wished he had, but for reasons having nothing to do with his brother.

Foolishness! He had worried about Darcy, not realizing that he himself was in danger of being taken in by the unprincipled jade. For such she surely was. A properly brought-up young lady would have swooned at what he had done to her. For that matter, she wouldn't have even allowed herself to be put in such a situation, alone with a gentleman. And at the very least, she would have run away rather than stay to calmly threaten her would-be seducer.

But as he thought about it, he wasn't sure he hadn't seen tears in her eyes as she left the study. Suddenly he was assaulted with the piercing apprehension of having wounded something young and innocent.

He fought it down. It could not be. He could not have been

so wrong. She had smiled at his overblown compliments and responded to his caresses—he was sure of it. No innocent girl would have behaved as she had. Only a brazen schemer would have been clever enough to recognize and foil his own scheme so quickly. He would have to think of some better plan to persuade Darcy to give her up.

He would also have to try to undo the damage from this sordid incident. He had been prepared to take the consequences if Darcy had walked in on himself and Miss Ashley, but now there was no benefit to be had from it. Only a deepening of the rift between him and his brother.

No doubt that was why Darcy was so late. She had probably met him in the hall and was even now pouring out her troubles to him, poisoning him against James. Darcy would come to his study, and he would have to try to explain his actions. Once again, they would argue over her.

James went back to the desk, sat down heavily, and tried to occupy himself with business as he waited for Darcy. But images of Miss Ashley intruded on his every thought, mocking him with his failure to protect his brother and with his own weakness. After several futile attempts to examine the papers before him, he crashed his fist down on the table, hard enough so that the pain of it brought him back to his senses.

He *would* find a way to thwart her. And he *would* find a way to combat his own growing obsession with her.

Seven

"I don't believe you, James. I can't believe you really did it!"

Darcy's words echoed loudly in the quiet study.

"I did," James answered bluntly.

"No, I don't believe it. You're just trying to frighten me."

"I am not. See for yourself." He arranged several papers on the other side of the desk for Darcy to examine, then sat back to observe his brother's reactions.

About ten minutes after Miss Ashley had left, Darcy had burst into the study, full of awkward apologies and the story of his horse throwing a shoe. Apparently he hadn't met Miss Ashley on her way out.

Perhaps James should have just made a clean breast of the matter to Darcy, but his sense of shame and defeat were still too strong. Instead, he had decided to take advantage of the brief reprieve and acquaint his brother with the estate business. Tomorrow would be soon enough to deal with the consequences of his failed scheme to expose Miss Ashley.

For now, he had the dubious satisfaction of seeing Darcy's expression turn from one of disbelief to stunned shock.

"You are serious, aren't you? You really have taken out a mortgage on Charlwood," said Darcy, looking with wide eyes at the neat summary of their financial status that James had prepared for the occasion. "Is that really the sum of my debts?"

Darcy's stricken expression seemed sincere. Had he really

been so unaware of the magnitude of the debts he and Lady Langdon had incurred?

"Yours," James answered. "And our stepmother's."

"I had no idea. Papa always lent me money to pay my debts and never said a word about it!"

"I will not do so, however."

"I don't expect you to," his brother retorted. "But you could have just told me about it, instead of lecturing me as if I were a simpleton or a small child."

James merely cocked an eyebrow.

"All right then! I should have taken greater care. But I didn't know this could happen. What's to be done now? We can't let Charlwood go out of the family!"

A frantic note had crept into Darcy's voice. This was promising. Should he reassure him? Or would it be salutary to let him fret a little more?

"I hope to be able to prevent that from happening. But if we are to do so, I must have your word that you will not outrun the allowance provided to you."

"You have it. What else?"

"You may familiarize yourself with *this*," said James, waving toward the pile of papers and ledgers littering the desk. "I am getting rid of Lytchett, and until I can replace him I can use your help. That is, if you feel up to the challenge."

"I can do it. Just tell me where to start," answered Darcy, eyeing the desk bravely. "And, James . . ."

"Yes?"

"I *am* sorry. About my debts and for calling you a miserly pinchpenny."

"I am sorry too. I have not dealt with you as I should. I hope we shall do better in the future," said James, forcing a smile, even as a stab of sadness went through him. This new-found rapport with his brother might not last. He must enjoy it while he could. Perhaps he could even risk a subtle warning. "And, brother . . .

"Yes?"

"I hope—that is, I trust you will think carefully before making any important decisions while our situation is so precarious. Do you understand?"

There was an odd look of determination on Darcy's face as he answered. "I do. I promise you, James, I will not disappoint you."

As he got into bed that night, James reflected on Darcy's promise. Under any other circumstances, he would have been elated at the progress he had made that day with Darcy. But all he could think now was how fragile, how tenuous the bond between them really was.

Darcy had patiently sat with him for several unexpectedly productive hours, helping him go over tenancy agreements and accounts. Conversation that evening had flowed almost pleasantly for the first time since they had all been reunited, although James couldn't quite remember what had been said.

Unfortunately, there was no assurance that this brief period of cooperation would continue. He feared that Darcy would grow bored and restless with the tasks he'd been assigned. Now he might never find out if his brother had the tenacity to follow through on his promises. Darcy's willing assistance would likely end the day he found out how his brother had kissed Miss Ashley.

Damned young fool! Not that he, James, was any better. If Miss Ashley hadn't broken off the kiss first, would he have had the good sense to do so once it was clear that Darcy was late? It didn't seem likely, for just the memory of her in his arms was enough to bring on the insane wish to do it all again.

He jumped back out of his bed and began pacing about the room, but the exercise only inflamed him further. He stopped, and leaned down over the fireplace mantel, resting his head against the marble, hoping its coolness would bring him back to his senses.

He had responsibilities. He had let himself become perilously close to forgetting that. The situation could easily have gone from mildly scandalous to downright compromising, and he might have been obliged to marry the girl himself. The fifth Earl of Langdon caught in his own snare, by God!

How could he have so totally lost his self-control?

The answer was only too clear. He was no better than his father had been, no more able to govern his passions, no more able to resist the allure of the wrong sort of female.

He'd been eleven years old when he first learned his father's true nature. He remembered it clearly. He'd run into the study to boast about having successfully cleared an oxer on one of his father's new hunters. Then he saw the earl sitting in the window embrasure, fondling a woman.

James never saw her face, but from her opulent if rumpled dress he knew it was a highborn married lady, one of their houseguests. It was not his mother! He ran away, not knowing what else to do. Later, his father found him in the stables and convinced him not to tell his mother, for it would only upset her. James finally agreed, for of course he didn't wish Mama to cry. And so he had become an accessory to his father's crime.

When he grew up, he swore he'd always be master of his own passions. Whatever he did, he would never allow lust to overcome his sense of responsibility. Once married, he would never betray his wife, never give her cause for grief or jealousy.

Now he seemed on the verge of forgetting all he owed his brother, his estate and his dependents. It was his duty to protect Darcy from the consequences of youthful infatuation. It was also his duty to marry an honest, caring woman, one who would be his helpmate and a good mother to his children.

He lifted his head from the mantel and walked over to the open window, gulping in the cool night air. He gazed out over the gardens and the lake, silvery in the moonlight, with the dark contours of the woods looming beyond. A nightingale was singing somewhere, the liquid trills of its song bringing back memories of more carefree times.

He *would* do better than his lecherous sire. He wouldn't make a botch of his marriage the way his father had. He'd seen enough faithful couples among his fellow officers and their wives to know it was possible.

Harry and Juana Smith. He'd met them at an impromptu

ball the soldiers had arranged several winters ago. James had
even had the good fortune of dancing with Juana. She had
been a graceful and charming partner, yet when Harry re-
claimed her afterward, anyone with eyes could see that neither
gave a fig for anyone else.

Of course, there were the Dalbiacs—his colonel of a few
years past, with his frail-looking, sweet little wife. They were
inseparable, Susannah riding with the colonel at the head of
the regiment, whether on the march or under fire. After Salamanca, she had searched tirelessly for her husband in the dark
among the dead and dying. She'd rescued her seriously
wounded cousin before being reunited with the colonel, who
had mercifully come through the bloody day unscathed.

Juana Smith and Susannah Dalbiac. They were wives to
make a man proud. Both small, dainty women with a strength
of character that sustained them through gruelling marches and
cold, rainy bivouacs. Never too busy to invite a tired, hungry
soldier into their tents for dinner, never too squeamish to tend
the goriest wound. And unselfishly devoted to their husbands.

If he could find such a woman, surely he would no longer
have a desire for anyone else. Or at the very least, his sense
of duty would prevent him from acting upon it. Where was
she to be found?

A slight breeze blew up, bringing the mingled scent of the
gardens into the room. Without warning, a vision intruded
upon him. Lush gardens and shimmering water. A rosy face
framed in gleaming chestnut curls. Tilted upward, lips half
open, ready for a kiss.

With a wrench, he dismissed the tantalizing image. Whatever she was, she was not for him.

Today was the day Darcy would ask her to marry him, Nell
thought as she put on her bonnet and spencer. Her fingers
trembled a little, and she couldn't decide if the flutter in her
stomach was excitement or apprehension.

She examined her reflection in the little mirror hanging in

the hall. Her new spencer, and the ribbons decorating her old hat, were both of a shade like new leaves. Lady Langdon had said it would emphasize the green in her eyes.

Despite her smart new apparel, she still looked the same old Nell. But she felt as if a stranger was looking back at her. The same stranger who had just yesterday surrendered to Lord Langdon's embrace for a few fevered moments. Her lips didn't *look* bruised— and yet she couldn't forget his kiss. Or the frightening knowledge that he could exert such control over her as to make her forget, even briefly, all that she stood for and cared about.

She had met Darcy on her way home from Charlwood. Although she'd meant to tell him about the earl's kiss, when the moment came, she couldn't do it. Instead she had just hastily accepted Darcy's invitation to go driving this morning, then hurried home. When she got back to the vicarage, she had retreated to her room, telling Hannah she still felt weak from the aftereffects of the influenza.

In the privacy of her room, she had finally let flow the tears that had been threatening ever since she had fled from Lord Langdon's study. But she had felt no better afterward. Now she knew exactly what Lord Langdon thought of her and how ruthless he would be in thwarting her hopes. Worse, she didn't know what he had thought of her hesitation in breaking off the kiss. Did he realize it was just shock? Or did he still think her the sort of female who would shamelessly fall into his arms just because he had greater wealth and influence than his brother?

She had roused herself to go down to dinner and talk to her father as if nothing had happened. She still felt a twinge of guilt about it, but somehow she couldn't bring herself to distress Papa with the tale of yesterday's events. And what, after all, could he do about it? She hated to imagine the results if he confronted Lord Langdon.

And she still thought she had done right in not telling Darcy. Lord Langdon surely wouldn't, since the knowledge would almost certainly provoke Darcy into rebellion. She didn't know if Lord Langdon had the good sense not to accept a challenge to fight his younger brother. Although Darcy was brave enough for anything, he would be no match for one who was both taller and heavier and a seasoned soldier.

No, it would be dangerous to tell Darcy the whole truth. It wasn't as if she had done anything wrong herself. Surely she could welcome his advances with a clear conscience.

She and Darcy *did* need to discuss his brother's likely objections to their marriage. They could defy family opposition and find happiness, as her parents had done, but they would have to work together to accomplish that goal. And if they didn't succeed in gaining Lord Langdon's approval, they would just find a way to do without it. The earl might succeed in tainting the joy of the present moment, but she was determined not to let him ruin the rest of their lives.

Soon enough, she saw Darcy drive his team of high-bred chestnuts up to the vicarage. Her father came to see them off, wishing them a pleasant drive. Nell felt a slight pang to see the vicar hiding his fatherly anxiety behind a kindly smile.

In all too few moments, Darcy helped her up into the curricle, and they set off. At first, Darcy was fully occupied in keeping his horses under control through the narrow village lanes. Nell could see that they were still very fresh, the distance between the Charlwood stables and the vicarage being too short for them to have worked off any of their excess energy.

The day had dawned very bright and clear, only a few clouds enlivening the vividly blue sky. They left Smallbourne, and Darcy let his chestnuts stretch into a canter down a comparatively straight stretch of road, bordered on each side by mature trees, now sheathed in the luxuriant green of early summer.

"What a perfect day this is!" she forced herself to say. She wouldn't let thoughts of Lord Langdon spoil it.

"Only as perfect as the company!" was Darcy's gallant response.

For some minutes they drove on in silence, as Darcy concentrated on handling the spirited team. When the horses had gotten rid of their excess energy, he settled them into a gentle trot.

"Dearest Nell," he began. "You must know the reason I have wanted to be private with you."

She nodded and tried to smile encouragingly.

"Then promise you will marry me and make me the happiest man in England," he said, slowing the horses to a walk. Holding his reins and whip in one hand, he took her hand in his free one and lifted it to his lips. She didn't resist, but she couldn't answer either. Somehow it all felt unreal. His kiss, even the bright sun and the green trees about them—they were all part of a dream.

He released her hand and slid his arm about her waist. He bent his head down to her, but on the verge of kissing her, he stopped. Perhaps he was troubled by her silence, or perhaps he saw the indecision in her face.

"What is wrong, Nell?"

She looked down at her hands, then back up at him. She couldn't explain. She wasn't sure she knew what was happening to her either. Perhaps it was Darcy's unfortunate resemblance to his brother, reminding her painfully of yesterday's disastrous interlude with the earl.

Darcy was still watching her anxiously. She had to say something. Perhaps it would be wisest to stick to her previously chosen course, to confide her concerns to Darcy.

"I am sorry. I am very worried about your brother. I believe he will use all possible means to prevent us from marrying."

"Are you honestly going to refuse me over such a trifle?" he asked hastily.

"No, of course not! But you must believe that I do not wish to come between the two of you, and if he has control of your fortune—"

"No, you don't understand him, Nell. I am sure he will come around to our engagement," he said, giving her a slight squeeze that did little to reassure her. How could he sound so confident? But then, he was still blissfully ignorant of how Lord Langdon had insulted her yesterday.

She stiffened, and he released her, looking indignant.

"What? Are you still worried about James? I tell you, he won't give us any trouble."

"I hope you are right," she answered. "I am sorry if I seem nervous."

He looked at her thoughtfully, then said, "I should explain why I don't think James will object."

Darcy looked oddly embarrassed. She couldn't imagine what he was going to say next, but nodded for him to go on.

"Well, I know about your uncle and your inheritance."

"You do? How—oh, I suspect Lytchett told you!"

"Are you very angry, Nell?"

"No, not with you, that is. With Lytchett, yes, I am angry. I asked him not to tell anyone. Does your brother know?"

"No, I haven't told him, but I hope to do so, if you will allow me. Why did you do such a thing? Giving Lytchett part of your allowance to give to our pensioners, but not wanting anyone to know?"

"I didn't want people like old Matthew to feel your family had forgotten them. One has to consider their pride, you know. They are so devoted to your family, it pleased them inordinately to think that your brother remembered them in these hard times," she said, unable to keep the sarcasm entirely out of her voice. "Actually, the most difficult part of the business was keeping Lytchett from pocketing the money for himself."

"That was dashed good of you, Nell. I have never met anyone so generous or thoughtful!"

"You are too kind," she answered, smiling. When Uncle Joshua had sent her a hundred pounds at Christmas, she had thought herself quite wealthy. Although she'd spent a portion of it to furbish up her wardrobe, she'd had almost equal pleasure in using the remainder to supplement the pitifully small estate pensions. Now Darcy's approval was another reward for her efforts.

"Tell me, Nell. Does it bother you that I've known about your fortune?" he asked, looking seriously at her.

"No, why should it? Oh, Darcy, I do not suspect you of being a fortune hunter! Why, the first day we met you had just come down from London. You could have had no idea that I had any money at all."

Darcy didn't laugh in response. In fact, she couldn't quite read his expression. Was it relief or embarrassment or guilt she saw there?

"The existence of your fortune *does* make things easier now," he said.

"You speak as if it were some wonderful sum. I am sure Lord Langdon will think it paltry."

"Why should he?" said Darcy, raising his eyebrows. "He's not so greedy as all that, you know. It's just that what with how things are going on the estate, I think he'll be glad to hear about it."

"I don't understand. What do you mean?"

Darcy looked away. Nell sensed that he was embarrassed again. Finally he turned back to her and answered her in a more sober voice than she had heard him use before.

"James has been obliged to mortgage Charlwood. To pay off my father's debts—and mine."

She stared at him, dumbfounded. Darcy had run into debt?

"I hope you don't judge me too harshly, Nell. But James was right to lecture me before. I have been spending a trifle too freely and playing too deep. But believe me, you need have no fear that you are marrying a hopeless gambler. I have promised to be more moderate in the future, and I mean to keep my word. So please tell me you do not despise me!"

Surprise kept her silent for a few moments. Darcy, a gamester and a reckless spendthrift? But no, she'd seen no signs of it in the time they'd been together. True, there was little opportunity for him to run into trouble in their quiet village, but he really hadn't seemed bored playing for imaginary stakes with her and Lady Langdon. Nor did he drink to excess, and his dress was elegant, not flashy. He did have fine horses, but so did every other young gentleman in his circumstances.

"Are you sure Lord Langdon was not exaggerating your debts, perhaps in order to frighten you?" she asked, finally.

"I did think so at first. Now I'm pretty sure he's in the right of it."

Nell wasn't so certain. She wouldn't put it past Lord Langdon to try to frighten his brother into submission. If Darcy was so far under his brother's influence, there was nothing she could say to counteract it.

"Nell, please say you don't despise me for it!" Darcy reiterated.

"How could I despise you? And if you *have* been foolish in the past, I am sure you will go on much better now," she said uncertainly.

"Please don't look so distressed, dear Nell! Honestly, I'm no gamester at heart. I know I'm unworthy of you, but believe me when I say it's the greatest wish of my heart to make you as happy as you deserve to be!"

She had been longing to hear just these words. Now she only felt numb, incapable of reacting or making a decision.

"Dash it, you're not refusing me, are you?"

She felt a rush of mortification at Darcy's shocked tone. What sort of missish fool was she, encouraging him, then succumbing to doubt at the crucial moment? She couldn't help it though. She was too full of questions, too overwhelmed by the enormity of the decision she was about to make. She needed time to think, to make sense of what he had just told her about himself and his brother.

"N-no, I am sorry I am being so foolish, but—but we really have not been acquainted for very long," she said at last. "Please, will you give me some time to think about my answer?"

She looked up at him, half fearing to see his reaction. The incredulous expression on his face quickly transformed itself into a confident smile.

He gave her hand a little squeeze and said, "Dear Nell. I've rushed you, haven't I? Very well then I will give you time to think about it."

She thanked him, profoundly grateful for his quick understanding and for the way he kept up an easy, lighthearted conversation all the way home. Gradually, she began to relax. He was so truly kind and gentlemanly, so unlike his brother. This was the Darcy she had fallen in love with.

However, she still couldn't understand why he was so sanguine about their prospects. Try as she would, she couldn't shake the suspicion that the challenges ahead were more formidable than either of them had previously suspected.

Eight

"I called at Southcott today. Miss Nettlehurst has accepted my offer of marriage."

Darcy and Lady Langdon both stared at James, their spoons suspended over their soup for several moments. Clearly they hadn't expected such a response to Lady Langdon's polite inquiry about his day.

Darcy recovered first.

"Congratulations, James," he said. "I wish you happy, but—well, isn't it all a bit sudden?"

"I see no reason to delay an inevitable duty. I must marry someday, after all, and I believe Clarissa will make me an admirable wife."

Not for the world would he reveal the real reason behind his haste—his conviction that a commitment to a lady of undoubted character was the surest defense against his dangerous attraction toward Nell Ashley. Although he did plan, after dinner, to tell Darcy about yesterday's ill-fated encounter with that scheming young woman. It would be bad, but not as bad as leaving it to her to tell the tale.

He had been lucky not to have been called to task for his actions already. After a restless night, he had overslept. When he had arisen, Darcy was already gone. His brother must not have seen Miss Ashley, though, for why would she have avoided using the incriminating story against James?

"I am sure she will," said Lady Langdon warmly. "Clarissa is a very beautiful and amiable young lady."

It took James a few seconds to remember that they were speaking of his intended bride. But he turned his attention to Lady Langdon and nodded.

"She's to inherit Southcott and its lands, isn't she?" asked Darcy.

"No. There is a cousin who will inherit. Clarissa will have a modest dowry, however."

Darcy looked surprised. Did he think James had planned to marry a fortune? Not that James might not have considered it if he hadn't been able to secure a decent loan, although his prospective bride's character would still have been a paramount consideration.

"But what did Nettlehurst say about the mortgage? Did you tell him about it?" asked Darcy, persevering in his curiosity.

His brother, though lacking in tact, was no fool. Lord Nettlehurst *had* looked nervous when James had made his circumstances clear. But he had evidently been carefully coached by Lady Nettlehurst to approve James's suit. It was no surprise to James that the fretful, invalidish old man had not dared to deviate from his assigned role. In her triumph, Lady Nettlehurst never thought to question James's resources after the deed was done. There was no need to tell Darcy all that, however.

"Yes, I told Lord Nettlehurst all about it. He raised no objection."

Darcy looked dubious, but returned to sipping his soup.

James followed suit. There was no reason to discuss Lady Nettlehurst's probable reaction once she knew James's financial status. In fact, he didn't know if his title or his reputed wealth mattered more to her.

He didn't feel guilty. James knew, on Adam's authority, that Clarissa was innocent of her mother's mercenary motives, and he knew he could support her in reasonable comfort. Moreover, he suspected she was not happy at Southcott, with such a distant, reclusive father and such a restrictive, overbearing mother. Adam had often fretted about his sister's plight in such an unhappy household. It seemed only fitting that James would rescue her from it, while she rescued him from his baser nature. Indeed, he had told her that Adam would have wanted them to marry, and the thought had clearly given her pleasure. He had vowed they would make a better home together than either had known before.

"James," said Lady Langdon, interrupting his thoughts again.

He looked up from his soup. His stepmother's polite smile seemed a little strained.

"Yes?"

"Perhaps I should consider setting up a separate establishment. You will not wish me to be in your way here at Charlwood once you are married."

Was she annoyed at the prospect of being supplanted as the mistress of Charlwood? he wondered. Or perhaps she saw this as an opportunity to escape from his control. But she did not look annoyed, or eager. If anything, she seemed rather forlorn. He couldn't mistake the expression, and felt a sudden, unexpected rush of pity for her.

"Nonsense!" he answered. "This is your home."

"Thank you, James," she replied, looking relieved. Still, her smile did not seem quite happy. It occurred to him that it must be a strange situation for her, to be dependent on her stepson's goodwill. Although he didn't know her very well yet, anyone could see she was not fit to live alone. She had no idea how to manage a household budget, and solitude threw her into the dismals. Why hadn't she remarried?

"Uh, James?"

This time it was his brother breaking into his thoughts. Why did Darcy sound so hesitant? Ruefully, James realized he hadn't been very good company at dinner today. Or ever since he had returned to England, for that matter.

"Yes, Darcy?" he asked, forcing himself to smile.

"I asked Nell to marry me today."

James's gut twisted in a mix of anger and revulsion. How could Darcy do that, when just yesterday he had promised not to do anything foolish? No wonder the hussy hadn't bothered to say anything! She hadn't had to. She had won already.

With a Herculean effort, James mastered his fury. Darcy deserved to be soundly thrashed, but it would do no good.

While his brother was still unmarried, James might still find a way to put a halt to it. Something less drastic than throttling Miss Ashley, which he would heartily enjoy at the moment.

"So have you decided on a date?" he asked, forcing himself to speak calmly.

"Well, not yet. Actually, she hasn't accepted me."

"She hasn't?" he asked, stunned.

"Oh dear! What a shame!" said Lady Langdon. "I was so sure you were both so amazingly fond of each other."

"She hasn't accepted me yet," said Darcy confidently. "I'm sure she'll come round to it. She is dashed fond of me - as I am of her, of course! She just needs a little time to get used to the idea."

James realized he had somehow been granted a reprieve. But why? What possible reason could Miss Ashley have for delaying her acceptance of such a flattering offer?

"James, I know you don't approve, but I think perhaps you will change your mind when you hear what I have to tell you."

"I am listening."

"Perhaps you don't know that Nell's uncle is going to provide her a handsome dowry?"

"Actually, I learned that in London. However, I do not see how it alters the case."

"You don't?" asked Darcy, in a puzzled tone.

"Not at all. Are you thinking you could set up your own establishment on such a sum? You would squander it within a year or two!"

"No, really, James!" Darcy answered, looking shocked and a little hurt. "I know I've been extravagant, but I'm not so bad as all that. All I meant was, her dowry would be a big help in getting Charlwood back in order, wouldn't it?"

James softened a little as he listened to Darcy. Perhaps his young brother was naive enough to think Miss Ashley's modest dowry would be a valuable addition to the family fortunes.

"Not enough to signify," he answered. "In any case, there is no need for such drastic measures."

"So it's still her character you're still worrying about? Didn't I tell you you were wrong? But you'll learn for yourself. Just give her a chance. You'll realize what a good and generous person she really is, if you just get to know her better."

"It seems I will have to do so."

James ate in silence for the rest of the meal, barely aware of the small-talk between Lady Langdon and Darcy. He couldn't stop wondering why Miss Ashley hadn't jumped at Darcy's offer. Try as he would, he could see only two reasons.

Perhaps she had sensed how strongly she had aroused him, despite his cold treatment after the fact. Perhaps she thought she might still win the greater prize? If so, she was going to be disappointed when she learned of his engagement. He had found the perfect answer for that scheme.

But it was a hollow victory. For as soon as she knew James had offered for Clarissa, she'd settle for second best and agree to marry Darcy. James would have to think of a way to prevent that, even if it meant discussing the matter with her father. He didn't wish to act the grand lord over the vicar, but he would do it to save his brother from a disastrous marriage.

James didn't like to think about the other reason Miss Ashley might have for not immediately accepting Darcy's offer. But he had to face up to it. He might have been wrong all along. Miss Ashley might truly love Darcy, in which case she might hesitate to make trouble between him and his brother. And he, James, might have frightened her, with his rough kisses and his threats.

Was she the virtuous lady Darcy claimed? Had he committed an atrocious sin against her and his brother? Had he, in the heat of his own lust, merely imagined her response to his kiss?

He must get to know her better. If he could just restrain his unruly passions, he would learn the answer to his questions. Perhaps then he would find some peace.

Nell fastened the slender gold chain about her neck, and examined her reflection in the mirror. The white muslin, delicately embroidered at the neck, sleeves and hem in Peg Mullen's tiny, even stitches, was the best Nell owned. It would have to do for dinner at Charlwood. And the little pendant, in the shape of a swallow, set with tiny seed-pearls, added a nice touch, she thought. It gave her confidence to wear something that had been her mother's.

She was suspicious of this invitation. Not that this was the first time she and Papa had dined at Charlwood. But it was the first time Lady Langdon had dared invite them since Lord Langdon's return. He must have at least condoned the invitation. Why he had done so remained a mystery.

As she and Papa walked up to the House, he tried to soothe her doubts. Yesterday, he had seemed relieved when she told him of her decision to take some time to think over Darcy's proposal. Now he suggested that perhaps Lord Langdon approved such a course, and wished for them all to become better acquainted. In fact, Papa seemed quite content to be invited to Charlwood again, voicing his expectation of spending an enjoyable evening, and the hope that he might be permitted the pleasure of browsing in the extensive library after dinner.

As the dinner progressed, Nell began to think that his prediction had not been as far off the mark as she had expected. Lord Langdon had greeted them with all courtesy, if not warmth. The Nettlehursts were also present, but apparently Lady Nettlehurst was in such good humor over Clarissa's engagement that she was polite, if not cordial, only looking moderately surprised that the vicar and his daughter had been included in the small party.

Seated between Lord Nettlehurst and Darcy, Nell passed a reasonably comfortable meal, although she was obliged to spend much of it listening sympathetically to an account of Lord Nettlehurst's latest stomach disorder. The elderly peer waxed indignant when she suggested chamomile tea, and then Nell remembered that hypochondriacs were generally too fond of their ailments to actually wish for a remedy. It was a relief to turn back to Darcy, whose sparkling eyes showed an amused sympathy for her plight.

Her father, situated between Lady Nettlehurst and Clarissa, comported himself with his usual gentlemanly affability. Bless him! He seemed totally unoffended by the fact that Lady Nettlehurst addressed all her conversation to Lord Langdon, at the head of the table. Other than wincing a few times at the sound of her ladyship's rather strident voice, Papa was enjoying himself, addressing a few kind remarks to Clarissa, and savoring the fine meal, along with a delectable Burgundy from the previous earl's carefully chosen stock.

In fact, everything was going surprisingly well, except that Nell had the distinct impression that she and her father were both under observation. Lord Langdon spent most of the meal politely conversing with the Nettlehursts, seated on either side of him. Still, Nell caught his eye on her several times. It was all very disquieting.

Perhaps she should feel encouraged. It seemed he might be reconsidering his position regarding her suitability as a bride for Darcy. However, she found it rather lowering to be scrutinized like a horse at auction. Lord Langdon should relax his vigilance for the evening. Surely he would get more pleasure in gazing at Miss Nettlehurst instead. Clarissa was certainly looking lovely in her pale gray silk gown. However, Lord Langdon seemed to be in no danger of being obsessed by his fiancee, so perhaps he really was marrying Clarissa only for her connections and prospective inheritance. That would not be surprising, given what Nell knew of him. She could only wonder at Clarissa's acquiescence to such a plan.

She had the opportunity to learn more after dinner, when she followed the other ladies into the drawing room. Lady Nettlehurst engaged Lady Langdon in conversation, and Nell succeeded in exchanging a few words with Clarissa, starting by offering her felicitations on her engagement.

"Oh, thank you, Miss Ashley," said Clarissa. "Yes, Mama is most pleased that I shall become a countess."

"Why Miss Nettlehurst," she answered. "I hope you are pleased as well."

"Oh, yes. Lord Langdon, James, I mean, has been most kind and gentlemanly, and he was such a good friend to dear Adam. Why he even saved Adam's life once. But that was before Adam was killed, at Vitoria."

"I had often wished for a brother. It must have been terrible to lose him."

"You have no brothers or sisters, Miss Ashley?"

"No. My parents always wanted more children, but it was not meant, I suppose. We were very happy together, the three of us."

"Your mama is dead, then?" asked Clarissa shyly.

"Three years ago." Even now Nell found it difficult to say more.

"I am so sorry, Miss Ashley," said Clarissa, and impulsively grasped her hand. "May I call you Nell, please?"

"Of course," Nell answered, touched by Clarissa's evident desire to make friends. Then she remembered what Darcy had said about Clarissa's restrictive upbringing, and realized that the poor girl must be lonely, particularly during this past year when opportunities for making friends must have been few indeed.

"What are you two silly young girls talking about?" Lady Nettlehurst interposed sharply. Nell saw a calculating look on her face. It was easy enough to divine her ladyship's thoughts. She was clearly assessing the risks of allowing her daughter to make friends with a nobody against the chance of offending Lady Langdon by snubbing her guest.

"We . . . we were speaking of our families, Mama," answered Clarissa.

"Ah yes, Miss Ashley, I recall your father saying that your mother' s maiden name was Wilford? What was her Christian name?"

"Elizabeth, ma'am," answered Nell.

"I remember her well. Viscount Luddington's daughter. We were debutantes together. A most delightful girl, although of course, she did not have the perfect features to be deemed a true Beauty. And, you will pardon me for saying so, Miss Ashley, she was just a little too independent-minded."

There was no polite answer to this, so Nell remained silent. During Lady Nettlehurst's speech, the gentlemen entered the room, their footsteps muffled by the carpet. Nell was relieved to see that her father was not among them. No doubt he had escaped to the library as he had done on previous occasions, and would be spared this trial.

Oblivious to the gentlemen's entrance, Lady Nettlehurst continued her disparagement of Nell's mother. "So unbecoming of her to defy her parents and marry, if I recall correctly, her brother's tutor!" This time, she looked at Nell, probably hoping for some signs of mortification.

"You can hardly expect me to regret my parents' union, ma'am," answered Nell quietly, after a brief struggle with her temper.

Noticing that the earl was in the room, Lady Nettlehurst replied, "No, I suppose not, but no daughter of mine would be allowed to do anything so improper as to question her parents' authority. You have no need to fear, my dearest James, that Clarissa will ever disappoint you by behavior unbecoming to a lady of quality."

Lord Langdon did not reply. Nell had expected him to be in full agreement with Lady Nettlehurst, but she thought she observed a fleeting look of contempt on his face. It passed so quickly that she could not be certain of it. It seemed almost as if, for once, his contempt was directed at Lady Nettlehurst rather than her.

At that point, Lady Langdon hurriedly suggested that Clarissa entertain them with some music. This had the happy effect of diverting Lady Nettlehurst, who quickly seized the opportunity to boast to Lord Langdon of Clarissa's superior education and accomplishments.

However, Lady Nettlehurst was not exaggerating, Nell thought as she listened to Clarissa. Miss Nettlehurst clearly had been well-taught, and her high, clear voice had no difficulty reaching the higher notes of the Italian song her mother had suggested. She looked so angelically beautiful that it was no wonder that even Darcy, who had never professed much interest in music, was listening intently.

Nell might have felt a twinge of jealousy had he not, afterwards, pressed her to sing as well. She finally yielded to his and Lady Langdon's persuasion, although she suspected the simple old ballads that she knew best would seem quite rustic after Clarissa's elegant performance. She got through the ordeal as best she could, but the appearance of the tea tray was very welcome.

Another test was still in store for her. Darcy left the small sofa on which they had both been sitting to get more tea, and Lord Langdon walked over and abruptly took his brother's place. She looked up at him warily, her heart thudding uncomfortably in her chest as she remembered their last encounter.

He began with nothing more alarming than a compliment on her singing, and she told herself she was being foolish. There was nothing he could do to her in a roomful of people. He would not try such a trick again. Still, she was glad to see that he was sitting as far from her as he could.

"I thank you, my lord, but I know my performance is nothing beside Miss Nettlehurst's. *She* is truly talented," she answered politely.

He merely nodded in response. He shifted slightly, and sat in silence for a few minutes, looking away from her. This despite the fact that he had been watching her closely all evening. Why had he come here to sit with her, if he had nothing to say?

She wouldn't gratify his pride by trying to make idle conversation. It was impossible anyway. The memory of his kiss was still too vivid in her mind. She was uncomfortably aware of his proximity, of the faint aroma of the port he had drunk earlier. She could sense his every movement through the delicately built sofa.

At length, he addressed her again, in a lowered voice.

"Miss Ashley. I must apologize for my behavior to you on our last meeting. It was a most ill-considered action on my part."

So he had come over to make her an apology! She looked at him in surprise, and growing indignation. There was no remorse in his face, only his usual guarded look. She had never heard anything so curt and graceless. Why was he even bothering? How dare he refer to what he had done as merely an "ill-considered action"?

Then she understood. He feared that she would accuse him of having compromised her. That she would expect reparation, or cause a scandal by disclosing what he'd done. He thought she would stoop so low, the ingrate! When she thought of all she'd done to avoid causing trouble between him and his brother, she wanted to scream.

Lord Langdon was clearly in need of a lesson.

"I beg to differ, my lord," she answered sweetly, having brought her temper under control one more time. "I would think trying to ravish one lady the day before proposing marriage to another merits a rather stronger description. Some would call it foolhardy, even dangerous."

She saw his horrified expression, and realized she had guessed correctly; he was appalled at the thought of the trouble she could cause. However, she had no intention of carrying out the implied threat, so she decided to relent.

At the same instant, he recovered his tongue.

"You do not mean—"

"Do not disturb yourself, Lord Langdon," she interrupted. "I assure you, I shall do my utmost to forget the incident ever occurred."

She looked him in the eye, hoping he would finally understand that she was speaking the truth. But forgetting his kiss was impossible, at least while he was sitting just a few feet away from her, watching her with those disturbing blue eyes, so like and yet unlike his brother's.

He relaxed.

"Thank you," he said in a low voice that she felt more than heard. She detected an unexpected trace of warmth in it as well. He actually seemed grateful to her for not telling Darcy about their kiss. Perhaps he had been dreading the loss of Darcy's trust. It was the first sign of any feeling or vulnerability she had seen in the earl. Despite herself, she was intrigued to know more.

"I suppose I understand your reasons for behaving in such a manner," she said. "You were trying to protect your brother, were you not?"

"Yes," he answered, but his voice and expression were both distant and reserved, as before. Clearly he didn't trust her enough to reveal any more of his feelings or intentions.

"Has it occurred to you that your brother may be perfectly capable of making his own decisions?" she asked.

"I *have* considered the possibility," he answered.

Before she could protest Lord Langdon's lack of faith in his brother, Darcy and Clarissa joined them.

"James, we have just had the best idea!" said Darcy, looking boyishly excited.

Lord Langdon stood up and offered his seat back to his brother, then seated Clarissa and himself in some nearby chairs. With Darcy beside her again, Nell found her heart returning to its usual rhythm. She watched curiously as Darcy unfolded his plan to Lord Langdon.

"The Nettlehursts are planning an engagement party, but Lord Nettlehurst thinks a ball would be too fatiguing, so they're just going to hold a fusty dinner-party. Why don't we give a ball here?" he asked, eagerly looking at the earl.

"Please! It would be ever so grand!" added Clarissa, a hopeful smile on her face.

Nell looked at Lord Langdon. The earl's face was inscrutable. She had thought he would immediately reject the idea, but he seemed to be giving it his consideration. Surely he was not willing to undertake the significant expense of such an affair?

After the brief pause, he nodded. "Yes, brother. I think it an excellent idea. When Mama was alive, there was a ball held at Charlwood every summer, but perhaps you do not remember."

"Oh, don't I, though?" answered Darcy. "I remember how the house was full of guests, how we used to watch for them to arrive from an upstairs window, and how Mama always found the time to come up with a plateful of jellies and cakes just for us."

"Ah, you *do* remember!"

"Of course. I used to think Mama was the most beautiful lady in the world, in her silk gown and the Langdon diamonds."

"I did, too. It will be good to revive the tradition of hospitality at Charlwood," said the earl.

"Yes, and Mama says it is absolutely our duty to do so," added Clarissa.

During this interchange, Nell sat quietly trying to understand why Lord Langdon had agreed to the ball. Perhaps she had been right, and Lord Langdon really had purposely exaggerated the family debts to Darcy. It certainly seemed he had sufficient funds to indulge his intended. Or perhaps he felt such a display was necessary to uphold the prestige of Charlwood and his family.

His next words took her completely by surprise.

"Speaking of duty, I also recall that we used to hold an event for the tenants and laborers at about the same time every summer. We should do so again."

Nell realized he was watching her, and tried to appear indifferent as she gathered her thoughts.

"What do you think of the idea, Miss Ashley?" he asked.

She paused before replying, wondering if he was expecting her to change her opinion of him as a landlord. Then she realized his true motive.

Coolly, she replied, "I believe such events were much enjoyed at one time. However, I am afraid it will take more than a mere party to regain the trust and loyalty of your people."

"I am not a simpleton, Miss Ashley," he answered with a touch of anger in his voice.

"No, of course not. You are a lord."

Clarissa gasped and even Darcy looked uncomfortable at this exchange. Lord Langdon suggested they all rejoin the others and choose a date for the ball. Clarissa eagerly followed him to the other end of the room, but Darcy lagged, turning to Nell and asking her what was amiss.

"Forgive me," she said, putting up a hand to cool her cheek. "I did not intend to cause you or Miss Nettlehurst embarrassment. I am afraid I allow your brother to provoke me much too easily."

"You will soon learn James is not so bad," said Darcy confidently. "But are you not looking forward to the ball? You will be invited, I assure you."

"Thank you, but there is a small problem. I don't know how to dance."

"That is no problem at all!" he said, his expression clearing. "Don't worry, my stepmother and I shall teach you."

She was obliged to thank Darcy, and go along with him toward the others, but she could not be confident that he or Lady Langdon would be permitted to befriend her for much longer.

Not for one minute did she believe Darcy's airy assurances that her modest dowry was sufficient to appease Lord Langdon. The earl was proud; no doubt he would not wish his brother to marry one who regularly mingled with what he would undoubtedly call the lower orders. Well, she would not change in an attempt to please him. That would be a useless endeavor indeed, for he would never forgive her insults.

Perhaps the threat of a scandal gave her some protection. But she did not trust his apology for an instant. Lord Langdon was a dangerous man. He had taught her that sharp lesson, at least, leaving her wiser, and more wary. She would not be taken in again.

Miss Ashley was proving quite a puzzle, James thought as he settled down alone with some brandy after the guests had all left. The evening had given him much to think about, but he still seemed incapable of rational thought regarding her. He should be analyzing everything that she had said, and yet he found himself remembering the look in her eyes, how the little pearl ornament she wore rose and fell with her every breath, how the candlelight had cast pools of light and shadow over the creamy contours of her neck and bosom. What a fool he had been to think that merely becoming engaged would overcome his regrettable obsession!

He reminded himself that he was practically a married man. Indeed, the thought of Clarissa's trusting innocence gave him pause. No matter how tempted, he would never do anything to betray her. Adam would rise out of his grave to haunt him if he did.

He just wished he could avoid Miss Ashley, in person and even in his thoughts. For Darcy's sake, he forced himself to reexamine the evening's events. He had to admit Miss Ashley had shown unexpected dignity in the face of Lady Nettlehurst's attacks. Her response to his apology showed spirit, but no coyness or spite. She had looked him in the eye. That was usually a sign of honesty.

He took another gulp of brandy at the memory of her eyes, so large and even solemn beneath her wide forehead. Hers was not the face of a schemer, was it? Or was he just hopelessly bewitched?

He finally began to feel the pungent warmth of the brandy coursing through him. But it wasn't enough to dispel the suspicion that he was an even greater fool than he had thought.

Nine

A light drizzle fell from a pale gray sky, perfectly suiting James's mood as he rode home through the village early one evening. He'd spent the past few days continuing his inspection of the estate, and all he'd seen and heard only added to his conviction that it would take years to reverse its current state of neglect and mismanagement.

The weather reminded him of another dreary day, not long ago, and the accusations Miss Ashley had laid against him then. He tried to suppress the memory, for on its heels came the growing suspicion that he had gravely misjudged her. An unwelcome thought, for he had always prided himself on being a sound judge of character. It was a skill he needed now as much as he ever had in his military career.

Yesterday, he'd been to visit old Matthew Cowden. Mingled amongst Matthew's reminiscences, there had been much praise for Miss Ashley. At the time, James had told himself that of course a lonely old bachelor would think well of a pretty young female, if she only had a smile or kind word for him.

But today James had confirmed Miss Ashley's account of the Mullens' problems. It annoyed him to find that she was right, but whether or not her concern for the Mullens was genuine, James knew she was correct in laying the responsibility on his shoulders. He'd have to find a way to help them.

Certainly he had it in his power to provide some modest monetary assistance, but that would be useless, and possibly harmful, if Ned persisted in his heavy drinking. He found himself wondering what Miss Ashley would recommend, and stopped himself. He still wasn't sure she was to be trusted, after all, and he should be able to deal with his dependents without her assistance.

He was still trying to focus his thoughts back on the Mullens, when he heard a child cry out.

"Please don't hurt me! No, no, no, no, no, no, NO!"

The screams emanated from the half open door of a nearby cottage. James hesitated for an instant. He had no desire to interfere with the villagers in the upbringing of their children, but he would not tolerate cruelty. He would have to investigate.

He quickly dismounted, tossing the reins over a crooked bit of fence bordering the lane. Ducking to fit through the low doorway, he entered the cottage. Straightening back up, he blinked. Gloomy as it was outside, the smoky interior of the cottage, lit only by a small fire, was still darker. It took a few seconds for his eyes to adjust. The sight that met them was totally unexpected.

Miss Ashley sat near the fire, in the midst of what seemed a veritable bevy of ragged children, holding the smallest, a boy of perhaps three or four years of age, screaming and struggling in her arms. James couldn't imagine what she was doing there.

She glanced up, looking startled and then annoyed as the child broke free of her loosened hold. The little boy darted toward the doorway, but stopped when he saw James blocking his path, and Miss Ashley was able to recapture him.

Clutching the boy tightly against her chest, she gave James another cold look. James wondered what sort of greeting, if any, she would have made, had the child's frantic cries not filled the cottage, making speech impossible. She went back to the seat by the fire and sat down again, her face impassive now despite the child's vigorous writhing and kicking. She looked to her left, and James noticed the dark-coated, grizzled man kneeling beside her. Mr. Olden, the apothecary.

He looked nervously from James back to Miss Ashley. She and the apothecary nodded, in some wordless signal, and he swiftly pierced the child's arm with a lancet which had been wetted with some sort of liquid. The boy's screams hit a new, higher pitch. Miss Ashley deftly turned the child around to hug him against her chest, got up and walked to the other side of the small room, turning her back toward James and the others. Although he could see she was trying to soothe the child, he also got the distinct impression that she was avoiding him as well.

He looked back toward the group by the fire, and shifted slightly to avoid a trickle of rain coming down through a hole in the roof. From the shadows to his right, he now saw a lanky bearded man bowing awkwardly. Mr. Olden had scrambled to his feet and was also bowing.

"Good day, my lord," he said, smiling rather nervously. "My apologies for not greeting you immediately, but Miss Ashley and I had our hands rather full!"

"The fault is mine, for having interrupted you. I would not have done so had I not heard the child crying. I merely wished to assure myself that there was nothing amiss."

"Nothing at all. My colleague, Miss Ashley, and I were merely vaccinating Tom Wicke and his children against the smallpox."

So that was what he had just witnessed. The apothecary's words, and even more so, the rapport with which he and Miss Ashley had worked, certainly seemed to support Darcy's account of her charitable work. James frowned. He still didn't like the thought of having made such a serious error in judgment.

"I only hope we done the right thing, my lord," said the man who the apothecary had called Tom Wicke. Gaunt and shabbily clad as the children, nevertheless he seemed respectful, showing no sign of the understandable resentment James had lately encountered in some others of his class.

"I am certain that you have done the right thing. So you are Tom Wicke? I understand you are a shepherd. And these are all your children?"

"Yes, my lord."

With the exception of the youngest, the children stood quietly grouped around their father. It seemed they were motherless. Five pairs of solemn eyes watched James from five thin, pixie-ish faces. Their scrawny bodies and thin clothing brought Miss Ashley's earlier accusations to mind. This time he felt their force all the more strongly, but his remorse would do the children no good. All he could do was start making amends.

"I would very much like to meet your children," he said to Tom, with his most cordial smile.

One by one, the children were introduced to him, and James took care to address each one by name, going down on one knee to speak to the smaller ones. They responded politely but shyly. He did manage to win smiles from a few of them.

At some point during the introductions, Miss Ashley had turned around and was now watching him with a puzzled expression.

"And that is my youngest lamb, Davey," said Tom, and Miss Ashley stepped forward, still holding the smallest child and again wearing her earlier, distant expression.

Davey was quiet now, but still clung to her, monkey-like, his thin legs wrapped around her waist, and sucking his thumb. If James needed any more proof that she was a frequent visitor to this cottage, the boy's confiding attitude supplied it. This was no act put on to impress him. Neither had the other occasion when he'd seen a child in her arms, he now realized with a pang of conscience.

He realized Tom was looking at him expectantly, and said, "You have a fine set of children. But what of their mother? Who cares for them while you are working?"

"Jenny here has watched the younger ones since I lost Emma," said Tom, indicating the oldest child, a tired looking girl in her teens. "That was over three years ago, now."

"Mrs. Wicke died of the typhus," said Mr. Olden. "The same spring that it claimed poor Mrs. Ashley. A strange woman came begging in the village, and before we knew she had the disease, it was too late for the kind souls who helped her."

Good Lord, had Miss Ashley's mother died from doing the same sort of charitable work that Miss Ashley was doing now? James looked back at Miss Ashley, and saw that she had averted her face from his gaze.

"I am sorry," he said. "Their deaths must have been a grave loss." He hated how inadequate the words sounded, how they reminded him of well-meant condolences he'd received when his own mother had died. But it was the best he could do.

A few minutes later, he, the apothecary and Miss Ashley bade the Wickes a good evening and left the cottage, amid a chorus of high-pitched good-byes directed primarily at Miss Ashley.

The rain had ceased, but the sky was now a deeper shade of lead, the lane was muddy, and water still dripped from the cottage roofs. Instead of remounting his horse, James decided to walk with Mr. Olden and Miss Ashley for a while. It was vitally important that he learn exactly how far he had misjudged her. For his brother's sake, of course.

"My lord, you must congratulate us," said Mr. Olden. "Today, Miss Ashley and I have ensured that everyone in Smallbourne is protected from the smallpox. Although, praise God, we have not had a case in the past twenty or so years, since the Vicar and his good wife convinced the parish officials to institute yearly inoculations, and not wait for the threat of an epidemic. Of course, we are now following Lord Egremont's example and using Dr. Jenner's new vaccine. With excellent results, I might add."

"You are to be commended," he answered, while mentally adding her parents' example to the list of evidence for Miss Ashley's good character. Long-forgotten, half-observed conversations between his own mother and Mrs. Ashley came back to him then. Had their mothers collaborated on just this sort of undertaking?

Whatever the case, Miss Ashley had clearly been brought up to work amongst the poor. However, she looked tired; perhaps a life of unending charity palled on her. Did she see Darcy as a means of escape?

"My lord," she said, causing him to look at her again. "You will be pleased to know that this practice has proven less costly than nursing and burying the victims in the case of an epidemic."

He stared at her then, wondering what prompted that remark.

Her expression was guarded, but her tone had been decidedly defensive. Then he realized she must be referring to his position as the principal landowner, and hence principal taxpayer, in the parish. How could she think he would try to put an end to the practice? He felt a spurt of annoyance at the implied insult.

"Miss Ashley, I assure you I am not so callous as to object to the practice on grounds of cost."

"I am glad to hear it," she said, in a carefully polite, expressionless voice. He was not fooled, however. He could read the skepticism in her eyes.

"I am puzzled, however," he said, feeling stung. "You both claim the vaccinations have been performed annually. How comes it that Tom Wicke and his family were not already protected?"

The apothecary, looking nervous, hastened to answer.

"Your lordship must remember that many of our good Sussex folk are quite ignorant, I must say, even superstitious. Tom Wicke, like his father before him, has always considered it to be tempting God to voluntarily take infectious matter into one's body. And of course, many country people distrust the new cowpox vaccine. From the way they talk, you would think their children were going to sprout horns and udders from it!" he concluded, with a hearty laugh.

"I am glad you were able to convince him otherwise."

"Oh, no! It was not I. It was our good Miss Ashley whose persistence finally cured Tom of his foolishness."

"Please do not make game of Tom! He was only doing what he thought was best for his family," said Miss Ashley. Looking at James, she added, "He has not had the advantages of education, so it is no wonder that his views are old-fashioned. Without a proper school in the village, the poor are doomed to superstition and ignorance."

Clearly the education of his dependents was one more score she held against him. Perhaps she was right; but it didn't make her lecture any less irritating.

"Miss Ashley, I believe it is time you and I discussed this and several other matters," he said firmly, as they reached the

place where the lane intersected the main road through Smallbourne. "I shall escort Miss Ashley home, Mr. Olden."

"Thank you, my lord. Good evening, Miss Ashley," said the
apothecary, muffling her protest. He bowed, and quickly set
off in the opposite direction, where his own home lay, seeming
glad to have made his escape from a contentious situation.

"You need not trouble yourself, Lord Langdon," said Miss
Ashley with a frown. "I am perfectly capable of walking home
by myself."

"I am sure you are, but it will do you no harm to talk to
me for a few minutes."

He looked about, satisfied that no one was abroad at this
hour. They should be able to speak freely. Then he saw that
Miss Ashley had moved to the other side of the road, so that
his horse was between them. Undaunted, he repositioned himself to lead his horse from the off-side. She walked on briskly,
staring fixedly ahead.

He realized there might be some excuse for her prickly manner, and tried for a conciliating tone. "Miss Ashley, I understand you have been doing this sort of work for quite some
time."

"I began accompanying my mother on her rounds when I
was a small girl."

"What? She exposed herself and you to the risk of catching
any disease that was rife in the village?" he demanded, remembering how she had succumbed to the recent influenza
epidemic.

"Of course not! She loved Papa and me, and she knew how
many other people depended on her. She was always careful
never to set foot in a cottage where a serious infectious illness
was reported, or allow me to do so. Her death was . . . a tragic
mischance. No one knew that beggar-woman had the typhus.
Then it was too late."

He heard the anger in her voice turn to pain, and instantly
regretted his line of questioning. He could no longer doubt
her. Despite what she had said, it was evident that she was
willing to take a degree of risk to care for the needy, as had
her mother, for whom she clearly still grieved.

He felt an unexpected urge to take her in his arms and comfort her. However, she was once again briskly marching ahead of him. As he caught up, he contented himself with saying gravely, "I am sorry. It must have been difficult for you to carry on your mother's work."

She slowed, and shot him a hard, suspicious look. He had the feeling that he had erred somehow, but he couldn't imagine what he had said wrong.

"I mean you must often find it tiring and wearisome," he ventured.

She stopped to face him, her eyes fairly sparkling with anger. What on earth did she think he had said? He halted as well, his horse's shoulder bumping him as the gelding stopped an instant later.

"I enjoy my work, my lord, and I have no intention of quitting it," she said. "I do not care if you are so arrogant as to think it beneath the dignity of one who wishes to ally herself with your family. If Darcy does not mind, I do not see why you should. Indeed, you should be grateful, since it is your neglect that has made my assistance to your people so very necessary!"

The stubborn little shrew! he thought. He had tried to be friendly, and she answered him with more insults. Now she was running ahead again, not allowing him the courtesy of a reply. Quickly, he closed the distance between them.

"Miss Ashley, you *will* listen to what I have to say. I will not tolerate any more of your unreasonable accusations." He paused, deciding where to start. "For one thing, I was a child when Tom Wicke was of school age, so I cannot be held accountable for his education, or lack thereof."

"When your father died, you did not precisely rush home to build a school for Tom's children, though!" she interrupted.

"I had my reasons for staying in the army, none of which concern you. I believed my estate to be in good hands at the time." She merely raised an eyebrow at that, and he felt impelled to explain himself. "I had not realized that Lytchett had taken over for his father, nor that he would prove to be a thieving scoundrel."

"It is the business of a good landlord to be aware of such things," she retorted. "Papa even sent you a letter on the occasion of your father's death, trying to politely remind you of your obligations, but you ignored it!"

"I never saw it. If indeed it was ever written, it must have gone astray. Letters to the Peninsula often did. Many ships went down in storms that year."

"That may be true, but you have also ignored all your brother's representations. Perhaps you think you have fooled poor Tom Wicke, speaking to him and his children so kindly, but I cannot believe it is anything but empty words!" she said, looking away from him again.

Damn it, she *would* believe him! Swiftly, he stepped forward and whirled to face her, so that he and his horse effectively blocked her way forward. She almost collided with him in her blind haste, then she looked up. He saw the stubborn defiance in her face, and his annoyance swelled into unreasoning anger.

"Miss Ashley, I have every intention of restoring prosperity to this village, and to all my other lands, for that matter," he said, seizing both her arms. "I am not my father, and I am not going to repeat his sins! Why can't you believe me?"

As he looked down at her, however, his wrath softened somehow at the sight of her flushed, angry face and the beckoning curves that even her plain dress and worn cloak could not disguise. He realized he'd like nothing better than to silence her recriminations with a kiss.

Her next words felt like a deluge of cold water.

"Why should I believe you?" she snapped. "You tricked me into your study on the pretext of discussing your pensioners. How can you possibly imagine I would trust you after that?"

He dropped his hands to his sides, and stepped back, rocked by the memory of what he'd done to her in his study. Damn, he had almost lost control again, just now.

"I am sorry," he said in a low voice. "I should never have done it."

"Yes, I remember, it was an 'ill-considered act'."

He winced at her sharp words. "I deserve that. But I assure you I sincerely regret my actions!"

"Not more than I," she said, and ran the short remaining distance to the vicarage, her cloak streaming out behind her. He made no effort to pursue her, knowing he would only make matters worse by forcing any further apologies on her.

For his anger had faded fast, leaving him prey to a deepening sense of guilt. He could no longer deny the fact that he had blundered horribly in his treatment of Miss Ashley. Now he'd seen with his own eyes the charity of which Darcy had spoken. The compassion that made her go to such extraordinary lengths to help the Wickes, and the Mullens and countless others. Such selflessness had nothing to do with the ambitions he'd imputed to her. She was no fortune-hunter. Just a caring, vital young woman in love with his brother.

He should have seen it sooner. Why had he been so eager to judge her, to see impropriety in what was merely the expression of a warm, affectionate nature?

He groaned. In hindsight, it was simple enough. His own lust had betrayed him. He'd fought back against his desire by assuming the worst of her. Despite himself, he had become what he most abhorred. He was just like his father. Worse, for he'd wronged an innocent girl.

Then he had compounded his error by his curst scheme to expose her to his brother. No wonder it had failed. No wonder she hated him. He was damned lucky Darcy didn't hate him as well.

No. It wasn't luck. It was Miss Ashley's forbearance that had saved him there. Undoubtedly, she'd kept silence to prevent him and Darcy from fighting. Also to keep from embroiling her gentle father in a conflict with his patron.

James groaned again. He'd put her in an intolerable position. The fact that she'd faced it with courage and dignity did not make his actions any less despicable.

He would make amends, somehow. Somehow, he would convince her that she had nothing to fear from him. That she could marry Darcy with his blessing—

Here his rushing thoughts came to a sudden halt. Something still felt wrong. He remembered thinking his brother hadn't seemed to be truly in love. But then, he was probably wrong, never having been in love himself.

He was pretty certain Darcy hadn't set up a local ladybird, which must mean Darcy truly cared for Miss Ashley. And then there was Darcy's recent zeal in helping him with the estate business. All this was probably Miss Ashley's good influence. He wouldn't jeopardize that with his insane, misplaced passion.

Nor could he forget his duty to Clarissa. But now that he understood Miss Ashley's nature, surely he would be able to master his attraction to her. From now on, he resolved that she would see nothing from him but elder-brotherly friendliness. Surely there would soon come a day when that was all he would feel for her.

Ten

Was it folly to come here?

Nell entered the grounds at Charlwood, thinking of her stormy encounter with Lord Langdon the previous evening. Although he'd ended with an apology, how could she be sure it was sincere? It was hard to believe he would tolerate the way she had insulted him, particularly now, after the rumors she'd heard in the village on her way here.

She should never have allowed him to provoke her into such anger. Now she had her reward, in the guilty, anxious fear that she had gone too far, that at least some of her accusations were unjust. But mingled with her anxiety was an equal measure of curiosity. She longed to know the truth despite the inevitable awkwardness of their next meeting.

The day had dawned clear after yesterday's rains. The ground was still damp, but drying fast under a bright sun. A slight, playful breeze murmured through the trees, coaxing her into optimism.

She told herself there was no need to feel like an intruder; she was here to do a favor for Lady Langdon. With any luck at all, she would be in company with Lady Langdon and possibly Darcy by the time she had to meet the earl again.

She found Mudge, the head gardener, in the kitchen garden. A careful combination of flattery and sympathy secured his cooperation in Lady Langdon's ideas regarding floral decorations for the ball. After she'd completed her business, Nell found it was still rather ahead of the hour she'd promised to join Lady Langdon, who had solicited her help in making out the invitations.

The rose garden beckoned. She hadn't visited it since the disastrous day after Lord Langdon's return to Charlwood, but she longed to see how the work she had set in motion was progressing. The roses were probably just coming into bloom, if her own garden was any indication. Surely she didn't have to worry about meeting Lord Langdon there.

How angry he had been! she thought as she went through the gate in the boxwood hedge that enclosed the rose garden. And yet, at one point, she had had the oddest suspicion that he was about to kiss her again. But that was absurd. He was far too angry, and he had never really been attracted to her anyway. By his own admission, he'd only kissed her the first time to make trouble between her and Darcy. He would not do it again; she was not beautiful enough to tempt a man into folly, and the earl must be the last man in England to let passion get in the way of his self-interest.

Assuredly, it was a relief to know that, whatever else his lordship might do, he would not kiss her again.

Nell strolled down one of the paths, pleased by the sight of many buds in various stages of unfurling their petals of creamy white, pink, crimson, and gold and beaded with drops of dew that reflected the morning sunlight.

She leaned toward a bed of white cabbage roses, a variety she'd always liked despite what some called their coarse growth habit. She loved the flamboyantly large flowers and their abundant fragrance. As did the bees, she remembered, backing away as one landed on the bud she was examining.

She resumed her walk, but a few yards farther along, she abruptly stopped.

The hedge that surrounded the garden had been shaped into several bays on each long side, each containing a bench. On one of those benches sat Lord Langdon, a copy of the *Gazette* beside him.

What a stupid mischance! She never would have come here if she'd thought he was the sort of man to enjoy a garden. But he was leaning back, his eyes half closed. Perhaps he hadn't

seen her. She turned to leave, but was obliged to stop when
he called out to her.

"Good morning, Miss Ashley. Please do not run away on
my account," he said.

She turned back toward him, out of politeness. He arose
from the bench. Now that his eyes were open, Nell saw that
they looked tired.

"Good morning," she replied. "I would not be here if Lady
Langdon had not asked me to speak to Mudge for her. I am
sorry to have disturbed you."

"Not at all," he said. "Perhaps you will allow me to walk
with you?"

His tone was perfectly cordial, but it was unthinkable to
agree. She wasn't sure it was quite proper, and besides, all
their earlier private encounters had ended disastrously.

"I think Lady Langdon is expecting me," she demurred.

"She had not yet come down to the breakfast parlor when
I left it," said Lord Langdon. "Come. It will do no harm for
us to talk a little."

She paused, trying to think of another excuse while her mind
raced to try to understand why he wished to speak to her.
Surely he didn't mean to try to force her to listen to him, as
he'd tried to last evening.

She looked around. She saw one of the under gardeners
trimming the hedge at the other end of the garden and knew
that Mudge and the others were nearby as well. Perhaps she
need not run away. Lord Langdon could not attempt any sort
of coercion with so many others about.

Gently, Lord Langdon said, "Please, Miss Ashley. I would
very much like to talk to you. On my honor, I mean you no
harm."

"No, I did not think— I mean . . ." She stopped, feeling
the treacherous heat rise in her face.

"I know I have not behaved as I ought toward you, but can
we not make a new start? For Darcy's sake?"

She wavered, caught by the softness of his voice and the
unexpected appeal in his eyes. To be on good terms with
Darcy's brother was what she wanted after all, was it not? And

she did wish to learn the truth about what she'd heard in the village earlier this morning.

Finally, she nodded, and he came toward her. For an awkward moment, she thought he might try to take her arm. Perhaps he sensed her hesitation, for he did not. Instead, he merely walked beside her as she set off down a path that intersected the garden diagonally. For a few minutes, they walked in silence, except for the gravel crunching under their feet and the humming of bees.

"Miss Ashley, I have been wishing to speak with you regarding the gardens."

The earl's voice was grave, causing Nell to doubt again. Was he going to object to her interference in his gardens, to the expense that had been incurred under her advice? Silently she waited for him to continue.

"I hear I have you to thank for rescuing them from the state of neglect into which they had fallen since my mother's death. I am deeply grateful to you for having done so."

Her heart lightened, and she answered, "I hope that all is as you remember it, my lord. We found it necessary to replant some of the beds, and even Mudge, your head gardener, could not recall the original varieties."

"It is as lovely as in my mother's day," he answered, looking down at a bed of pink moss roses, a rare, softened expression on his face. Then he looked at her again and said, "Lady Langdon tells me that you have been an enormous help in dealing with Mudge. He knows his work, to be sure, but he was cantankerous when I was a child, and I cannot imagine that he has mellowed with age."

She relaxed at the compliment. "No, I believe he has not, but I understand him nevertheless. Mudge and I have much in common."

"Indeed?"

She looked at him sharply, but he seemed amused rather than contemptuous.

"Why, yes," she replied. "We gardeners toil and dig and plant, and then there is too much rain or not enough, or an untimely frost nips everything in the bud, or ants get into the melon beds. I am sure that when I have been gardening as long as Mudge has, my disposition will be quite ruined too."

He laughed. It was an unexpectedly hearty sound, filling the air. He looked younger then, and she remembered that he was not yet thirty, that the lines around his eyes were not the result of age, but of years of service under the harsh sun of the Peninsula.

"I take leave to doubt that," he said. "If you are not too busy, perhaps you would be willing to show me what you and Mudge have been doing in the rest of the gardens?"

She realized it was the first time she'd seen a genuine smile on his face, one that reached his eyes, as if a bit of the blue sky above was reflected within them. So Darcy was not the only Mayland possessed of a charming smile!

She stiffened, realizing Lord Langdon had once again beguiled her into lowering her guard. Whatever he might be doing now, this was the same man who had neglected his estates so shamelessly for the past several years. The same man who had kissed her so ruthlessly barely a week ago.

He must have seen the hesitation in her face. "I am sorry," he said. "I did not mean to inconvenience you. If you are busy today, perhaps some other time?"

His lack of insistence was somehow reassuring. The gentle tone in his voice reminded her of the unexpected tact he'd shown in dealing with the Wicke children yesterday. She had assumed his benevolence was just an act, but now she had reason to think otherwise. She remembered that the children really had liked him. She'd always believed children and animals knew whom they could trust.

So she nodded and took Lord Langdon on a tour of the vegetable garden and the herb garden. But despite his unusual courtesy, she couldn't help feeling rather unsettled by his presence.

When they came onto one of the narrower paths in the herb garden, his arm brushed hers. She flinched and inwardly scolded herself. There was no reason to be agitated by such a slight touch.

Instantly, he fell in behind her, giving her a chance to recover her composure. She thought she succeeded in hiding her unease by describing the work currently being done in that part of the garden and going on with the plans she and Mudge had for fall planting and introducing several young gardeners they met along the way to his lordship.

James was more than pleased with what he saw. He was not surprised that Miss Ashley had shown equal competence in dealing with his obstinate head gardener as she had in assisting Mr. Olden at the Wickes' cottage. Everything about her was remarkable, he decided. Her skill, her humor, her common sense.

As she led him through the orchard, he decided he even liked the way she walked, her stride brisk, purposeful, almost mannish. That is, if one ignored the graceful sway of her hips. And of course, one *did* ignore that.

She stopped at the gate and looked at him as if trying to decide whether to say something. He composed his face, hoping she hadn't noticed how he had been watching her. He'd been making such good progress in winning her trust and friendship, it would be a shame to ruin that now.

"Miss Ashley, did you wish to say something?" he asked kindly, hoping he sounded like an older brother or an uncle.

"My lord, please forgive me if I am being presumptuous. I have been hearing rumors in the village that you are making plans to rebuild some of the laborers' cottages, and I was wondering if that is true."

"Why, yes, Miss Ashley. I do plan to rebuild some of the cottages. I believe others merely require some repairs."

"I am glad to hear it," she answered. Rather awkwardly, she continued. "But I am sorry for having doubted you. In this instance, I am happy to have been wrong."

"Your doubts are quite understandable."

"Lord Langdon, if you really are planning to do something for the laborers, may I make a further suggestion?"

"Please do," he said, choosing to ignore the implied doubt in her question. Her expression was so eager. He wondered what she would suggest.

Her next words came out in a rush. "I think it would be an

excellent thing if you could arrange to allot a small amount of land along with each cottage. That way, the laborers' families could raise some of their own food and perhaps even keep a pig or a cow."

She stopped, and he read mingled hope and doubt in her large eyes. He looked away, the better to consider her suggestion. The more he thought about it, the more he liked it. His tenant farmers were reluctant to raise their laborers' wages in these uncertain times, and the current system of monetary relief to the poor was woefully inadequate and demeaning.

"It would not have to be very much land at all," she continued persuasively. "But it would make such a difference to those who cannot afford to buy fresh fruit or vegetables for their families. I would be more than happy to provide seeds from my own garden to help them get started, and— Well, I hope you will think about it, my lord."

"I certainly shall. Believe me, I have been concerned about my people's plight. Your plan would not only alleviate their wants, but it might very well restore their self-respect to be able to do something for themselves."

"Ah, you *do* understand!"

A look of elation swept over her face. He found himself unexpectedly moved by her smile. Her approval was balm to his aching conscience, but there was more to it than that. He searched her face for an answer. Her smile wavered a little, and a question crept into her eyes.

Something warned James that he had better look away. He was still trying to do so when he heard Darcy's voice from the kitchen garden.

"Oh, there you both are!" Darcy shouted, hurrying along toward the orchard. "Nell, my stepmother has been looking for you this past half hour. Shall I take you back to her?"

"Hello, Darcy," said Miss Ashley, looking bemused. "Yes, of course. I am sorry to be late. I was showing your brother about the gardens."

"That's grand! I'm happy to see you both getting along so well. James, are you coming with us?"

"No. I'm going to the stables. I just remembered there is something I must speak to Pluckley about."

"Very well," said Darcy.

"Good day, Lord Langdon," said Miss Ashley, giving Darcy a smile as he took her arm.

James continued to stand by the orchard gate, watching them walk back toward the house. He heard Miss Ashley say something to his brother and saw Darcy lean down and give her a quick kiss.

He looked away. Something churned inside him. No doubt he was just irritable from a restless night. It was annoying to have had his conversation with Miss Ashley interrupted just as they were finally beginning to understand one another.

He looked down, realizing he had unconsciously clenched his hands into tight fists. No. He couldn't deceive himself. It was no mere annoyance he was feeling. It was jealousy, pure and simple. He still wanted her. For himself.

Despite everything and everyone, he still wanted Miss Ashley.

He forced himself to think of Clarissa, but it was no help. He found himself remembering the single chaste kiss he'd given his fiancée after she had accepted his proposal. Clarissa had obediently submitted to it, but in their dealings since, she had never shown any desire for anything more. Thinking that in time she would grow more affectionate, he had restrained himself. Now he realized that it had been far too easy to do so. Did that bode well for their future as a couple?

He dismissed the question. Surely he and Clarissa would grow to care for each other. His feeling for Miss Ashley was a mere transient lust; as long as he continued to suppress it, it would soon die a natural death.

Eleven

As Darcy escorted her back toward the house, Nell was surprised to find herself wishing she could have stayed and talked longer with Lord Langdon. Now, of course, she could share her happiness with Darcy.

"Oh Darcy, I have heard such wonderful news from your brother. I am so happy you finally prevailed upon him to rebuild those wretched cottages!" she said, smiling up at him and squeezing his arm impulsively.

"I hoped you would be pleased. Now I expect a reward," he said and stopped. Leaning down, he gave her a quick kiss. He seemed about to give her another, but she pulled away, hoping Lord Langdon and the gardeners hadn't seen the first one.

"What is wrong, dearest Nell? Are you afraid someone will see us? Shall we go down by the lake?" he asked.

"No, please," she said, feeling oddly reluctant. "Lady Langdon must be wondering where I am by now."

"Very well, darling. But I warn you, I might fall into a decline if you continue to treat me so!"

She didn't know whether to be sorry or relieved that he hadn't insisted. Then she realized that it must be his way of being chivalrous, of not pressing her since she hadn't yet agreed to marry him.

Gratefully, she laughed and said, "I thought only ladies fell into declines!"

He laughed and continued to flirt playfully until they

reached the house. He escorted her to the drawing room and left her with Lady Langdon, who was happily compiling a list of guests for the ball.

"Dear Nell. Did you have a pleasant stroll in the gardens?" asked Lady Langdon with a twinkle that made Nell blush.

"Yes, very pleasant," she replied and described the progress of the gardens and her conversation with Lord Langdon. She was curious to see how Lady Langdon interpreted his lordship's recent actions.

Lady Langdon sighed and said, "I must admit I was very wrong about James. He has been so kind of late. I was never more shocked than when he asked me to plan the ball, saying he realized how much Darcy and I were pining for a party!"

"But what of the cost?" Nell blurted out.

"James assures us that we are not in such serious straits that we cannot afford a country ball. He says that what with the mortgage, and the sale of the hunting box in Leicestershire, there will be enough left from the improvements on the estate to permit some entertaining. He wishes to be on good terms with our neighbors, you see, and talks of wanting to revive the tradition of hospitality at Charlwood."

"It is all very surprising," said Nell with feeling. "But I truly am happy that things have become more comfortable for you here."

"Yes. You would not believe it, but James actually sat down with me several days ago and showed me how to keep an account book. He was so patient with me and never scolded me for being slow or stupid. He said he understood that I had never been taught how to manage money. He even apologized for scolding me about that silly hat! Then I had to admit that he was right to do so, that perhaps thirty guineas was a bit much to spend on just one hat."

Fortunately, Lady Langdon looked back down at her list so she could not see Nell's appalled expression.

Thirty guineas! she thought. That was more than Tom Wicke earned in a year. Perhaps Lord Langdon had some justification for accusing his stepmother of extravagance. It was not Lady Langdon's fault that she had been brought up in ignorance of the value of money, but it was quite understandable that the earl might find her improvidence rather exasperating.

If Lord Langdon had been right about Lady Langdon, had he been justified in scolding Darcy as well? No, it couldn't be true! It was Darcy's good influence that had inspired Lord Langdon's newfound generosity toward both his family and his dependents.

"Nell, have you decided what you will wear for our ball yet?" asked Lady Langdon, breaking in on Nell's thoughts.

"Not yet, ma'am," she answered, relieved to think about something else. "I don't think I have anything that is suitable. I was thinking of going in to Chichester to find a fabric and have Peg Mullen make a new dress for me."

"Shall we go together?" asked Lady Langdon eagerly. "I have a sweet Chantilly lace gown that only needs a new underdress to make it appear perfectly new. That would be a savings indeed over a new gown, would it not? Perhaps you can advise me as to which shops have the best prices."

Nell agreed, and a date was decided for their trip into Chichester. She spent the rest of the morning helping Lady Langdon write out invitations and discussing what plants and flowers would decorate the ballroom to best advantage. However, in the back of her mind, she continued to brood over the puzzle of Darcy and Lord Langdon.

She accepted Lady Langdon's invitation to join in their noon meal. When they reached the yellow parlor, Darcy was already there, liberally helping himself to the ham laid out on the sideboard. He greeted them with a bright smile, and Nell tried to banish her doubts of him. They all chatted amicably, and Nell couldn't help contrasting the relaxed atmosphere of this meal with the last time she'd eaten her nuncheon at Charlwood. Lord Langdon had not come yet, but this time, she thought, no one dreaded his arrival.

When he did come, however, he seemed rather grave. Had he seen Darcy kiss her? Surely he no longer disapproved. Perhaps some problem had arisen regarding the estate. Whatever the case, he was perfectly civil and even willing to listen to

Lady Langdon's enumeration of the guests to be invited to the ball.

"Of course we will send invitations to the Goodwood set. James, are you acquainted with young Lord March? Since you both served in the Peninsula together, I was wondering if your paths had crossed."

"Yes, ma'am. I would be very happy to see him here."

"Very well. Lord Egremont, although we cannot be at all certain of his attending. The Cardingtons and the Denthams and . . ." She continued to rattle off names. "And Lord Poxton, of course. Dullingham is quite near here."

"Poxton!" cried Darcy, who up until that point had merely been nodding his head. "That old man milliner! He's so fat he can't even ride anymore, but he thinks he's some sort of Adonis! And since he succeeded to his uncle's viscountcy and moved into Dullingham he has become so pompous there's no bearing it! It's a great shame old Poxton never had sons of his own."

"You are too hard on the poor man," said Lady Langdon. "He is a little fat perhaps, and I cannot deny that his elevation to the peerage has gone to his head a little. But he is very good-natured, and there is no harm in him."

"By all means, invite him then," said the earl, sounding indifferent. "But that does put me in mind of something I have been wishing to ask you. I have invited my friend Colonel Huntley for a visit. I have assured him that he is welcome under my roof at any time, but the silly fellow insists that I inquire with you as to whether he will not be an inconvenience! Shall I tell him he can come?"

Lady Langdon paused, looking down at her dish. Finally she asked, "Colonel Huntley, did you say?"

"Yes, Edward Huntley. You do not object to entertaining him, do you? He is perfectly gentlemanly. He has recently come into an inheritance and wishes to buy a country estate. He will probably spend much of his time riding about and inspecting properties. He won't expect any particular efforts to entertain him, I assure you."

"Of course, I do not object! I shall be happy to welcome any of your friends to Charlwood," said Lady Langdon.

The earl thanked her, and conversation went back to the plans for the ball. Nell left Charlwood soon after, having various errands in the village. Unfortunately, none of her tasks were engrossing enough to keep her mind from dwelling on the possibility that she had misjudged Lord Langdon and on the fact that she still didn't feel ready to accept Darcy's proposal.

Perhaps that was why she had felt so uncomfortable about Darcy's kiss today. It would be cruel to encourage him while she was still so unsure. It also would be very embarrassing to be caught behaving indiscreetly again.

He had been so kind and patient with her. Surely it was just a matter of time before she was sure of her heart. Surely then she would be able to enjoy his kisses wholeheartedly.

During the following week, Nell came no closer to a decision regarding Darcy's proposal.

It was a pleasant week, full of the usual errands and gardening chores that she had always enjoyed and enlivened by several mornings spent at Charlwood learning to dance under Lady Langdon and Darcy's instruction. Darcy was a droll and charming teacher, and she found she enjoyed a lively dance as much as riding or walking the Downs. She even received invitations to several parties. Although she knew these were due to Lady Langdon's sponsorship, she still looked forward to going, hoping to make a few more friends, like Clarissa Nettlehurst. She also looked forward to the Charlwood ball, since she had chosen a suitable satin under Lady Langdon's advice and commissioned Peg to make up a gown in the style recommended by her ladyship.

Several times, it occurred to her that she would have to give it all up if she refused Darcy's offer. It would be too awkward for her to continue any association with the Maylands beside seeing them at Sunday services, which would be difficult enough. On the other hand, these were not good reasons for committing herself to living with a man the rest of her life or bearing his children.

She didn't know why she hesitated. She couldn't decide whether to feel disappointed that Darcy's chivalry prevented him from making any further attempts to kiss her. She didn't know why she sometimes found herself thinking about Lord Langdon's kiss and the wanton feelings it had aroused in her. Surely, she was not so abandoned as to wish Darcy to do anything of the kind!

Sometimes she berated herself for being so indecisive. Darcy was proving his worth every day, accompanying his brother about their lands and assisting the earl in his plans and improvements. Construction was starting on the new cottages, a constant and happy reminder of the pains Darcy had taken to convince Lord Langdon of his duty.

Of course, Darcy couldn't have succeeded if the earl had been as bad as they had all believed him to be. Lord Langdon was clearly on the road to becoming a conscientious landlord. Perhaps he saw the wisdom in treating his people well and realized that healthy and happy workers would contribute to his prosperity in the long term.

Several times, she hoped to discuss the matter with him again, but the opportunity never arose to do so. Once again, Lord Langdon retreated behind his guard. He continued to be polite, but Nell wondered if she had merely imagined his brief show of friendliness. She could only conclude that he had decided to tolerate her for the sake of family peace, but still found her lacking in some way. Whether it was her birth, her disposition, or her occupation, she could not tell. The earl gave her no opportunity to find out. Somehow, that hurt more than she wanted to admit.

Perhaps, she told herself, he was just preoccupied with the estate and with preparations for bringing his bride home to Charlwood.

She still couldn't tell what to make of him and Clarissa as a couple. Not that either of them showed any signs of regretting their engagement; it was just that neither showed any sign of excitement over it either.

Even with her small experience of parties, she'd had to agree with Darcy that their engagement party had been the dullest affair imaginable. Lord Nettlehurst's love of seclusion had kept the party small, to the annoyance of Lady Nettlehurst, who clearly longed to be a fashionable hostess. The Nettlehursts seemed a dreadfully mismatched couple, and their house very little like a real home. Nell couldn't help wondering if Clarissa had accepted Lord Langdon's proposal merely to escape South-cott. It didn't seem to Nell that Miss Nettlehurst loved the earl.

Perhaps that was only right. Lord Langdon didn't show any loverly impatience to wed Clarissa either, despite her golden good looks. He must have chosen her for her birth and her docile good nature. Clarissa, poor girl, would surely never oppose his opinions or provoke him into losing his temper.

Nell shuddered at the thought of such a marriage; she wanted something far different for herself. But if that was the sort of lifeless, cold-blooded union Lord Langdon favored, she wished him joy of it.

For what seemed like the fiftieth time that day, James wished he could strangle Lady Nettlehurst. He'd hoped she would not accompany her daughter to the party he was holding for his tenants and laborers. He'd wanted to introduce Clarissa to his people, but he had been nearly certain that Lady Net-tlehurst would not wish to lower herself to mingle with the commoners who thronged the lawns, feasting on roast pork and other hearty fare and imbibing considerable quantities of the excellent local ale.

Almost as soon as he stepped out onto the lawn, with Clarissa on one arm and Lady Nettlehurst on the other, he had realized he should have kept the latter away at all costs. She'd started by telling one of the farmers' wives that she was dressed above her station in life and continued by preaching humility and economy to some of the poorer of his guests. Now she was admonishing Tom Wicke for allowing his children to run about on the august lawns of Charlwood.

Lady Langdon and Darcy had helped him smooth over the previous insults, but he was not going to tolerate any more.

"I believe you are looking fatigued, ma'am," he interrupted. "I cannot allow you to exert yourself any further."

With a smile and a reassuring word to Tom, he resolutely escorted his intended and her mother back toward the house. Clarissa came along meekly enough, but Lady Nettlehurst hung heavily on his arm, looking back with obvious regret.

"What can have put such an idea in your head? I am not at all tired," she protested.

"I beg to differ. You must be completely exhausted with the effort of defending the dignity of my house and family."

"Not at all, dear James," she said with the affected fondness that never failed to irritate him. "Indeed, I hope you realize that I would spare no pains to convince your dependents of the great good fortune they enjoy in living on your estate."

"Thank you," he said dryly. "I think they are perfectly aware of their fortune without your pointing it out to them."

"I am afraid you are wrong," she said. "The lower orders are too simple to understand such things on their own. They need the occasional reminder. Surely you cannot object to my providing it?"

"I do object, and I expect you to respect my wishes on this matter. I will not have you annoying my people to gratify your vanity. You will wait in the drawing room until we are free to rejoin you. Now, will you come along quietly or must I drag you there?"

"I am not accustomed to being spoken to in such a manner!" she retorted, letting go of his arm and raising her voice to a grating volume and pitch. But really, it was no more important than the buzzing of a fly.

James thought it a shame that Clarissa could not view her mother in that light. He felt her tremble and looked down to see her growing pale at the threat of another of her mother's tantrums. He gave her what he hoped was a comforting look, then turned back to Lady Nettlehurst, whose rouged face had now assumed an even angrier shade of red. Fortunately, she was still walking briskly in the direction of the house.

"I should have known you would take the part of those sniveling, improvident wastrels!" she shrilled. "When I think of how you are throwing money away on cottages for a parcel of ungrateful sluggards while you let the glory of Charlwood fade into dowdy decay, I vow I could scream!"

"I am desolated to disappoint you," he said in a bored voice. "But I have already told you that I do not care if the Egyptian style is all the rage. I have no intention of furnishing Charlwood with any of your ridiculous crocodile-leg settees or gilded palm trees. I believe Clarissa will agree with me when I say it is more important that my laborers' children have decent roofs over their heads." He looked down at his fiancée, hoping she would be brave enough to agree.

Nervously, Clarissa nodded and said, "Yes. I mean, when one thinks of those poor little children, it seems only just . . . " Her voice faltered, and James knew she was dreading her mother's reaction.

"I cannot believe my ears! My own daughter, my only living child, fast becoming a radical! I have no doubt as to where she learned such revolutionary notions—from you and that low, vulgar little parson's daughter you allow your brother to run wild about the countryside with!"

"That will be quite enough!" James let go of Clarissa to turn and face Lady Nettlehurst, who had stopped and was now staring at him with her mouth agape. "Not another word or I will personally throw you into your carriage and send you back to Southcott!"

"How dare you speak to me that way?" she said, recovering her voice much too quickly. "If I had only known, I would never have allowed my daughter to enter an engagement with a man with so little sense of pride in his birth and his noble heritage! A fraud too, for you cannot deny that you hid your true circumstances when you proposed to her!"

"I told Lord Nettlehurst about the mortgage when I asked for Clarissa's hand. He must have been convinced that I will be able to support her in reasonable comfort, or he would not have given his consent."

"I should never have trusted him to speak to you alone!" she muttered.

"Does that mean you intend to convince him to withdraw

his approval?" he asked calmly, knowing the question would give her pause.

Lady Nettlehurst's mouth gaped again, and this time, mercifully, she was silent for several moments. If he had been in the mood to be amused, he would have laughed at her expression of mingled fury and dismay. He could see her weighing the mortgage and what she saw as his faults against the earldom and the fact that Clarissa's chances of contracting another noble match would be lowered if their engagement were broken.

As he expected, Lady Nettlehurst schooled her face into a more moderate expression, although he could still see the hostility in her eyes. Nervously, she said, "My dear James, you mistake me. I was only trying to admonish you, as your own mother would have wished. I am sorry if I allowed myself to get carried away."

"Very well," he said. "But I believe you will be more comfortable at home, so I shall call the carriage for you."

Then he realized that Clarissa was gone. She must have slipped away at some point during the argument and was now probably weeping somewhere in the gardens. What a pity his meek and proper intended did not have enough strength of character to deal with this situation. If only she were more like— But he had best not think about that.

He looked back at Lady Nettlehurst. She was looking about, her lips pursed, her temper clearly rising again at her daughter's defection.

"I will find Clarissa and bring her home when the festivities are over," he promised, escorting Lady Nettlehurst swiftly into the house before she could start ranting again. He called for her carriage and came back out to find his fiancée. It was probably too much to expect Clarissa to go back out to mingle again, but he hoped at least that she wouldn't be crying when he found her. He didn't seem to have the knack of consoling her.

Well, at least she hadn't inherited her mother's voice or her small-mindedness. Perhaps she would do better once out of Lady Nettlehurst's immediate control. As he rounded the house and headed toward the gardens, he told himself it was far too late to start regretting his engagement.

He hadn't walked far before he saw Clarissa emerging from the rose garden on his brother's arm. Darcy must have seen her dart off and gone after her. As they came closer, James was relieved to see that although his fiancée's face was slightly tearstained, she seemed composed, even smiling slightly as Darcy spoke to her. He thanked heaven for the easy address that enabled Darcy to deal with such ticklish situations. He'd have to thank him later.

A few minutes later, he was back among his people. Clarissa was at his side, tongue-tied but shyly smiling at everyone to whom she was introduced. In time, he thought, her sweetness would win their liking, if not any particularly deep respect. A short distance away, Darcy and his stepmother were laughing and talking to other guests, who all seemed to be enjoying themselves quite thoroughly. He should feel some satisfaction in that, at least.

Yet something seemed wrong about the situation. Perhaps it was the thought of Nell Ashley intruding on his consciousness. In Clarissa's place, *she* would know exactly how to behave and what to say to everyone here. But that was unfair to Clarissa; she hadn't had the same upbringing.

He had best put Miss Ashley out of his mind. If anyone else noticed his attraction to her, it could end in disaster for all of them.

It was pleasant to have Darcy's arm around her waist, Nell thought, even if it was only to teach her to waltz under Lady Langdon's guidance. He had seemed a bit distant the past few days.

His touch was somehow reassuring, even though he maintained the correct distance between them. Still, Nell was glad Hannah was not here to see the new dance, for Hannah would undoubtedly think it scandalous. For herself, Nell decided that, if Lady Langdon liked the waltz, it must not be so very awful.

Indeed, it was very agreeable to be whirling so gracefully about a wide, empty ballroom in the arms of so accomplished a partner. As Darcy guided her deftly from one end to the other, the unwonted pleasure of the dance brought a smile to her face.

Suddenly, the music faltered and stopped. Nell and Darcy came to a standstill and in unison looked over toward Lady Langdon to see what had happened. Then Nell saw Lord Langdon standing in the doorway, a look of controlled fury on his face.

"Pardon my interruption, ma' am," he said rigidly to Lady Langdon. His voice echoed in the large empty space. "I merely wished to inform you that I have received a letter from my friend, Colonel Huntley. He plans to arrive here tomorrow afternoon. I hope that is not inconvenient."

"Oh," said Lady Langdon, looking flustered. "Yes, of course. No, I mean, not at all! I will ask Mrs. Marden to have a room ready for him."

"Thank you. Good day," he said. Then he bowed and left without a further glance at Nell or his brother.

The three looked at each other in bewilderment.

"I wonder what ails him?" Darcy asked.

"I do not know," answered Lady Langdon. "Perhaps he disapproves of the waltz. Many people do, you know, but I am surprised that he should be one of them. I had heard that Wellington's officers are famous for dancing whenever they are not fighting."

Nell looked down and kept her tongue. It would only upset Darcy and Lady Langdon if she voiced her conviction that she was the cause of the earl's displeasure. Neither did she want to betray the hurt she felt at his brusque treatment.

"Well, I hope he permits it to be danced at our ball, or it will be the dullest affair imaginable!" said Darcy.

"Oh, dear!" exclaimed Lady Langdon. "I should have thought of this before we began our dancing lessons. Nell, I am afraid I must counsel you not to waltz at our ball. You are too new to society, and there are those who would call you fast for waltzing before you are properly out and accepted, so to speak."

Darcy seemed ready to argue the matter, but Nell forestalled the argument by assuring Lady Langdon she would do nothing the countess did not think proper. The lesson ended there, since none of them felt inclined to continue, and Nell took her leave.

Darcy escorted her home, but his rather forced conversation did not succeed in lifting her spirits much. Somehow, this was far different from how she had felt on previous occasions when Lord Langdon had treated her with coldness. Then, she had merely been angry. It was easy enough to tolerate unkindness from someone one despised. But she no longer despised Lord Langdon. His recent actions had shown that he was capable of justice and compassion. So why were those qualities so absent from all his dealings with her?

James left the ballroom and hurried out of the house. The sight of Nell in his brother's arms had kindled a blind rage within him, but he still retained enough control not to wish anyone to witness his frenzy.

Perhaps a ride would help him master himself. He set off for the stables, where an undergroom hastily saddled Jack for him. But soon, he realized that even fresh air and a fresh horse were not enough to cure his black mood. He reined Jack in after a long, hard gallop. He would not ride his horse into the ground in a vain attempt to escape the source of his fury.

He allowed Jack to walk on a loose rein, only vaguely realizing that they were heading for the top of the nearest down. His anger had cooled to the extent that he could begin to wonder who he most wanted to kill: Darcy or himself.

The thoughts of a blackguard and a coward! Darcy was his innocent if sometimes foolhardy little brother. How many times had Mama trusted him to care for Darcy during their childhood rambles and adventures? He would not lift a hand against Darcy; he might as well put a bullet through his own head. And that would be the most craven course of all. Too many people depended on him.

Still sickened by his anger, he rode out into the clearing

atop the hill he had just climbed and dismounted, letting his horse graze freely. Bow Hill, he realized. It had been a favorite childhood place, open and breezy, crowned with several burial mounds dating from Saxon times. From here, one could see for miles.

He sat down on the sloping side of one of the barrows, gazing out blindly over the countryside below.

Why could he not be content with matters the way they were, with the fiancée he had chosen? Most people would not hesitate to call Clarissa more attractive than Miss Ashley. His betrothed was an accredited Beauty, with her fairy figure and angelic face. Like one of the Sevres figurines that populated his stepmother's drawing room mantel, he thought. And just as beddable.

No, it was Nell Ashley he wanted. Nell, with the hazel eyes that could be so solemn or so merry depending on her mood, with the trim waist and lavish curves he so wanted to explore. Nell, her insights, her courage, her warmth. She was what he needed, what he had unconsciously been seeking.

He loved her.

He let out a hoarse, bitter laugh at the irony. He had tried so hard to convince himself that this was a mere transient lust. He had thought he was like his father, incapable of a faithful, enduring passion. Now he knew better.

He found it painfully easy to imagine what life would be like with Nell. He could picture her as a trusted helpmate, a generous lover, a devoted mother to their children. He would never want or need any other woman.

He bowed his head, covering his face with his hands, trying to thrust aside the tantalizing dream. For that was all it was, all it could ever be. Duty demanded that he honor his engagement to Clarissa. Duty demanded that he take care of his brother. He had failed Darcy these past few years. He would not fail him again, not now when Darcy had shown such unexpected good judgment in his choice of bride. And what could he do, after all? To forbid their marriage would only hurt Nell. That would be the worst crime of all, after all she'd already endured at his hands.

We'd Like to Invite You to Subscribe to Zebra's Regency Romance Book Club and Give You a Gift of 4 Free Books as Your Introduction! (Worth $19.96!)

If you're a Regency lover, imagine the joy of getting **4 FREE Zebra Regency Romances** and then the chance to have these lovely stories delivered to your home each month at the lowest prices available! Well, that's our offer to you and here's how you benefit by becoming a Regency Romance subscriber:

- **4 FREE Introductory Regency Romances are delivered to your doorstep**
- **4 BRAND NEW Regencies are then delivered each month (usually before they're available in bookstores)**
- **Subscribers save almost $4.00 every month**
- **Home delivery is always FREE**
- **You also receive a FREE monthly newsletter, *Zebra/Pinnacle Romance News* which features author profiles, contests, subscriber benefits, book previews and more**
- **No risks or obligations...in other words you can cancel whenever you wish with no questions asked**

Join the thousands of readers who enjoy the savings and convenience offered to Regency Romance subscribers. After your initial introductory shipment, you receive 4 brand-new Zebra Regency Romances each month to examine for 10 days. Then, if you decide to keep the books, you'll pay the preferred subscriber's price of just $4.00 per title. That's only $16.00 for all 4 books and there's never an extra charge for shipping and handling.

It's a no-lose proposition, so return the FREE BOOK CERTIFICATE today!

Say Yes to 4 Free Books!
Complete and return the order card to receive this $19.96 value, ABSOLUTELY FREE!

If the certificate is missing below, write to:
Zebra Home Subscription Service, Inc.,
P.O. Box 5214, Clifton, New Jersey 07015-5214
or call TOLL-FREE 1-888-345-BOOK
Visit our website at www.kensingtonbooks.com.

FREE BOOK CERTIFICATE

YES! Please rush me 4 Zebra Regency Romances without cost or obligation. I understand that each month thereafter I will be able to preview 4 brand-new Regency Romances FREE for 10 days. Then, if I should decide to keep them, I will pay the money-saving preferred subscriber's price of just $16.00 for all 4...that's a savings of almost $4 off the publisher's price with no additional charge for shipping and handling. I may return any shipment within 10 days and owe nothing, and I may cancel this subscription at any time. My 4 FREE books will be mine to keep in any case.

Name _____

Address _____ Apt. _____

City _____ State _____ Zip _____

Telephone ( ) _____

Signature _____
(If under 18, parent or guardian must sign.)

RN040A

Terms and prices subject to change. Orders subject to acceptance by Zebra Home Subscription Service, Inc.
Offer valid in U.S. only.

‖⸗⸗‖‖‖‖‖⸗⸗‖‖‖⸗⸗‖⸗‖‖⸗‖‖‖‖⸗‖‖‖‖‖‖‖‖‖‖‖‖‖

REGENCY ROMANCE BOOK CLUB

Zebra Home Subscription Service, Inc.

P.O. Box 5214

Clifton NJ 07015-5214

PLACE
STAMP
HERE

No, he thought as he straightened up and got to his feet. He would give his blessing to their union. The two people he loved most in this world would find true happiness together.

As for him, he would have the cold satisfaction of having behaved with a proper sense of duty and honor.

Twelve

Dear Nell,

You and your father positively must come to dine tomorrow. Colonel Huntley arrives tomorrow, and I know the gentlemen will all be wanting to talk forever about the war and hunting and other horrid things, and I shall be bored to tears if I do not arrange for some female companionship!

I have invited Clarissa as well, for James will undoubtedly wish to introduce her to his friend. Of course, I am obliged to invite Lady Nettlehurst as well. I am sorry for it, but I trust you will be able to overlook her toploftiness and lend me your support!

Lady Langdon

After such a note, it seemed strange to Nell that, when she and her father were conducted to Lady Langdon's drawing room on the appointed evening, Lady Langdon was not yet come down from her room. The only person there was Darcy, looking elegant but restless. As he greeted them, Lady Langdon hurried in, full of apologies for her belated arrival.

"What a first-rate rig, ma'am! You look magnificent. You will make the Nettle green with envy when she sees those emeralds!" exclaimed Darcy as he saw her.

Indeed, thought Nell, Lady Langdon had outdone herself on this occasion, wearing an elegantly simple gown of dull gold silk and the emerald necklace and earrings Darcy had mentioned.

"You must not talk that way, dearest Darcy!" protested Lady Langdon while trying not to laugh. "You make it sound as if I were overdressed for the occasion. I merely wished to make a proper welcome to James's friend—that is all!"

Soon after, the sound of masculine voices and laughter was heard in the hall. A minute or two later, Lord Langdon and Colonel Huntley walked in, but their mirth seemed to have been quenched as soon as they walked into the room. The earl's face in particular took on a rather masklike expression.

As Lord Langdon introduced his friend, Nell observed that Colonel Huntley was a hearty-looking gentleman, of perhaps forty years of age, average height, a compact, powerful build, and brown hair touched with gray about the temples. His movements were quick and decisive, but Nell noticed that he seemed a bit stiff when using his right arm, perhaps from some past injury. He was not strictly handsome, but his lively brown eyes, beneath bushy brows, looked both kindly and good-humored. He seemed rather ill at ease, however. Perhaps after army life, he was not accustomed to society and was feeling shy.

Nell was surprised to see Lady Langdon giving him a regal nod and welcoming him to Charlwood with words as formal as her attire. Perhaps the countess was behaving in the socially correct manner for the situation, but it seemed strange that she did not, as usual, exert herself to make a guest comfortable. It was clear from Colonel Huntley's rigid stance that her stately manner had had quite the opposite effect.

When Nell herself made his acquaintance, she smiled in a friendly manner, hoping to set him more at ease. He smiled back more naturally then, and she decided her first impression was not wrong. He did have kind eyes.

At dinner, Nell was seated between Darcy and Colonel Huntley, and she found no reason to change her mind about Lord Langdon's friend. He was a gentlemanly dinner companion, and he entertained her very well with stories of army life and descriptions of places he had seen that she had only read of. Still, beneath his liveliness, she sensed some sort of tension.

Her enjoyment of the evening decreased considerably after she and the other ladies left the gentlemen to their port. As usual, Lady Nettlehurst dominated the conversation, devoting most of her efforts to criticizing Nell.

"My dear Miss Ashley, I must wonder at your walking about the countryside all by yourself, without so much as a maid to lend you consequence. Are you certain it is quite safe? As a friend of Lady Langdon's, I must object to your causing her such concern."

Nell saw Lady Langdon preparing to protest and quickly retorted, "It is quite safe, I assure you. I am well known and have so many friends in the village. If I do go farther afield, I always take my dog with me. I am sure he is much better protection than a servant could be."

"But, Miss Ashley, surely such behavior is unbecoming in one who aspires to friendship with such a noble family as this," said Lady Nettlehurst. "On my dear daughter's behalf, I hope you will reconsider these habits before you embarrass us all!"

This time, Clarissa looked pained as well, but too frightened to voice a protest.

"I am sorry if I cause offense," answered Nell. "But I see no reason to give up the work that I have been brought up to do and which is so badly needed."

At that point, Lady Langdon joined in to defend her, but Lady Nettlehurst stubbornly continued to justify her own position until the gentlemen rejoined them. Nell wondered at Lady Nettlehurst's vehemence. Then she remembered some of the things Darcy had told her about Clarissa's mother and realized that this was Lady Nettlehurst's way of trying to protect the dignity of the earldom her daughter was marrying into.

Sadly, she supposed Lord Langdon was in agreement with his prospective mother-in-law's views. It really was of no particular consequence, was it? Later, she and Darcy would laugh at Lady Nettlehurst's unpleasantness. For now, however, Nell was sorry to see that both Lady Langdon and Clarissa were upset over it.

Things were little better when the gentlemen rejoined them. Lord Langdon's manner was even more forbidding than usual. He ignored her completely and divided his time between talking to the Nettlehursts and Colonel Huntley. After a brief, low-voiced exchange with Lady Langdon, Colonel Huntley gravitated back toward Lord Langdon and spent the remainder of the evening talking to him and the Nettlehursts. Nell heard the name Adam mentioned several times and realized they were talking of Clarissa's brother, which would certainly account for the total lack of merriment exhibited by that whole group. Lady Langdon seemed subdued, and although Darcy circulated and conversed as usual, Nell sensed a strain about him as well.

Although she did her best to hide it, Nell was confused and troubled by the undercurrents of emotion she sensed in the room. She was relieved when Lord Langdon effectively broke up the party by informing them all that Colonel Huntley's shoulder was paining him after his journey from London and wished to retire.

"Thank God that's over," said James, pouring Colonel Huntley some brandy in the library. "What could have possessed my stepmother to organize such an affair for your first evening here?"

"What indeed?" said his friend in an odd, hard voice. James stared at him, but instantly Edward resumed his usual manner. "By the way, thank you for making up that story about my shoulder. Ah, this is better," he said, lounging back into one of the library's deep, comfortable chairs and taking a gulp of the brandy.

James was glad to see Edward looking more at ease, and he finally relaxed himself, staring into the depths of his glass. He had known it would be a trial to see Nell tonight, but he hadn't realizing how agonizing it would be to watch her talking and laughing with Darcy. He'd even suffered a pang of jealousy to see her enjoying a lively conversation with Edward.

As he had walked into the drawing room after dinner, his eyes had met hers briefly. Had he only imagined a hurt look in hers as he looked away? He hated to cause her pain, but at least he hadn't betrayed himself.

He looked back at Edward. It was a comfort to have his friend here. Bleak as his own mood was this evening, he could see that Edward was not quite himself either. He hoped his friend's shoulder was not really paining him, but Edward would not wish to have a fuss made over it.

They drank their brandy in friendly silence until Edward interrupted it by congratulating James on his engagement.

"Your fiancée is just as beautiful and amiable as our poor friend Adam described her."

"Thank you."

"So you must tell me about this Miss Ashley. I take it she's the parson's daughter you were telling me about?"

"Yes."

"She seems a very pleasant young lady. Since she is invited here, can I take it you've changed your mind about her?"

It was like Edward to ask so many questions. He had always been quick to sense trouble and as quick to try to help. However, tempting as it was for James to confide in his friend, it would be dishonorable of him to discuss Clarissa or Nell with another gentleman.

"Yes," he said without further elaboration.

Edward obligingly took the hint and began to talk of horses. James pushed himself to discuss the colonel's plans to purchase a high-bred team and sporting carriage. Several glasses of brandy later, he asked Edward if he was still hoping to buy a country place nearby.

"I don't know. Perhaps," answered the colonel pensively. James could not understand his friend's mood.

"New horses, new carriages, and now an estate!" he said in an attempt at humor. "Next we will hear you are looking for a wife!"

Perhaps it was the brandy or the flickering candlelight, but

James thought his friend's ruddy complexion took on a deeper hue as he made haste to answer.

"Nonsense! You know I am a confirmed old bachelor."

Although he adhered to his resolve not to tell Edward about his love for Nell, James was nevertheless glad of his friend's presence over the weeks that followed. They spent much of their time out-of-doors, riding on either estate business, accompanied by Darcy, or on a quest for a property that might suit Edward. James sensed that Edward too concealed some sort of trouble or concern. He did not pry, seeing that Edward also found some relief in their silent rides together.

Meanwhile, there was satisfaction to be had in the progress being made on the new cottages and a numb sort of comfort in throwing himself into the work of the estate, from reviewing tenancy agreements and hiring a new steward to participating in the annual sheep washing. He would long remember Lady Nettlehurst's annoyance when she discovered that he, Edward, and Darcy had all plunged into the stream to help in the task. Shocking Lady Nettlehurst was one of his few pleasures lately.

He certainly did not enjoy the occasional country dinner parties and balls that were beginning to spring up now that some of the Beau Monde were trickling back to the countryside and the Nettlehursts were out of mourning. He wished he could avoid them, for Nell was usually invited along with his family. However, there was no way to refuse these invitations or to forbid his stepmother to entertain in turn. He did not wish to offend his neighbors or embarrass Clarissa by not attending the parties to which they were both invited. If he could not give her love, at least he owed her courtesy.

As for Nell, it was all he could do to keep up ordinary civilities, exchanging a few meaningless words with her now and then, but for the most part, avoiding her as best he could. Sometimes he was tempted to go to her or even ask her to dance when she seemed uncomfortable among a new set of people. He was pretty certain that she had hoped to resume the discussion Darcy had interrupted in the gardens; no doubt she was eager to offer further advice and suggestions. At times he even thought she seemed hurt or puzzled by his reserve.

No doubt it was better so. His longing for her was still too great, his pain too raw, to make any further attempts at friendship possible. At some point she would be bound to smile at him, and he couldn't be answerable for the consequences.

He could see that society regarded Darcy and Nell as a courting couple. No doubt it was only a matter of time before an announcement was made. When he knew they were walking or riding together, images of their kisses and caresses arose to torment him. He couldn't stop imagining Darcy and Nell as he had seen them together in the folly the day after his return to Charlwood. Happy, eager for each other. But now, God help him, he would not interfere.

"Why shouldn't I buy him? I think he's well worth the price the owner is asking."

Nell looked again at the horse Darcy was riding. At sixteen hands, the handsome roan dwarfed her own mare, Magpie, and his deep chest and sturdy limbs promised endurance on the hunting field. But three hundred guineas for a horse still seemed an overwhelming sum, even worse than thirty for a hat. It revived unwelcome suspicions about Darcy's spending habits, suspicions she had been trying to suppress over the last few weeks.

"He is a fine fellow," she answered cautiously. "But surely three hundred guineas is rather dear, even for a hunter?"

"Well, he is not quite dirt cheap. But James has sold the hunting box in Leicestershire and most of the horses that were kept up there. I need something decent to ride if we're to have any sport with the local hunts."

After a short pause, she said, "I see that, of course, but can you afford him?"

"I can if James gives me an advance on the next quarter's

allowance." Darcy's voice sounded matter-of-fact, but she couldn't read his expression, for he was looking away.

"Do you think your brother will be willing to do so?" she asked, and a happy thought occurred to her. "Does that mean things are not so desperate as he claimed? Perhaps he just invented the mortgage to persuade you and Lady Langdon to spend more moderately?"

"No, the mortgage is real enough," he answered, sounding suddenly glum.

"But then, I don't understand—"

"To hell with the mortgage! I'm tired of being good and sensible and frugal. I've worked hard to help James. Don't I deserve to have some pleasure as well?"

Darcy spurred the horse into a gallop, and the high-bred hunter soon left her and Magpie far behind. He was usually not so rude, Nell thought as she urged the mare to her best possible pace. Nevertheless, it hurt to think that her companionship might not be enough to console him for the few things he'd had to give up.

It was a few minutes before she caught up, on the other side of the meadow they were traversing, and by the time she did, she had composed herself.

"Of course you deserve to enjoy yourself," she said, hoping to pacify him. "I am sure you have been a great help to Lord Langdon. You have done so much good, encouraging him to undertake all the improvements that have been so badly needed here and—"

"No, I haven't," he interrupted.

She stared at him now and saw mingled frustration and guilt on his face.

"I had best tell you the truth," he said, looking at her directly now. "I never did talk to James about those blasted cottages. He was planning it all even before he went up to London. You were so pleased with me, I couldn't bear to tell you it was his idea, not mine. But I can't let you think that any longer. You are right about the horse too. I am stupid and selfish to think of plaguing James to buy it when he has so many other worries."

She looked at him in shocked silence, trying to read his expression. It was difficult to believe she had so completely misunderstood both him and his brother. However, Darcy seemed deadly serious, in stark contrast to his usual liveliness. His story must be true.

"I suppose you no longer have any wish to marry me, now that you know what a wretched liar I am," said Darcy, looking away again. He sounded so dispirited that she couldn't help wishing to comfort him.

"You are telling the truth now," she said. "It is not an easy thing to admit one is wrong."

She realized then that she had been just as wrong. But surely there was some excuse for her and Darcy's mistake. Remembering Lord Langdon's forbidding manner on his return to Charlwood, she thought that nothing could have been better calculated to arouse their hostility. If he had just been more conciliating, how much more readily Darcy would have started to mend his ways.

It was to Darcy's credit that he made such a sincere effort to do so, giving up the luxuries to which he was accustomed. If he sometimes found a life of moderation difficult, it was not the place of one who loved him to criticize. Rather, she had to find a way to encourage him and reward him for his efforts.

"Whatever you say, I know you have been a wonderful help to your brother," she said warmly. "You have a good heart, Darcy. I have always known that."

"But you still haven't said you will marry me."

She felt an inward chill at his words. It seemed that her praise meant little to him. Had her prolonged wavering cooled his affection?

"Please forgive me. I had not meant to make you wait so long." She took a deep breath and continued. "If you have changed your mind, please tell me. I will not hold you to your offer if you don't still wish me to be your wife."

"I still wish it," he said. Their eyes met, but there was no joy in his look, just a grim determination. She could almost have wept. She hadn't realized how deeply her continued indecision had wounded him.

"Dear Darcy, I . . ." She paused again, taking another deep breath. "I promise you I will give you an answer very soon."

That evening, as Nell prepared herself for sleep, she wondered if she should have followed her first impulse to accept Darcy's proposal then and there. Yet as she was on the brink of it, something had stopped her. What was wrong with her? Surely her love for Darcy was not so feeble as to wither at the discovery that he had a few faults? It could not be. She *did* care for him; she enjoyed his company, rejoiced in his achievements, ached for his frustrations. Was this not love?

Still, she couldn't help being glad she had not jumped at his first offer. Papa was right. She and Darcy had needed to become better acquainted before committing themselves to a life together.

However, most of society did not share Papa's enlightened attitude. She wasn't sure how many people knew Darcy had actually proposed, but most seemed to regard her and Darcy as practically engaged already. Lady Langdon's sponsorship had ensured Nell a welcome into local society, but Nell was shrewd enough to know that, while many people were sincerely friendly, others would be very much amused to see her fall from grace. If she did not accept Darcy's proposal now, she would either be pitied for being jilted or, worse, branded as an unconscionable flirt.

Of course, she couldn't marry Darcy just to avoid society's disapproval, but it was one more reason why she should make her decision, and quickly. She had wavered before, in part from uncertainty about Darcy, in part from concern over Lord Langdon's objections.

That obstacle, at least, seemed to be gone. Darcy had assured her that his brother had given his approval to their courtship. She had to believe him, despite the fact that Lord

Langdon had avoided any personal conversation with her since their talk in the gardens.

Weeks had passed, but it still hurt to think how close she and the earl had come to a real reconciliation that day. More than that, a budding friendship, she thought, wondering why it had come to naught.

As she thought about it from Lord Langdon's point of view, however, matters became painfully clear. What must he have felt to come home to a neglected estate, to a stepmother and brother both deeply in debt? He had dealt with all these problems with promptness, justice, and even a commendable degree of sensitivity toward his erring family.

Since he was beset by so many problems, was it any wonder that he had distrusted her as well and tried to separate her from Darcy? Certainly his methods were wrong, but his intentions had been good. She was willing to forgive him, but perhaps he couldn't forgive *her* for the horrible, unjust things she had said to him. Would an apology assuage his male pride? She would make it if it would help. But would she even be given the opportunity?

She had to laugh at the irony of it so she wouldn't cry. Just a few short weeks ago, she had wished that Lord Langdon would leave her and Darcy in peace. Now that she had her wish, all she wanted was a few minutes alone with the earl to try to recapture the friendship she still felt was possible between them.

"Lord Langdon is here, miss. He says he wants to speak with you privately, but won't intrude if you are busy."

Nell looked up from the sock she was darning. Lord Langdon come to visit her here, wishing to speak with her privately? What could it mean? Perhaps this was the chance for which she had been hoping. She composed herself, knowing she could not miss this opportunity.

"Thank you, Betty," she said. "Please show him in, but leave the door open and stay in the hall while he is here."

As Betty left, she stuffed the sock back into her sewing basket and looked swiftly about her small sitting room. The sprigged wallpaper was a little faded and the curtains were of a cheap white dimity, but at least all was tidy.

A moment later, Lord Langdon walked in and bade her a good morning. She arose and returned his greeting, trying to judge his mood from his countenance. But it told her little; the invisible wall was still there between them. If anything, his face was set in even more than ordinarily forbidding lines.

She seated herself again after offering him the chair on the other side of the worktable. He ignored her invitation, instead pacing about the room, making it seem even smaller by his size and restless energy. However, Nell thought he seemed more ill at ease than hostile.

"What was it that you wished to speak to me about?" she asked in a helpful manner.

"Miss Ashley," he began, stopping to stand in front of her. Stiffly, he continued, "In going over the estate accounts, it came to my notice that Lytchett has received funds from you for the purpose of supplementing the estate pensions. I have come here to express my gratitude and to reimburse you."

He handed her a folded piece of paper. She looked down, seeing her name scrawled on it. Apparently it was a letter enclosing the sum she had disbursed for the pensioners. She remembered that Lytchett had told the Maylands the story of her inheritance and of her anonymous gift. She hadn't thought much about it before, but she should have expected the earl would wish to pay her back.

"This is not necessary, my lord," she said with a smile. She held the letter out toward him, although she was prepared not to press the issue if he insisted.

"I beg your pardon, but it is most necessary," he answered, going over to the window. "Do not think me ungrateful, but I can take care of my people."

Provoked by his tone, she retorted, "As they have been cared for these past several years? I am sorry if you think I have interfered or if my actions have offended your pride! I only did what I thought was right and necessary."

He glanced back at her then. She saw regret, even sadness in his eyes, and the sight of it made her instantly repent of having snapped at him again.

"I am sorry. It was unkind of me to say that," she said softly. She got up from her chair and took two steps to join him by the window. "Please forgive me."

He looked down at her, and she realized she'd unwittingly put a hand on his arm. She saw his fists clench, and his face harden again.

"There is nothing to forgive," he said, his voice still rough. "I will disturb you no longer. Good day, Miss Ashley."

He bowed and left the room too swiftly for her to reply.

She stood for a few minutes trying to recover from the brief, disturbing encounter. How could she have lost her temper so easily, despite all her good intentions? She had always thought herself fairly even tempered, if not quite such a saint as Papa. But Lord Langdon provoked her to a degree of anger of which she hadn't thought herself capable.

She brushed away a tear and told herself she had been foolish to hope she and Lord Langdon could become friends. There had been too much ill feeling between them. She knew that now. She had seen in his eyes how deeply he regretted the errors he'd made, had probably regretted them ever since his return to England. His conscience would have suffered enough without her unreasonable accusations. She wished she could help, but alas, she now knew she was nothing but a thorn in his side.

He should never have gone to see Nell, James thought as he rode off down the lane. He could have just had the money sent to her. He'd told himself that she deserved to be thanked personally, but really he had just been looking for an excuse to see her and speak to her again.

Then she had greeted him with a charming, shy smile, and like a rude oaf he had hidden his feelings behind cold formalities. It was only natural that she'd lost her temper in return, but her angry words had barely wounded him. It was her apology that tormented him. It was the way she had come to his side, the artless touch of her hand and the lilt of her softened voice tempting him to forget all his noble intentions and take her into his arms again.

He had mastered himself, but just barely. He knew she was probably hurt by his brusque exit, but what else could he have done?

Stayed and accepted her apology like a gentleman, was the inexorable reply from his conscience.

Then, like a blow, he realized that his own cold behavior might be the reason she and Darcy were not yet engaged. He knew the importance Nell placed on family ties. She would marry Darcy eventually, whether James befriended her or not, but perhaps she was still hoping they could marry with his sincere approval.

Meanwhile, Darcy had been showing all the signs of frustrated love. He was moody, forgetful, and disinclined to confide in James as he had earlier. He could only be suffering from Nell's hesitation in accepting his hand.

James had vowed not to stand in the way of their happiness. It was time he remembered his resolution to treat Nell as a kind elder brother would. She was a forgiving person; she would undoubtedly respond to his attempts at a reconciliation. Perhaps one day he would even find some consolation in her friendship, even if the task of earning it would be harder and more painful than anything he'd yet endured. Merely avoiding her had been child's play by comparison.

Thirteen

Nell couldn't believe it. But she could not deny the evidence of her own eyes. She'd entered the Mullens' cottage only to see Peg in the act of packing up her family's meager belongings. No, it couldn't be. Less than a week ago, Lord Langdon had assured her he would care for his people, and Nell had come to believe that meant helping families like the Mullens, not getting rid of them.

"Dear Peg, what has happened?" she asked softly, mindful of Alice sleeping nearby.

Peg turned toward her, and Nell saw a broad smile on her friend's face.

"Good morning, Miss Nell. Please sit down. I have the best news! Old Hinkson has agreed to take Ned on as an apprentice. We are to move into the rooms above the smithy tomorrow."

"I am so happy for you, Peg! But how does this come about? It seems very sudden."

"It was decided just two days ago. Can you believe it was his lordship that convinced Hinkson to do it?"

"How very kind of him," Nell said softly. So she had not been wrong!

"Of course, Ned is older than what most apprentices would be, but Lord Langdon talked Hinkson into taking him on anyway and even assured him Ned wouldn't drink so much once he had employment again. I shouldn't tell you this, but Lord Langdon also came here and talked to Ned. He pretty much threatened his life if he should get so much as tipsy again.

But Ned won't. He only drank before because he felt so bad about Alice and me."

"I know, Peg. Times have been hard for you. But I am sure things will be much better now, and this is such an excellent thing for Hinkson as well. It was such a tragedy when he lost both his sons in the war. I'm sure he always expected them to take over for him. It will do him a world of good to have a family about again. I hated to see him turning into a bitter old man."

"To be sure, he's a bit crusty. Mayhap he'll do better with a woman to cook for him and a babe to play with. Don't you think so, Miss Nell?" asked Peg, fondly looking down at Alice. "Of course, I *am* glad Alice has outgrown her colic, just like you said she would."

"I knew it would only be a matter of time." Nell smiled. But when she looked at the baby, she felt a little pang of envy for Peg's newfound happiness in motherhood. Was she a fool for not reaching for the same joy herself?

"But you have come about the dress," said Peg. "I almost forgot, what with all the excitement. Here it is."

She opened the wrappings and pulled out a satin ball gown. As Nell expected, Peg had outdone herself, faithfully recreating a design from one of Lady Langdon's fashionable periodicals. When Nell tried it on, it was seen that only a few very minor adjustments were needed for it to be a perfect fit.

"Ooh, you do look a picture! I'm sure you'll shine them all down in this gown, Miss Nell."

"Thank you, Peg. It is a lovely dress." Nell smiled at the compliment, which she was in no danger of actually believing. It was no matter; she didn't aspire to shine anyone else down, but she did think she would look nice.

She paid Peg, who promised to have the altered dress brought to the vicarage the next day, and then left the cottage in an oddly troubled state of mind. She should have been happy for the Mullens' change of fortune and excited at the prospect of the ball, which was only two days away.

However, all she could think about was Lord Langdon's kindness to the Mullens and the astute way in which he had dealt with their problems. More than ever, she longed to be on friendly terms with him, so she could commend him for it and apologize for having doubted him. But she didn't suppose he would value either her praise or her penitence.

Nevertheless, her heart skipped a beat when she turned onto the main street of Smallbourne and saw the earl's phaeton and bays coming toward her. A minute later she realized they were being driven by Darcy and not Lord Langdon.

He pulled up and offered to drive her back to the vicarage. She accepted willingly, but couldn't help asking why he was driving his brother's horses.

"I've sold the chestnuts," he replied.

"Your beautiful horses?" she asked, amazed he had found the resolution to part with his famous team. "That must have been so hard for you! To whom did you sell them?"

"Colonel Huntley. He's made no secret of wanting such a team, and I decided they were costing too much to keep up. When he heard I was selling, he made such a generous offer for them I almost didn't want to accept it. But how could I refuse? It's the least I could do to help James."

"Is such a sacrifice really necessary?" she asked, knowing what this meant to Darcy.

"I don't know. James told me it wasn't. But he's been so glum lately. I'm afraid he's not telling me everything."

"I'm sure things are not as bad as you fear," she said. "You are such a good brother to worry so."

"I am not," he said, and his face twisted in an unwonted look of self-loathing.

"But you are," she reassured him. "I am certain Lord Langdon appreciates all the efforts you've made to help him."

"It's little enough compared to what he's doing for us."

Nell looked at him inquiringly, and he gave her a rather forced smile. "I was meaning to tell you. James has said that, if we marry, he will give us Broadoaks as a wedding present. It's a property we have in Kent that came into the family several generations back through some marriage or other. It's not entailed, so he can give it to us outright."

"How very kind of him," she answered with an attempt at

brightness. It was a clear signal that Lord Langdon approved of their marriage and a wonderful opportunity for Darcy. So why didn't she feel any elation at the news?

"Yes. Although the land is in need of better management, and the manor house was badly damaged in a fire last year. But there is an empty dower house on the estate, where we could live quite comfortably until the main house can be rebuilt. I didn't think you would mind that."

"No, I would not," she said absently, only half listening to what he had said. She couldn't quite banish the suspicion that Lord Langdon had chosen this gift as a means of moving her a whole county away. She decided that was ridiculous and forced herself to attend to Darcy's description of the estate.

"Broadoaks is a beautiful place. It's named for some fine old oaks that grow on the grounds. I'm sure the gardens are a disaster, but you would enjoy setting them to rights, I expect. What do you think?" He looked at her, and she thought his expression seemed hopeful. His words were certainly persuasive.

She thought of them living there, busying themselves with estate improvements and various country amusements. She would miss Papa, but they would be close enough to visit often, she thought. She couldn't ask for a more perfect plan. So why did she feel such a lump of apprehension in her throat?

"It sounds lovely," she said, forcing the words out.

"You don't sound very thrilled." He turned and took her hand and gave her a pleading look. "Please don't tell me you're planning to refuse me. I am not wrong to hope, am I?"

She looked down at their hands for a moment. Looking back up, she weakened at the appeal in his eyes and the determined set of his chin.

"No," she said softly. "Not at all."

"I am so glad," he said, taking her hand up to his lips. With a mixture of excitement and apprehension, she knew she had pretty nearly committed herself.

At that point, they reached the vicarage. He helped her down from the carriage and held her hand tightly for an instant as they parted. Nell watched him drive away, then went around to the garden, avoiding the house. She was too restless and puzzled to talk to Hannah, or even Papa, about what had just happened.

She went to the little shed and donned her gardening gloves. Then she threw herself into the unending task of weeding the flower beds, now bright with summer flowers.

Once again, she had been on the verge of accepting Darcy's proposal, and once again, she hadn't quite done it. Was it just prenuptial nerves that had made her hesitate? Surely if Mama were still alive, that was what she would have told her. She would have said it was only natural to feel nervous at such a change in her life and the prospect of moving away from her home.

Perhaps she should talk to Papa, but she knew he still had reservations about Darcy. Of course, all Papa had said was that she should listen to her own heart. But lately her mood had been shifting about so much, between joy, depression, confusion and apprehension, that she could not tell *what* her heart was saying.

She only knew she could not bear this wretched state of uncertainty for much longer. She had to make a decision soon.

"Nell, forgive me for interfering, but I must speak to you about Darcy."

Nell looked inquiringly at Lady Langdon as the two walked together, cutting roses to decorate the rooms for the evening's ball. The countess had seemed particularly cheerful and energetic this morning, despite the sultry weather. No doubt she was thrilled at the prospect of such a grand social event. But now, her dark eyes were full of friendly concern.

"I am afraid he has been rather out of sorts lately, dear. I'm afraid he is quite pining away over you."

Lady Langdon's voice was nothing but kind, yet Nell still felt the heat rise in her face.

"I am so sorry. I never intended to make him wait so long for an answer. You must think me the most abominable flirt!"

"No, not at all. I am certain you had no intention of causing

Darcy any pain. I merely wanted to assure you, if you had any doubts, that Darcy does love you quite deeply."

"I know he does."

"But is there any other problem? You can't possibly still fear James's disapproval anymore, can you?"

Nell shook her head.

"Dear Nell, forgive me if I pry a little further! It is only because I am so very fond of both you and Darcy. I can't help wanting to promote such an excellent match. Am I right in suspecting that your papa and your good housekeeper do not approve of Darcy?"

"Yes," she answered.

"Then let me give you some advice, based on my own experience," said Lady Langdon with a strange urgency in her voice. "I know you value their opinions, Nell. But I beg you not to let anyone else's advice stand in the way of your happiness. I must tell you that I . . . once loved a man of whom my family disapproved, for he had no wealth or worldly consequence at the time. He asked me to wait for him, saying he would come for me once he'd won his fortune, but my parents told me he was just toying with my affections. I allowed myself to be convinced of that, and so I married Lord Langdon, for I could no longer bear living in my parents' household. He was older and so kind, and he did not expect me to give him my heart as a younger man might have done. He only wanted a companion, for he was tired of his many . . . flirts. We got along very comfortably, but I never forgot my first love. I would not wish you to make such a mistake."

"Thank you for telling me this," said Nell. "It must be terribly painful for you to speak of it."

The countess embraced her and said, with an odd little smile, "Thank me by accepting Darcy's proposal. Otherwise, the time may come when you regret every day that you missed that could have been spent with him. If you love him, tell him so, and do it soon!"

Gruffly, Nell answered, "I will."

Fourteen

"I am positively convinced this color is too young for me!" Lady Langdon lamented, looking critically at her reflection in the mirror.

Nell had never seen her friend so agitated about her looks before. The countess was always so effortlessly elegant. It was hard to believe she was nervous now when she positively glowed in a figured lace dress over a rose pink satin slip. A delicate diamond tiara sparkled in her dark curls, matching her necklace and earrings, but the jewelry could not outshine the light in her dark eyes.

"No, not at all, ma'am!" Nell answered. "You know perfectly well you are even more exquisite than ever."

"Thank you, dear Nell." Lady Langdon laughed, blushing a little. Remembering how the countess had struggled to maintain her spirits during her early months in Sussex, Nell was glad to see that holding a ball at Charlwood had thrown her friend into such a pleasant flutter.

"But I am wasting time," Lady Langdon said and called her dresser over to help Nell into her gown.

A short time later, Nell was doubly thankful to Lady Langdon for offering the services of her dresser. Certainly, Hannah or Betty could have helped her out of her day dress and into the cream-colored satin ball gown decorated with little knots of pale green ribbon. But neither of them could have arranged

her hair in such a charming fashion, with a profusion of ringlets around her face, the back twisted up á la gréque, and
ornamented with more of the pale green ribbons. Long gloves,
her mother's pearl pendant, and a pair of earrings kindly lent
her by Lady Langdon finished off her ensemble.

As Nell gazed in the mirror, she knew she had never looked
so good. The soft shade of the gown was much more becoming
to her than a pure white, and the green ribbon contrasted nicely
with her chestnut curls and emphasized her eyes. She was almost beautiful.

"Lovely!" pronounced Lady Langdon.

"Thank you," she answered, smiling. "But beside you,
ma'am, I feel like an overblown daisy next to an orchid."

"Nonsense, dear. You will win hearts tonight. At least one
heart, I'm sure! Shall we go down and dazzle the gentlemen
now?"

Nell followed, feeling a pang of uncertainty. A second glance
in the mirror had shown her that even elegant apparel could
not disguise her commonplace features or her overbuxom figure. What had Darcy's golden good looks to do with such
ordinary prettiness? But such thoughts were vain and foolish.
Darcy was not so shallow; he had said she was beautiful
enough times. She had to believe she *was* so in his eyes.

She and Lady Langdon were greeted by a blaze of scarlet
as they entered the drawing room. Lord Langdon and Colonel
Huntley had chosen to wear their dress uniforms, perhaps in
tribute to Clarissa's brother. Nell didn't imagine either of them
were vain enough to realize how splendid they would look in
scarlet and gold.

She couldn't help staring at Lord Langdon for a moment.
The bright color of his coat emphasized his height and the
breadth of his shoulders and the gold in his hair. Who would
have thought he could look so magnificent?

Still, there was something like grim determination in his
face as he politely complimented her and Lady Langdon on
their appearance. Clearly he was making a great effort to set
aside their differences and act the kind host; the least she could
do was not embarrass him by gaping like a yokel.

To distract herself, she looked at Colonel Huntley and realized that he'd been standing tongue-tied ever since she and Lady Langdon entered the room. At about that point, Lord Langdon nudged his friend with an elbow.

As the colonel recovered from his admiring trance and made his bows to them, Darcy entered the room, looking elegant and rather rakish in his black evening attire. With a graceful flourish, he presented Nell and Lady Langdon with several small bouquets.

Nell smiled at him as she thanked him, but he seemed unwilling to meet her eyes. Guilt stabbed her then; how could she have toyed with his affections so? But surely it was not too late; she could still make him happy.

The Nettlehursts arrived then—Lady Nettlehurst arrayed in crimson satin with rubies; Clarissa in a pale blue silk with diamonds and sapphires around her neck and in her hair. They made Lord Nettlehurst's excuses; apparently he was not feeling strong enough for such a lively party.

Soon after, other dinner guests began to arrive, and Nell realized she would have to wait for her chance to speak with Darcy privately.

Lady Langdon had apologetically told Nell that she would not be seated near Darcy this evening. There was no helping it; as a son of the household, Darcy was obliged to entertain some of the more exalted guests. Although she would have preferred to be near him, Nell had to content herself with sitting between Colonel Huntley and Lord Poxton, whom she had previously met at a party.

This time, she was better able to maintain her composure while conversing with the viscount. On the previous occasion, she had been both stunned and appalled by Lord Poxton. She'd never seen anyone so huge or so ornately dressed. But now she experienced only mild wonder at his green coat, his vividly striped waistcoat stretched over an enormous stomach, and the diamonds and emeralds winking in his cravat and in the many rings that adorned his fingers.

She couldn't help deploring such wasteful display or thinking that his eating and drinking would be the death of him before long. However, unlike some dandies she'd heard of, he was meticulously polite and good-natured in an indolent sort of way. She suspected that he enjoyed the thought of how honored the recipients of his attention must feel. She listened politely to the story of his recent elevation to the peerage, but turned gladly to Colonel Huntley when Lord Poxton seemed sufficiently distracted by the food set before him.

As always, she enjoyed talking to Colonel Huntley, who seemed to be in a ripple of good spirits, drinking and laughing much and obviously looking forward to the dancing later in the evening. Nell noticed that the strain she had sensed in him on his arrival at Charlwood seemed to be gone, and she was happy for it.

Despite all this, her eyes couldn't help occasionally wandering toward where Darcy sat. He seemed to be laughing a bit louder than usual and drinking more. Nell lost her own appetite, feeling a rising anxiety to be dancing with him, to be close enough to tell him what would surely soothe and gladden.

She was obliged to be patient a little longer. For the first few dances, Darcy continued to do his duty by some of the higher-ranking ladies present. When he finally led her out, Nell realized that while the lively music and complex figures of a country dance might provide many opportunities for flirtation, the mood was not right for more serious revelations.

Afterward, they were both obliged to dance with other partners, and Nell endured the penance of dancing with Lord Poxton. Although he was surprisingly light on his feet for such a rotund gentleman, his constant maneuvers to catch his own reflection in the tall pier glasses set between the ballroom windows disrupted the figures of the dance and caused much confusion and embarrassment for his partner.

Although she didn't lack more graceful partners afterward, Nell had to force herself to pay attention to them. Between dances, her eyes roved restlessly about the room, now spotting Lord Langdon bowing to one of his partners, now alighting on Darcy smiling at yet another elegant partner with overly bright eyes. She thought that under other circumstances she might have enjoyed the ball very well; now she felt too warm and longed to be out of doors, alone with Darcy away from the distractions of this glittering crowd. Well, this was what she deserved for thinking she would find an opportunity to declare herself at a ball.

Midway through the evening, the musicians struck up for a waltz. Mindful of Lady Langdon's warnings, Nell had refused all requests for this dance. She looked for Darcy; perhaps they could sit and talk now. But no, he was dancing with Clarissa. Even Lady Langdon had gone onto the dance floor on Colonel Huntley's arm, despite having said earlier that she had no intention of dancing.

Nell sought a place to sit down, meanwhile encountering a few disdainful looks from some of the other ladies who were not dancing—an unpleasant reminder that there were those who resented her friendship with the Maylands.

She settled herself into an out-of-the-way corner of the ballroom, hoping she didn't look as awkward as she felt. She tried to ignore it when a couple flitted past her, headed for the doors onto the terrace, which were partially screened from view by a flower-bedecked trellis erected in front of them. Lady Langdon had said the screen would keep the older chaperones from complaining about drafts, but Nell could see that it also furnished a discreet exit for the amorously inclined among the ballgoers. She felt a slight pang at the thought. Darcy had made no attempt to lure her out onto the terrace.

She looked away from the trellis and concentrated on watching the dancers and so started with surprise at the sound of Lord Langdon's voice.

"Miss Ashley, I hope you are enjoying our ball."

She looked up to see a rather rigid smile on his face. But there was a warmer expression in his eyes. He must have seen she was feeling just a trifle forlorn. She was grateful for his kindness in coming to speak to her, but oddly, she felt her unease growing rather than fading.

"Very much," she replied, her pulse quickening uncomfortably. "I had not realized how much I would enjoy dancing."

"You have not had as many opportunities for such pleasures

as you deserve. I am glad we have been able to make one for you now," he said, seating himself in an adjacent chair.

She wondered at his paying her such an attention. Why would he risk offending his more noble guests just to sit with her? Surely their tête-à-tête would be remarked. She looked about anxiously, but the dancers all seemed engrossed in one another. The music was just loud enough that no one would overhear her conversation with Lord Langdon, imparting an unexpected intimacy to their situation.

She looked back at the earl. He was gazing at her with an unfathomable expression in his eyes. She felt an odd sense of danger, which was foolish. Even if he did not care for her personally, she no longer had anything to fear from him. But this silent exchange of glances was unbearable. There was much she needed to say to him if only she knew how to start.

"Lord Langdon," she began and stopped when she realized he had simultaneously said her name as well.

"Please go on," he said.

"Lord Langdon, I must tell you how very glad I am that you have offered an estate to Darcy. I know it will mean the world to him to have his own place to care for and manage."

He looked away. Gruffly, he said, "I am only doing my duty to my brother. He was shown himself worthy of the gift by the help he has given me and the good sense he has shown in offering for a lady of such good character as yourself. I expect you will both be very happy there."

She bit her lip. His words were kind, as before, but the tone in his voice made his feelings perfectly clear. Even if he approved of her now, in his heart he still wanted her and Darcy sixty miles away. Or was she being presumptuous to think he cared so much about her one way or the other?

In any case, she owed him an apology. Perhaps it would ease the ache she felt over the awkward distance between them.

"Lord Langdon," she began, faltering. He looked back at her and, again, smiled that odd, twisted smile. She continued, struggling for the right words. "I have been meaning for some time to apologize for the horrid things I said to you outside the Mullens' cottage and the evening after we visited the

Wickes. I wanted to do so when you visited last week, but I am afraid I lost my temper. I am . . . deeply sorry for what I said on all those occasions. I have since found that I was very wrong. I hope you will forgive me."

"There is nothing to forgive," he said, looking down. "I treated you far more contemptibly, with less justification. It is I who should be begging forgiveness."

The depth of regret in his voice shocked her. She studied his profile, seeing the faint lines of care about his eyes and on his forehead, his resolute chin, and his firm, commanding mouth. She could not help remembering how he had kissed her with those lips. What chaotic feelings he had aroused in her then!

But as she watched him, she realized that it was that kiss as much as anything that had disordered all her hopes and plans. Finally, she knew the true danger he represented. Vainly, she tried to summon up the anger she had felt at all his past insults, like a shield against more treacherous emotions.

Then he lifted his head. When she saw the sad, rueful expression in his eyes, the last vestiges of her distrust crumbled, and she was defenseless.

"I have long since forgiven you, my lord," she said.

He heaved a deep sigh. He sounded relieved, but she saw that his eyes had darkened, and she was transported back to that day in his study. She could almost feel again the force of his tongue intimately exploring her mouth, the strength in his arms molding her body to his. Worst of all, she couldn't repress the thought of what it would be like if he did it again.

She looked down, clasping her hands tightly in her lap. Surely this was a temporary madness, fostered by the heated atmosphere and too much champagne. She was merely confused because Lord Langdon had unintentionally awakened the passions that Darcy should have taught her. Once she and Darcy came to an understanding, she would forget this lunacy.

She straightened up, noticing the waltz had ended.

"Will you dance the next dance with me, Miss Ashley?" asked Lord Langdon.

She started in surprise, then took a deep breath, trying to

calm herself. A wanton part of her longed to dance with him, but with her newfound knowledge, it would be dangerous, even wicked to do so. Desperately she looked for Darcy and saw his blond head and dark coat at the other end of the ballroom. He was escorting yet another young lady onto the floor. Dear God, why was he intent on dancing every dance when she needed him?

She saw Lord Langdon was patiently awaiting her reply. She had no reasonable excuse not to accept. To refuse would be rude. A mischievous voice inside her asked what harm could come from just one dance.

She took another deep breath and voiced some conventional words of acceptance.

When he arose and offered his hand to help her up, she knew she'd made a mistake. Even through the thin fabric of her glove, the simple clasp of his hand, hot and strong, set her pulse racing again. His powerful scarlet-clad body radiated a masculine heat, bringing a fiery blush to her cheek.

She lowered her head. This was dreadful. Could she hope he would attribute her unruly color to the warmth of the room? If he knew the real cause he would doubtless think her a worse hussy than he had when they had first met.

He continued to hold her hand tightly as they started to walk toward where the new set was forming. She wondered if this was customary and if there was still time to turn back. She sought the will to tell him she had changed her mind, even as her feet carried her inexorably along beside him.

However, they had not gone more than five steps before they encountered Colonel Huntley and Lady Langdon headed in the opposite direction. Lord Langdon released her hand as the colonel accosted them.

"There you are, James! And Miss Ashley too, I see. A capital party, is it not?"

Nell saw Lady Langdon beside the colonel. Hastily, the countess said, "I do hope you are enjoying yourselves, my dears. But I am *so* hot. I vow I nearly fainted away just now! Colonel Huntley has kindly offered to escort me on to the terrace to see if some fresh air cannot revive me. There are still a few dances before supper. I hoped I would not be missed for a few minutes. Do please join us!"

Nell didn't know why Lady Langdon was chattering so, but she decided that a stroll on the terrace under Lady Langdon's chaperonage would be far safer than dancing with the earl. Perhaps the night air would cool her face before anyone saw the desire emblazoned upon it.

"Please, Lord Langdon," she said. "I hope I do not disappoint you, but I am feeling rather warm as well."

His expression was unreadable, but he nodded and offered her his arm. She hadn't realized he would wish to accompany them, but all she could do was place her hand on his arm and hope he did not notice her agitation.

Under cover of the beginning of the next dance, the foursome slipped out of the ballroom. As they stepped onto the terrace, a light breeze wafting up from the gardens brought the scent of roses. A large golden moon hovered over the grounds. Nell could still faintly hear the music from the ballroom.

A few steps along the terrace, a few more breaths of the cooler air, and she felt more peaceful, almost mistress of herself again. She risked a glance at Lord Langdon's face. He was looking calmly ahead to where Colonel Huntley and Lady Langdon preceded them. His stoic demeanor helped steady her. The alarming thrill she felt at his proximity was tapering off to a strong but more bearable pleasure. She would get through this evening, and tomorrow, surely, she would be sane again.

Then the quiet of the moonlit night was broken by a muffled cry.

Fifteen

The cry was followed by an oath from Colonel Huntley and a gasp from Lady Langdon. Nell and Lord Langdon quickly caught up with the other two. They were struck dumb and motionless with shock at what they saw.

Sitting on a seat, screened from view by a large potted shrub, were Darcy and Clarissa. Nell felt a sudden chill inside. Numbly, all she could think was that it must not have been Darcy she had seen in the ballroom.

Darcy sprang up and blurted, "Clarissa—Miss Nettlehurst, that is—was feeling a bit faint after our dance, and . . . and I thought the fresh air would revive her, so we . . ." His voice faltered. He looked quickly around at each of them, although he avoided meeting Nell's eyes. "Oh, damnation! I admit I was kissing her," he said finally.

His cravat was mussed. Clarissa looked like a fallen angel, her hair tumbling down out of its pins, and her bodice falling off one shoulder. More than just a kiss had happened here, Nell thought, feeling the chill spread through her body. She gripped Lord Langdon's arm tightly to keep from shaking. She felt his arm stiffen under hers, until it felt more like an iron bar than a human limb.

She looked at him and saw her shock mirrored in his face and almost instantly transformed into a look of demonic fury.

"You lecherous cur!" he growled. She let go of his arm as he started toward his brother, his hands clenched into fists.

Clarissa and Lady Langdon shrieked simultaneously.

"James, for God's sake, restrain yourself!" shouted Colonel Huntley.

But his warning was unnecessary. Lord Langdon stopped just short of his brother and turned back toward the others.

With frightening calm, he said, "Do not worry, Edward. I know this is not the time or place to deal with my brother as he deserves."

"You don't understand, any of you," said Darcy. "I love her, and . . . and . . . I mean to marry her!" Clarissa rose shakily, and Darcy put his arm around her protectively. She buried her face in his shoulder, sobbing.

The rest of them stared, struck mute by this second shock.

No, Nell thought, her inward shivering developing into a sense of nausea. This must be some grotesque dream. But when she looked at Darcy's defiant expression and the way Clarissa clung to him, the magnitude of her own blindness appalled her. How could she have been such a fool?

She looked down, clenching her hands tightly at her sides. Not in pain or anger, although surely those feelings would come soon. She must suppress them for the time being, before she lost the last shreds of dignity she possessed.

"What is this nonsense?"

Nell looked up and saw Lady Nettlehurst forcing her way into their group, her expression even more predatory than usual. Her rubies glinted in the moonlight like dozens of baleful eyes.

"Clarissa, come here at once, I say!" she commanded. Clarissa obediently disengaged herself from Darcy's clasp and went to her mother, her head downcast. Darcy watched, looking stunned at her instant capitulation. Then Lady Nettlehurst addressed herself to the earl.

"Lord Langdon, I do not know what came over my daughter just now, but I can assure you that this is not at all like her. I promise you that I will spare no pains to ensure that in the future she will behave herself in a manner not unbefitting the Countess of Langdon."

"That will not be necessary," said Lord Langdon. "I want no unwilling bride."

"But your betrothal has been announced. Everyone knows about it. You cannot jilt my daughter in this manner!" protested Lady Nettlehurst, but the heightened pitch of her voice showed growing desperation.

The earl ignored her, addressing himself to Clarissa. With cold gentleness, he asked, "Do you still consider yourself betrothed to me?"

Clarissa looked up briefly. Tears streamed down her face, but she managed to shake her head.

Lady Nettlehurst erupted. "How could you do such a thing, you foolish, irresponsible child? My only daughter, the hope of my life? After all my efforts—"

"Be quiet!" interrupted the earl. "Or is it your wish to draw the attention of those in the ballroom?"

Lady Nettlehurst shut her mouth tightly, glaring at him.

"Thank you. Now I suggest that you both leave quietly. We will tell everyone that your daughter was overcome by the heat and was obliged to leave. Then, in a few days, Miss Nettlehurst and I can inform the world we have mutually decided to call off our engagement. You may trust my family, and Colonel Huntley, not to gossip about this evening's events."

Lady Nettlehurst sniffed. "Small comfort!" she complained. "This will undoubtedly give rise to all sorts of rumors. Your brother has ruined my poor daughter's prospects of another respectable match!"

"Then let *me* marry her!"

"*You!*" she answered, glaring at Darcy. "My daughter, marry a paltry younger son! A wastrel and a rake, to boot! She'll be an old maid before I permit such a thing!"

Her head held high, she stalked back toward the ballroom, dragging her daughter along with her. Clarissa gave one unhappy look back at Darcy, but made no attempt to escape her mother's clutches.

Darcy took a few steps after them and called out, "Darling, never fear! I shall find a way!"

Nell shuddered at the bereft sound of his voice. Then she felt Lady Langdon's arm around her. "Nell! You poor dear! Is there anything I can do for you?"

Nell stiffened. She had managed to maintain her composure while everyone was preoccupied with Darcy and Clarissa, but Lady Langdon's soft words nearly broke through her control.

"No, I thank you," she said. Strange how her own voice sounded so odd and distant. "I only wish to go home."

Finally, Darcy looked at her. "I am sorry," he said. "I never meant to hurt you, I promise. I couldn't help it. Please forgive me!"

Even through her numbness, she saw he was sincere. *Why could you not have told me sooner and spared me this?* But she would not berate him aloud; once she started, she wouldn't be able to conceal how his betrayal wounded her.

"I forgive you," she said, lifting her chin. She was pleased to hear that her words sounded so cool and calm.

"Thank you!"

"There, Darcy. You have gotten much more than you deserve," said Lord Langdon. "Now I suggest you all go back to the ballroom. I will make sure Miss Ashley is conveyed home safely."

The others went back into the ballroom, and Nell found herself alone with the earl.

"Please come with me, Miss Ashley."

She obeyed, having no idea where he planned to take her, but content for the moment to merely follow orders. She didn't want to think; that was too close to feeling, and she was determined not to break down until she was safely home at the vicarage.

They walked the length of the terrace and entered a door at the other end of the house. Nell realized they were in the library.

"I will send my man to order the carriage for you, Miss Ashley. I thought you would be more comfortable awaiting it here."

She thanked him, sat down in one of the leather-covered chairs, and looked about her. The library was her father's favorite room at Charlwood, but she had only been here once before herself. She couldn't remember the colors of the furnishings; now, lit only by the moonlight streaming in through the windows, all she could see was soothing shades of gray. Being at the opposite end of the house from the ballroom, the library was also surprisingly quiet.

How kind it was of Lord Langdon to bring her here, she thought. She could never have endured a return to the noise and brightness of the ballroom. He must have known that. She was grateful, but amazed at his composure. After his initial blaze of anger, he had firmly taken control of the situation. This despite the fact that his life had been turned upside down as much as—perhaps even worse than—hers. Perhaps his feelings for Clarissa had not really run very deep.

He returned to the library more quickly than she expected. Nervously, she stood up as he came in. A shadow across his face hid the expression in his eyes; but she could see the tension around his jaw and in his stance. Despite his self-control, he was suffering.

"Farley will return here when the carriage is ready. He has been with me for years; you may rely on his discretion."

She realized Lord Langdon was speaking of the fact that they were alone together in a dark, unfrequented part of the house. There would be gossip enough after this ball; she should be grateful he was taking pains to make sure not to add to it. At the present moment, reputation seemed worth little while her plans had all gone so far awry.

"You are pale, Miss Ashley," he said in a softer voice. "Is there anything I can do for you? Shall I fetch you a glass of wine?"

He came a step closer, and the moonlight was full on his face. His eyes were filled with sorrow and compassion. She could not bear it. She wished he would go back to issuing orders in that grave, impersonal manner that had steadied her through the recent ordeal. His warm sympathy only reminded her of what had just happened, of what she had lost.

What she had never really had, she corrected herself. Darcy had never looked at her as he had at Clarissa. Perhaps practical, humdrum Nell Ashley was not the woman to inspire such passion in any man.

The cold shivers came upon her again, along with the empty,

fluttery feeling in her stomach. She struggled for control, telling herself that an emotional scene would be a poor way to repay Lord Langdon's kindness. But it was no use. She covered her face with her hands, as her shoulders shook with the effort of suppressing her tears.

She hoped he would go away.

Instead, he gently pried her hands away from her face, then put an arm around her, drawing her up against his chest. She stiffened, knowing she should not allow him to comfort her so. With his other hand, he lightly pressed her head down onto his shoulder and began to stroke her hair.

That last tender touch was her undoing.

She gave herself up to the gush of tears welling up from the hurt, empty place inside her and clung to Lord Langdon, shamelessly seeking the blessed solace of his warm, strong embrace.

Sixteen

James held Nell close, cursing Darcy for having brought her to this. Gradually, she stopped crying, but continued to lean against him trustingly, apparently too distraught to resist his embrace. He continued to caress her hair, temporarily forgetting his brother's betrayal in the pleasure of consoling her.

Tentatively, he moved his hand down from her silky curls to rub her neck. She gave a little sigh, but it did not sound like a protest. He moved his hand in little circles down the back of her neck, past the slender chain that held her little pendant, and gently stroked her shoulders.

How wonderful, how very right she felt in his arms. It was a painful joy to know he had succeeded in comforting her. God help him, he was also treacherously aware that she no longer felt cold and shivery, that he held a warm, vital feminine form in his arms. By chance, his hand reached the place where her sultry, velvety skin disappeared under the cool satin of her gown. He pulled his hand back, conquering the heady urge to slip it inside the delicate fabric and feeling guilty to be so aroused when she was so miserable. He would do nothing to distress her, but was it so wrong to enjoy holding her while he could? It would all be over soon enough.

Then a voice within him protested. Why should he despair? He was a free man now. Clarissa and Darcy's betrayal had given him that, at least. He'd finally won Nell's trust and friendship, or else she would not rest so easily in his arms. In time, when she healed from this blow, might he not be able to teach her to feel something more? It would require patience and restraint. While there was hope, however, he could wait as long as necessary for the chance to win her as his own.

She gasped.

He realized he had unconsciously tightened his embrace. *Damn!* How could he have been so careless? She looked up at him, her eyes wide and dark, then made a move to disengage herself.

No, he wanted to scream even as he instantly released her.

"I am sorry, Miss Ashley," he said before she could speak. "I assure you, I had no intention—no desire to take advantage of your distress. Please believe I only wished to comfort you!"

In a low voice, she replied, "Yes, I understand. Thank you."

He looked at her sharply. In deepening dismay, he read only fear and confusion in her face, before she averted her eyes completely. His explanations had failed to reassure her. What else could he do or say to convince her of his integrity?

Then she looked past him, toward the doorway. James turned, and saw Farley waiting there.

"The carriage is ready, my lord," said Farley. There was no way of telling how much of the scene he had observed. But it was no great matter; Farley would not gossip.

"Good night, my lord," she said, still in a subdued voice. She gave a quick curtsy and nearly ran past him to follow Farley out of the room.

James watched them leave, longing to go with Nell, knowing it was useless. It was clear she wanted nothing better than to get away from Charlwood, from Darcy, from *him*.

He sank down into the chair Nell had just vacated, overwhelmed by the futility of his dreams. He'd been a fool to think of winning her after all she had endured at his brother's hands and his own. They were true sons of their father. Like him, they would bring an honest woman nothing but grief.

He knew he should rejoin his guests and try to act as if nothing very momentous had happened this evening. There would be plenty of gossip later—some of it on his own broken engagement, some on the sudden end of Darcy and Nell's courtship. It was his duty to minimize it by behaving as normally as possible.

To hell with his duty! He went to a sideboard and poured himself a brandy. He tossed it off mindlessly, then stared at the empty glass. Perhaps a few more would dull the ache of his despair. And then he would go for a long walk until he was too exhausted to feel. Yes, that was what he would do. If he couldn't have the desire of his heart, did it matter what else he did?

He slumped, then straightened back up again. Grimly smiling, he twitched his uniform back into place, and walked resolutely back through the house, back toward the ballroom, toward the hideous brilliance of chandeliers and the grotesque sounds of music and laughter.

"You are yawning, Edward. Go to bed. I assure you, I will not shoot myself or my brother or throw myself in the lake just because you are not here to prevent me."

"Are you sure? Frankly, you are looking rather grim," said Edward, looking sharply back at James.

"You're not such a pretty sight yourself, you know," James answered wryly. "Go on. I shall do."

Obediently, Edward put down his glass, heaved himself up off his chair, and left James alone in the library.

What a horrible evening, he thought, downing the last of the brandy in his glass. At least it was over now. He'd done his duty, and little enough satisfaction had come of it. But he hadn't expected duty and responsibility to bring happiness; their role was to ensure right conduct and prevent harm to others. If only his brother had one ounce of either virtue!

As if summoned, Darcy looked in the doorway. Seeing James, he advanced a few steps into the room.

"James, can I talk to you?" he asked in a small voice.

Oh, Lord. His ne'er-do-well of a brother wanted to apologize. As if he hadn't endured enough trials this evening. Now he would have to try to keep from thrashing Darcy the way he deserved.

"This is not a good time," he said.

"Please. You must let me apologize."

"I must? Very well then." He leaned back in his chair, trying to ignore his brother's restless pacing about the room.

"I'm so sorry, James," Darcy blurted out finally, stopping in front of his brother's chair. His voice sounded convincingly pathetic. Was it a ruse to get James's sympathy? Or did Darcy really think mere words could absolve him of what he'd done this evening? "Well, aren't you going to say anything?"

"What would you have me say?"

"I would like your forgiveness."

"You think it's that simple, after all you've done?"

"I couldn't help it! I love Clarissa."

"And always will, no doubt, until another attractive woman comes within your sphere to make you forget *her* as well."

"How can you say that? *Your* life isn't ruined! You never loved Clarissa. You can find someone else to bear you an heir."

"My feelings for Clarissa are none of your business. But since you think betraying my trust is no great matter, what of Miss Ashley's?"

Darcy did not answer immediately. This time, he at least had the grace to look a little guilty. But after a pause, he said, "I don't think she was ever going to accept my proposal anyway. She wouldn't have taken it all so calmly if she had."

"You are mistaken. She cried her heart out over you afterward."

"If that's true, I am very sorry for it. But Nell is strong. She's not like Clarissa. She doesn't *need* me. I'm sure she'll come about."

"It will be no thanks to you if she does. It's a pity she does not yet realize she's well out of a very bad bargain."

Darcy winced and said, "She forgave me, James. Can't you?" Again, the pleading note tugged at James.

I could on my account. But on hers?

"First I must know this," James said aloud. "When you decided you were in love with Clarissa, why did you not come and tell me or make a clean breast of it to Miss Ashley? You might at least have spared her this mortification. It was cruel of you to continue to deceive her and keep her hopes alive. *Why* did you do it?"

"Damn you, I did it to please you!"

James laughed harshly. "Now why do I find it so difficult to believe that?"

"It's true! I know how much you approved and how good it would be for the estate and—"

"Stop already! You've never had an unselfish thought in your life, have you? That's what's ailing you now, isn't it? It's the first time you've been denied something you thought you wanted."

"No, that's not true. I wanted a pair of colors, but you were too scaly to purchase them for me and wanted to have all the adventure for yourself!"

James could sit no longer. He sprang up from the chair and began pacing himself.

"Do you think army life is some sort of picnic or a drill in Hyde Park? I'll tell you what it's really about. It's about having to stop your men from stealing grain when both they and their horses are starving. It's about killing brave men who might have been your friends under other circumstances. It's seeing friends die and going on because you must, because you know an insane egotist like Napoleon must be stopped."

"I'm sorry, James. I didn't understand," said Darcy, looking down.

James stopped pacing by the glass doors that led onto the terrace, feeling infinitely weary. "No. God help me, I didn't want you to. Now I know I was wrong. I should have sent you into the army. Perhaps a good dose of military discipline would have made something of you. I know *I* have failed to do so."

"You have failed to make something of me?" he heard Darcy say angrily from the other end of the room. "Why should you have anything to do with it? You're not my father!"

"No, more's the pity, since he taught you to be just like himself."

"What do you mean by that? Papa was kindness itself. He wouldn't have knowingly hurt anyone."

"I wonder if Mama thought so when he was conducting his vile affairs in this very house."

"He didn't. He couldn't have done anything so cruel!"

James turned around, the bitter weariness blazing back into anger. "No, he gave you ponies and later horses, and opera dancers and as much blunt as you wanted to gamble away. So he was perfect, wasn't he? Let me ask you another question. If I had married Clarissa and you had married Nell, how long would you have waited before seducing my wife and betraying yours? A month? A week? *How long?*"

"Damn you, James! If that's what you think of me, I'm leaving!"

"Go."

James could barely see or breathe, the smoke was so thick from the fires that had started in the dry grass of the battle-field. But the order had been given to charge, and so he continued to urge his horse forward and exhort his men in a strange, raspy voice unlike his own.

Their own infantry parted, and the three cavalry regiments passed through to the disordered French column. The French tried to get into square, but it was too late. A few of his own men fell under a terrible volley of enemy fire, but James and most of his troopers galloped on.

They were close, close enough to see the variously brave, desperate, or panic-stricken faces of the enemy. Now they were upon them.

He couldn't breathe anymore. His sword felt unbearably heavy. Mechanically, he raised it and brought it down upon a French infantryman. In his dying moment, the young man looked up at him. As he'd done before, James looked down into the face of the valiant youth who was about to sacrifice his life for the monster Bonaparte.

James woke up, covered in sweat. His mouth tasted of ashes.

He hadn't dreamed of Salamanca in a long time. The dream had faded in the years that had passed since that famous, bloody charge. But now it was back, and it was different. This time the eyes in that ghostly young face were blue, not brown, and the face was his brother's.

Seventeen

Nell woke with a start, not quite knowing why. She looked about and realized it must still be very early. A faint gray light shone at the window, but the rest of her room was dark.

Then she remembered what had happened the last night.

She rolled over, curled up in her blanket, and tried to recapture sleep. Later, when the sun was up, she would face the new day and decide her next course. Now she craved oblivion.

Sleep eluded her, however. Once set in motion, scenes and voices played back through her restless mind. Darcy and Clarissa springing apart before them, then desperately holding on to each other. Darcy's apology. Lord Langdon's kindness. Her own tangled, confused reactions . . .

She thumped her pillow and rolled over again, trying to banish the images from her mind. She felt too tired, too feverish to be rational. But she still couldn't sleep. The room felt warm and airless despite the open window. Irritably, she pushed away the blanket, which had gotten twisted uncomfortably around her, and got out of bed.

She went to the window and looked out, taking in the cooler air. There was not a breath of wind to bring it inside. A mist lay over the garden below and the fields beyond. Through the mist, the moon still faintly glowed, but near the horizon another pale gleam heralded the dawn.

She no longer felt tired, only restless. She looked down into the garden again and made a quick decision.

She splashed some water on her face and hastily tidied the

thick braid in which she slept. She smiled wryly as she remembered how Hannah had stayed up to help her to bed. She had told Hannah what had happened in a cool, dispassionate manner, too drained for tears or anger. Poor Hannah must have been disappointed at the scant heed Nell had paid both her words of comfort and her I told you so's.

Hannah would probably be shocked if she knew what she was about now, Nell thought as she silently slipped into one of her oldest dresses. But what she contemplated wasn't scandalous, only mildly eccentric.

She slipped downstairs into the kitchen and put on her gloves and an old apron. Odysseus lifted his head and thumped his tail on the floor upon seeing her. She stepped out into the garden, and he padded out after her.

This was better, she thought, enjoying the cool fresh air. Strange how familiar things looked so different at this hour. A thick dew coated the plants, all their colors muted to shades of gray green. Every blade of grass was slick with moisture, shimmering in the eerie light.

She went to the vegetable garden and dropped to her knees. The light was good enough for weeding, she decided. Absorbed in her foolish plans, she'd neglected the garden this past week. She would do so no more.

She had let herself get distracted by a silly fantasy. Darcy had shattered it, irreparably. *Why* had he done so? she wondered, fiercely tugging at a stubborn weed. Had he tired of her naivete, her lack of pretense to fashion, her well-meaning attempts to reform him? Was it Clarissa's superior beauty, breeding, and style that had attracted him? Could he really be so shallow?

Or perhaps his pursuit of her and then of Clarissa both stemmed from a desire to annoy or undermine his brother.

If either was true, he was no great loss to her.

Then she remembered the stricken look on his face when Lady Nettlehurst pulled Clarissa away from him. No, he must sincerely love Clarissa. If only he had been man enough to tell her sooner!

Nell brushed away a tear, then realized she'd done so with

her dirty glove. She must be a sight. Anyone would take her for a lunatic if they saw her now, chuckling as she brushed away another tear. Then she realized it was not the loss of Darcy that made her weep. It was merely the passing of a youthful dream.

Still she felt strange and disoriented. Of course, she didn't know what to do from here. It would probably be too awkward for her to continue her association with the Maylands after all that had happened. But why should that make her feel so bereft?

The sound of Odysseus's barking interrupted her thoughts. She looked up to see him running back and forth along the inside of the stone wall that separated the orchard from the pasture behind the vicarage. Perhaps it was some animal that had excited his attention.

Then, through the mist and the trees, she saw a tall figure moving along the old right of way that skirted the pasture alongside their wall. Who could it be? It couldn't be one of the shepherds; she couldn't see or hear his flock. Could it be a gypsy or a chicken thief?

No, she thought as the figure paused and stopped across from the back gate. A rogue would have been frightened off by Oddy's deep-throated growls. He would not just stand there. Although she couldn't see him clearly, something seemed wrong about his posture. Perhaps he was injured or sick. Perhaps he needed her help.

She walked warily toward the gate, and Oddy came back to her. Putting her hand on his head, she called out, "Who's there?"

"It is I. Lord Langdon."

Lord Langdon! What was he doing here at this hour? She hastened toward the gate.

"I am sorry if I frightened you, Miss Ashley," he said, looking as surprised to see her as she was to see him.

"No, you did not," she assured him. He was looking sharply at her. Then she remembered her old dress, her braid, and the smudges on her cheeks and hurried to explain. "I know I must appear perfectly demented. I was just doing some gardening.

I could not sleep. The dawn comes so early at this time of summer."

"I could not sleep either," he said. In the dim light, she saw he looked haggard, as if he had lost sleep on more nights than this last. He was no longer in his uniform, but he had dressed carelessly, and there was a faint aroma of brandy about him. Was he drunk or just sad and tired?

His voice sounded thick, and there were deep hollows under his eyes. Nell realized he must be suffering at least twice as much as she had, and she found herself silently cursing Darcy and Clarissa for having brought him so low with their careless betrayal.

"You look dreadful, my lord," she said impulsively. "Will you not come and sit down in the orchard. Perhaps I can fetch you some water?"

"Thank you, but I must not impose on you. If someone should see us——"

"No one will see. This part of the garden is not visible from the lane, and it is unlikely that this pasture will be used for some time. Please. You look ill."

"I am perfectly well, Miss Ashley," he said, squaring his shoulders. Typical of a man to be so stubborn, she thought. But he *would* let her help him. She couldn't let him stagger about the neighborhood. What if he fell into a ditch somewhere?

She gazed at him with equal stubbornness. Finally, after looking about to be sure no one was stirring, he submitted. "To please you, I will have some water."

She smiled and opened the gate. Quickly she pulled off her gardening gloves as she led him to the bench under the apple trees. Seeing it was wet, she stripped off her apron and laid it upon the seat. He protested again, but sat down at her urging.

She ran to the well, and drew a bucketful of water as quickly as she could. She poured a little of it over her soiled hands and splashed a little on her face, hoping to clear some of the grime. Then she scooped some water into a dipper to bring back to Lord Langdon.

She handed him the dipper, and James drained it quickly,

like a man dying of thirst. He had been feeling parched, he realized. Wordlessly, Nell went for more. He watched her run to the well, trying to understand why she had welcomed him into her garden at this strange hour. After last night, he'd expected her to want nothing to do with him or his family ever again.

As she hurried up to him with another dipperful of water, he saw the concern on her face and knew the answer. He knew why she would risk the damage to her reputation if anyone saw their encounter. She couldn't help herself in the face of another's suffering.

It was something.

This time he drank more slowly. With a nervous glance at him, she sat down on the bench a mere few feet away. He realized it was to prevent him from feeling a gentlemanly urge to get back up too quickly.

She was still watching him anxiously. He must look pretty ghastly. But he was starting to feel better. It was a good thing she didn't know how her proximity coaxed his senses back to life.

Last night, she had been lovely in her satin ball gown with the ribbons in her hair. This morning, in her plain dress and the youthful braid, she was simply adorable. It was all he could do not to pull her onto his lap and wrap his arms around her. To hold her, to caress her, to make her forget all his cursed brother had put her through. . . .

He closed his eyes and leaned back, trying to relax his body, now tightening with a new, more pleasant tension. If he could not rid himself of these urges, at least he would have the good sense not to act upon them.

Then she moved closer. He felt a cold, wet, gentle hand upon his forehead. He hadn't even realized how his head had been aching. This was bliss. He almost protested when she drew her hand away. An instant later, it was back, brushing more cold water over his forehead and temples, fingers light, gentle, infinitely soothing.

Her warm solicitude was not what he had wished for, but it was more than he had any right to look for. Unexpectedly, piercingly sweet. He wished he could go on sitting with her like this, accepting her gentle attentions, but he knew that was not possible. He opened his eyes and stopped her hand, taking it into his.

"Thank you," he said.

"Are you feeling a bit better?" she asked briskly. Then he remembered that what she did for him she would have done for anyone, regardless of what she suffered herself. It was difficult to believe that just a few hours ago, she had lain sobbing against his chest.

"Yes," he answered, giving her hand a squeeze. "But I should be asking *you* the same question."

She met his eyes for a moment. Then abruptly, she wrenched her hand away and jumped up. He stood up, watching in anguish as she staggered over to one of the apple trees and leaned against it, still facing away from him.

Nell held on to the tree, shaken by potent, confused emotions that threatened to make her legs buckle under her. Lord Langdon's proximity, the touch of his hand, and the softness in his voice all brought back the same tangle of feelings that she'd felt last night as he had comforted her with his warm embrace. But now, she finally realized the depth of her self-deception.

I love him. I love Lord Langdon. I should have known it before, she thought. *He is everything I ever wanted, everything I deluded myself into thinking Darcy to be. Strong, kind, forthright.*

She heard grass swish behind her. He was right there behind her. She must calm herself. There was no telling what he would think if he knew what she was feeling.

"Damn Darcy!"

She heard his voice behind her. Oddly, the raw pain and rage in it steadied her. She realized some of this bitter emotion was on her account. Perhaps she could relieve him of at least that worry. Anger such as his was like an infection, eating away at a person. She couldn't let that happen to him. She had to remember that they were friends, and it was the place of a friend to reassure and console.

"Lord Langdon," she said, turning around and composing her face. "Please do not worry about me. What Darcy did was wrong and weak. But I do believe he could not help himself and is sincerely sorry for it."

"Do you care for him so much? After all he has done, do you still defend him?" he asked roughly.

She recoiled from his harsh words, but persisted. "No, I do not defend him. I will try to forgive him though."

"You are kinder than he deserves. I know this has wounded you more than you admit."

"If I am upset it is because I have been foolish. I am afraid I allowed myself to become infatuated with your brother. I don't think we would have suited."

"Is this true?" he asked, and she knew he watched her closely. She met his eyes briefly and nodded, then looked away. She could not bear such close scrutiny for long. She let go of the tree and walked back to the wall, knowing Lord Langdon followed her. She looked east, across the pasture, and saw the sun had appeared at the horizon. It was rising and would soon burn away the mist. The dewy grass shimmered in the slanting light.

The sight steadied her, bringing a measure of peace to her soul. She realized that what she had said was true. Darcy's betrayal had wounded her pride, but not her heart. She couldn't say it, but as surely as the sun was rising, her heart was with the man standing beside her. At least she understood herself now.

She looked at him, hoping he too was drawing some serenity from the dawn. He glanced from the rising sun back to her. Did his expression seem a trifle less grim?

"Miss Ashley, I must apologize for speaking so intemperately," he said.

She was confused for a moment, then realized he referred to having cursed Darcy. "It is no great matter, I assure you. I have assisted Mr. Olden in setting broken bones before. I have heard worse."

As she'd hoped, Lord Langdon smiled. She *had* succeeded in cheering him.

"I must leave you soon," he said in something more like his usual, decisive voice. "But before I do, I have a favor to ask."

"What is it?"

"My stepmother has become very fond of you. I think she would regret losing your friendship. I know my family and Charlwood must seem hateful to you just now, but I hope very much you will be so kind as to continue visiting her as you have been accustomed to do."

This was totally unexpected. How could she agree after everything that had happened? On the other hand, how could she refuse without giving offense?

"I don't know. I am afraid . . ."

"Darcy will not be there," he said, some of the roughness back in his voice. "No, I did not send him away if that is what you are thinking. When I rose this morning, he was gone."

More softly, he continued, "I only wish to assure you he will not be there to make things awkward for you. You need not answer now, but please think about it."

She couldn't resist him when he used that gentle, coaxing tone.

"I will," she answered.

"Thank you," he said, looking pleased. "May I say I hope you will also continue to advise me regarding the estate and my people?"

She nodded. Dear heaven, she was powerless to refuse him, even when she knew this could lead to disaster.

"Thank you. Good morning, Miss Ashley." He bowed and let himself out the gate.

She leaned over the stone wall, watching him go, glad to see his usual brisk, long stride had returned, admiring the breadth of his shoulders and the glint of sunlight on his hair.

Oh, she was assuredly a fool! How could she have agreed to visit Charlwood again? She would never be able to hide her yearning from him. Sooner or later, she would betray herself. And then he would think her silly and fickle.

No, worse! she thought, remembering his earlier suspicions.

He would think she was blithely setting her cap at him now that he, the greater prize, was available.

She couldn't bear for that to happen. Somehow she would prevent it.

She had maintained her composure through this meeting by concentrating on helping him. She would continue to do so. She would be his friend, his adviser, just as he had asked. It was no new role for her. Surely she could play it and play it well enough that no one would suspect.

Perhaps, perhaps in time . . .

Firmly, she stopped herself before she began to dream again. She had made such a botch of things with Darcy. Perhaps this was not love, after all. This could be just another foolish infatuation. So what if it felt utterly, compellingly different from her feeling for Darcy?

She'd played the fool once already. She swore she would not do so again.

As he crossed the dew-drenched fields, James couldn't stop seeing Nell's face, kissed by the dawn light. So beautiful, at least to him, so very dear. Had she truly taken so little hurt from Darcy's violation of her trust?

It was possible, he assured himself. She had a steadfast common sense despite her innocence. Perhaps all along it had warned her against accepting Darcy's suit. Perhaps that was the real reason she had wavered.

Perhaps he should not despair. She was willing to continue her friendship with him and Lady Langdon. Surely that was a start?

Or was he a fool to hope?

That afternoon, Lady Langdon called at the vicarage. When Betty showed her into Nell's sitting room, the countess walked in shyly, for the first time looking uncertain of her welcome.

Nell got up quickly and came forward to greet her friend with a reassuring smile.

"Nell, my dear! I was afraid you would not wish to see any of us again after last night," said Lady Langdon, folding Nell into her soft, fragrant embrace.

"I do not blame you for what happened, ma'am."

"But it was I who advised you to accept Darcy's suit, encouraged you to think he was in love with you! Please believe I was as misled as you were. I never wished you to be hurt so!"

Lady Langdon broke into tears. Nell patted her back, feeling both moved and embarrassed by the countess's sympathy.

"Please don't cry, ma'am. I am not so deeply wounded as you believe."

"You are not truly?"

"No, indeed. I am almost ashamed to admit it, but I have realized that Darcy and I would never have suited."

To Nell's relief, Lady Langdon backed away a little, cocking her head back to study Nell's face. She must have been satisfied with what she saw, for she gave a relieved smile and visibly relaxed.

"Dear, sensible Nell! You do not know how relieved I am to hear you say so." After a pause, she asked, "You *will* come back and visit as you have before? Darcy has gone to Brighton to visit friends, the poor foolish boy, so you need not fear any awkwardness."

Nell thought wryly that being obliged to hide an unrequited passion might certainly be called awkward. But it seemed she would have to do so; both Lord Langdon and his stepmother were determined for her to continue her friendship with them.

Lady Langdon must have seen the doubt in her face.

"Nell, please say you will. James is very concerned that you not pine in isolation after what has happened."

"How very kind of him," Nell answered. Odd how this morning Lord Langdon had stressed that he wished her to remain friends with his stepmother to keep *her* from being lonely.

"Yes, he is very kind, isn't he? But aside from the fact that

I would miss you sorely, there is another reason we should continue our friendship. There is bound to be a great deal of gossip about the breakup of James's engagement and about Darcy's sudden departure. No one will know exactly what happened, but I do believe there may be fewer rumors regarding *you* if we are all seen to be still on good terms."

Nell nodded her understanding. She was tempted to go into seclusion for the next few weeks, for she would undoubtedly be obliged to repulse numerous attempts to discover the truth of what had happened. But clearly it would be in all their best interests for her not to do so.

Like it or not, she was going to continue to be a part of the society at Charlwood.

Eighteen

Magpie's lips tickled Nell's hand as she fed the mare a lump of sugar. Having finished the treat, Magpie nuzzled Nell's pockets.

"I'm sorry, darling. There is no more," she crooned, stroking the piebald cob's glossy neck.

The groom at the Fox and Hounds had clearly expended extra effort this morning to have Magpie looking her best. The mare's black patches shimmered starkly against her creamy-white coat. Her tail was trimmed and serious attempts had been made to coax her mane to lie flat on one side of her neck.

Turning, Nell smiled at the groom, who was adjusting Magpie's girth.

"She looks lovely today, Jem. Thank you so much."

"We do our best, Miss Nell," he answered with a wink and a grin. "Especially knowing you are going riding with the folk from the House."

Nell blushed. It was abundantly clear that the annoying rumors that were currently circulating were not confined to the local gentry. Still, it was touching that her friends at the inn held her chances so high and were clearly doing their best to turn her out in style.

However, no degree of grooming could disguise the fact that Magpie was no thoroughbred. Just a sturdy, beloved little mare who was as easy to ride as she was to drive, whose surefootedness and gentle disposition made her equally perfect for

Papa's absentminded horsemanship and Nell's occasional solitary rides on the Downs.

Jem led Magpie over to a mounting block and held her while Nell mounted. She thanked him and, leaning over, handed him a modest coin.

Jem grinned again, and this time he added a wink.

"Good day, Miss Nell, and enjoy your ride!"

"Thank you. I will!" she answered as she set off on the lane leading to Charlwood.

She allowed Magpie to warm up along the lane at a brisk walk. When they reached the path through the woods that was a shortcut to Charlwood, she urged Magpie into a gentle trot.

She hadn't had a chance to ride much recently, and she was also eager to visit Bosham, the picturesque coastal village that was their destination. Sufficient reasons for her to feel so light, so restless with excitement. That she would soon be riding in a party with Lord Langdon, that he had organized this outing after she'd mentioned a wish to see Bosham, was all completely irrelevant.

Only a few weeks had passed since he had been betrayed by both his brother and his betrothed. Impossible that he should be developing any affection for *her*.

"He is merely being kind again, isn't he?" she murmured.

Magpie flicked her ears backward in response and snorted.

"You are right, Magpie. To read anything more into it would be folly of the worst sort."

Indeed, she had seen the earl only a few times since the morning after the ball. He seemed very busy, yet on the occasions when they did speak, he always had a warm smile for her. Although he never mentioned Darcy or Clarissa, he always had at least a question or two about some family or other on his estate on which he wanted her advice. She was grateful for the questions, for they gave her something to do besides dwelling on the unexpected sweetness in his smile or the way her pulse raced every time he sat down next to her.

As they had all expected, speculation about Lord Langdon's abruptly terminated engagement had abounded. However, while he, his stepmother, Colonel Huntley, and Nell herself maintained a polite silence on the subject, no one could do anything but speculate.

Still, there was enough malicious scandal broth brewing to set Nell's teeth on edge. Remembering how he had suspected her in the past, Nell could only hope Lord Langdon hadn't heard the worst rumors. Perhaps he hadn't or at least he hadn't believed them. Otherwise why would he have been so quick to include her in this expedition?

Comforted by the thought, she rode out of the woods into sight of Charlwood. Riding around to the stable yard, she saw Lord Langdon, Colonel Huntley, and Lady Langdon standing there, as grooms brought out their respective mounts.

A few minutes later, they had all mounted and set off down the lane, which they soon left for an ancient bridle way. Passing through patches of woodland, traversing sheep pastures, and skirting cultivated fields, they started to make their way slowly through the Downs toward the coast. Lady Langdon enjoyed riding her sweet old gelding, but preferred a sedate pace.

Eventually, they reached the flatter lands nearer the coast. Reaching a patch of woodland between several of the numerous farms, they saw the bridle way stretching ahead of them, straight and level for perhaps a half mile, shaded by tall, pale beech trees on either side.

"What a place for a canter!" Nell said as they approached the wood.

"James, why don't you go on ahead with Miss Ashley? I will stay behind and keep Lady Langdon company," said Colonel Huntley, guiding his horse to be near the countess and her mount.

"Thank you. I will. Miss Ashley, are you ready?"

She nodded, and he urged his horse into a canter. The big chestnut, having obediently maintained a gentle pace throughout the ride, looked happy to be given his head for once and lengthened his stride into a full gallop.

Magpie perked up her ears, eager to follow his lead, if not quite capable of keeping up. Nell let her gallop on, enjoying the speed and the feeling of wind in her face.

They reached a bend, and Lord Langdon slowed to a trot.

As Nell came around, she saw that a good-size tree had fallen across the bridle way at a little distance ahead of them.

"Do you wish to jump it?" he asked, turning slightly in the saddle.

"Yes, please," she called out. She'd jumped similar obstacles on Magpie before and knew the mare wouldn't refuse. Besides, it seemed awfully tame to ride into the woods just to skirt a log.

"Very well!" he said and brought his horse back into a brisk canter toward the fallen tree. The lordly beast took the obstacle in his stride. Nell followed, experiencing a rush of pure delight as Magpie flew over the log. When they slowed to a walk at the other edge of the woodland, to allow the others to catch up, she was beaming with pleasure.

Lord Langdon looked as if he had also enjoyed it. "Well done, Miss Ashley! You have a very nice little mare there."

"Yes, she is a dear, isn't she? I've ridden her ever since I outgrew my pony."

"I understand how you feel. I will always have a special fondness for Jack here. We have been through many a campaign and grueling march together," he answered, giving his horse a pat.

"So that is his name—just Jack?" she inquired, admiring the big horse's powerful limbs and large, kind eyes.

"He has never had another to my knowledge, and I saw no reason to give him a fancier one. We have been together since Salamanca. I was lucky to find him. There are not many horses that are up to my weight!" he said, smiling.

She smiled back. Their eyes met for an instant; then she looked ahead again. They continued in silence for a few moments.

Then Lord Langdon said, "Miss Ashley, there is something particular that I must ask you. I hope you will say yes."

Nell's heart skipped a beat as she looked at him, awaiting his reply. He looked so grave and earnest it must be a matter of great import to both of them.

"I have been thinking for some time that we should have a

school in Smallbourne," he said. "I was hoping you would be willing to assist me in establishing it."

Her shoulders sagged as she realized what he was asking. Of course. What had she thought he would do? Profess his undying love for her?

"Why, yes," she replied. "I would be most happy to help you in setting up a school."

"Are you certain?" he asked, and she realized he was wondering why she had hesitated.

"Of course. I have been wishing for such a thing for a long time."

To prove it, she launched into some of the ideas she'd had about a school: its situation, the subjects she thought should be taught. Lady Langdon and Colonel Huntley caught up, but Nell and Lord Langdon continued to ride together, discussing the school. The earl listened politely, but he had a rather odd smile on his face. Perhaps he found her enthusiasm amusing.

"I am glad you find this an interesting project, Miss Ashley. I look forward to working with you on the plans."

"I do too," she said. "It will also furnish an explanation for those who question the time we spend together."

"Please explain. I don't understand."

Nell blushed. How could he be oblivious to the rumors that were circulating? Now she would have to tell him at least some of them. She took a deep breath before starting.

"Lord Langdon, there are those who are beginning to link our names together. They say I am setting my cap at you."

"It's only gossip," he said, reassuringly calm. "Do you mind so very much?"

"Of course. I do not like being labeled a fortune hunter," she said quickly. He winced, and her blush deepened as she realized how he had construed her statement. "Without at least some evidence," she added, hoping her smile did not look as strained as it felt.

"No one who knows you or has a morsel of good sense would heed such slanders. But come. You still seem worried. What else has been said about us?" His tone brooked no re-

sistance. She decided he had a right to know. He might hear
it from someone else anyway.

"Someone has been hinting that I am the reason you and
Clarissa broke off your engagement."

Now he looked angry, as he had not at her earlier revelation.
"Who has said so?" he barked in a voice that did not bode
well for the culprit.

"No one of consequence actually. I think she just said so
because I was not willing to tell her what happened the night
of the ball. I don't think anyone really believes it."

"I should hope not!"

"Perhaps if it is known you and I are working together to
set up a school, that will still some of the mischievous tongues.
When enough time passes, they will be obliged to give up
their silly inferences about our friendship, don't you think?"

"Undoubtedly," he said, but his expression was still grim.

After a few moments, he changed the subject, making an
obvious effort to shake off his irritation. They came to more
open land, an area of flat, windswept fields, marshes, and
meadows, not picturesque in the ordinary sense, but pleasant
and quiet under the midday sun. Soon the village of Bosham
was within sight.

Nell found it delightful: the tidy village, the old Saxon
church with its rather squat tower, the harbor glistening in the
noonday sun and studded with various craft. Although she had
never learned to draw herself, she was not surprised to see
several artists sketching various views of the church and harbor.

The meal Lord Langdon ordered for them at the best inn
was also very good; and both Colonel Huntley and Lady Langdon were in the best of moods, full of lively conversation. But
beneath her enjoyment, Nell couldn't help thinking about her
conversation with Lord Langdon. She soon came to the realization that it was not actually the gossip that had sparked his
anger; it was her reference to his broken engagement.

Outwardly, he seemed to be recovering well from the dual
betrayal he'd endured. But she was sure he suffered more than

he would admit. Had he, despite all appearances to the contrary, really loved Clarissa so much?

Nell was still thinking about Lord Langdon the next morning when she and Hannah went shopping in Chichester. After they had completed their shopping, Hannah went to visit a cousin of hers who lived in George Street, while Nell took a short stroll in the vicinity of the cathedral.

She was walking down West Street when she saw Lady Nettlehurst and Lord Poxton coming at her from the direction of the market cross. She had no desire to meet with either of them, so she quickly turned right and slipped into the cathedral.

Although she had been to the cathedral many times before, she didn't mind the chance to revisit some of her favorite spots. It was a hot day, and the dim coolness within the heavy stone walls was pleasant after the heat and glare of the streets.

She walked through the nave, and toward the south transept. Pausing to admire the lovely stone tracery of the south window, she made her way toward the Lady Chapel. There, she discovered that she was not the only one seeking refuge in the cathedral that day.

As she entered the chapel, she caught sight of Clarissa, wearing a striped walking dress, a stylish bonnet, and the expression of a startled rabbit. Clarissa darted behind one of the old tombs that lay in the chapel. Nell walked toward her and softly called her name.

"M-miss Ashley!" whispered Clarissa, cowering in her hiding place. "Please go away! If you see her, please don't tell my mother I am here!"

For a few moments, Nell stared at her, thinking of the last time they'd seen each other. She still thought Clarissa weak and foolish, but it was hard to stay angry with so pitiful a creature.

"What are you doing here?" she asked gently. "Is there anything I can do to help?"

"No, nothing! I have been very silly!"

"I must tell you that I saw your mother and Lord Poxton coming in this direction. Are they looking for you perhaps?"

"Yes, they must be," said Clarissa, biting her lip. "Mama and I were shopping. Then she saw Lord Poxton a few shops away, and she insisted on calling him over. I didn't wish to speak to him, so while she was waving to him, I slipped away. I shouldn't have done it—she will be so very angry with me!"

"But why would you be afraid to speak with Lord Poxton?"

"He . . . he has become most particular in his attentions, and Mama has high hopes that he will offer for me. Indeed, I think he will, for he told me he has not found any other lady who would so perfectly adorn his arm and his home. But I love Darcy! Oh, I am sorry. I should not have said that to you!"

"Never mind. I have realized I mistook my heart where Darcy is concerned. I'm persuaded we would have been a wretched match."

"So kind of you to say so! Truly, I am very sorry for what happened. If it's any consolation, I have my punishment now. Mama says I must marry Lord Poxton, for few other men will be willing to overlook the fact that I broke my engagement to Lord Langdon."

Nell's first impulse was to say that Clarissa had gotten her just deserts for breaking faith with as honorable a gentleman as could be found. However, she saw the guilt and anxiety in Clarissa's eyes and softened. Clarissa was clearly a pawn in all of this. She must have accepted Lord Langdon's offer under her mother's instruction; now she would probably allow herself to be forced into marriage with that fat, self-indulgent dandy.

"I am sorry to hear that," Nell said finally. "But surely no one can force you into marriage. You have only to refuse him and stand firm by your commitment to Darcy, and your mother will have to relent. Otherwise, you can wait until you are of age and can marry anyone you please. My own mother did so, you know."

"Do you truly think so?" asked Clarissa, wide-eyed, as if the thought of directly opposing her mother had never occurred to her.

At that point Lady Nettlehurst and Lord Poxton entered the chapel.

"Ah, there you are, my naughty child!" exclaimed Lady Nettlehurst. "My dear Lord Poxton, you see, it was just as I thought. Dear Clarissa saw one of her friends and wandered off to inspect the cathedral, quite forgetting to tell me about it, didn't you?"

Clarissa, obedient to the commanding gaze of her mother, nodded her agreement. Lady Nettlehurst smiled graciously at Lord Poxton, who seemed to be satisfied with her smooth explanation. Then she inclined her head stiffly toward Nell. She glanced back at her daughter in a manner that left Nell in no doubt that a royal scold awaited Clarissa at home.

"Ladies, can I interest you in a little refreshment?" asked Lord Poxton with ponderous grace. "There is a place I know of nearby where they serve some very tolerable ices."

Lady Nettlehurst eagerly accepted his invitation for herself and her daughter. Nell made her excuses, for it was time for her to rejoin Hannah and she had no desire to stay and watch Lady Nettlehurst coerce her daughter into accepting Lord Poxton's attentions.

She made her way back to George Street, almost wishing that there were some way for her to help Clarissa. It seemed improbable that Clarissa would help herself. What *had* Lord Langdon seen in her?

Nell could no longer believe that he was the sort of person who would coldly choose a wife simply on the basis of suitable birth, style, and submissiveness. But the only answer was that he had loved Clarissa.

That wasn't a very satisfactory explanation either.

She told herself to stop thinking about him before she totally lost her common sense, which plainly told her that she was no proper bride for the earl. Nor was he in love with her.

But still she wanted to know.

James had thought it a masterly stroke to enlist Nell's aid in setting up the village school. It was far too soon for trying flowers and pretty words on her; besides, that was more Darcy's style, and James wanted his own courtship to proceed on far different lines. For a start, he wanted her to feel easy with him. She always seemed most natural and comfortable when they discussed parish affairs, so this had seemed like the perfect answer.

Now he wasn't so sure it was the right idea.

They were sitting together at one end of the drawing room; Lady Langdon was playing the piano at the other, Edward having obligingly volunteered to turn the pages of her music.

He and Nell were properly chaperoned, and he had been scrupulously and painfully careful to make no move that might distress her. But still she seemed uneasy; he'd been obliged to repeat several of his questions to her, and her answers seemed a trifle disjointed.

Was she still fretting over that malicious gossip, he wondered, wishing he could wring the necks of those who had spread it. But most at fault were Clarissa and Darcy, for setting them all up for this stupid situation. He couldn't bear to see Nell looking so ill at ease.

"Is anything amiss?" he asked gently.

"No, not at all," she replied. "I am sorry. You must think me quite scatterbrained this evening."

"I do not think that. But I know something is troubling you, and I wish you would tell me what it is."

She hesitated, then seemed to make some sort of resolution.

"Lord Langdon," she began. He waited for her to continue, wishing she could call him by his Christian name. "Lord Langdon, I met Miss Nettlehurst in Chichester the other day."

He frowned, realizing he was on dangerous ground. He wondered what Clarissa had said to upset her.

"How is she? What did she have to say for herself?" he asked in a carefully neutral tone.

"Her mother is trying to make a match between her and Lord Poxton. Clarissa is very unhappy about it."

"She should just refuse him then."

"I am afraid she does not have the resolution. I never

thought I would feel this way, but I find myself feeling truly sorry for her."

"That is very Christian of you. I trust you do not expect me to do the same?"

She looked away, but he knew she was troubled. He wished she hadn't brought up this topic, but perhaps it was time to let her know at least some of the reasons he'd proposed to Clarissa. He couldn't let her think he still pined for his lost fiancée.

"I am sorry. I should not have expressed myself so harshly. I should be grateful at having been spared an unhappy marriage." She still looked sad, so he corrected himself. "I *am* glad. Perhaps I should tell you why I proposed to her in the first place."

Nell nodded without quite looking at him.

"I believed it my duty to marry and get an heir," he started, noting how she seemed to stiffen at his words. But she deserved to hear the truth, so he cautiously persevered. "I thought, based on how my friend Adam described her, that she would prove a virtuous and proper wife. I also felt sorry for her, living in such an unhappy household as Southcott. But I was mistaken. None of those are sufficient reasons to marry. I've realized I want something more in the woman I marry. I want a lady with true strength of character, one who can be a help and a companion to me, not a mere ornament to my name and home."

As he was speaking, Nell had turned her head and watched him closely. He tried to judge her reaction to his words, but her face, usually so expressive, seemed carefully controlled. He hoped he'd said the right thing, without revealing enough to frighten her off.

"If I seem bitter," he concluded, "it is because of the manner of her betrayal and the harm that has come to you in consequence."

Nell's expression softened, and she said, "Thank you again for being so kind, but please do not concern yourself about me. I have also escaped a bad match, and for that, I find I can forgive much. I don't think Clarissa was at all malicious, you know. It would have taken great courage to break off her engagement sooner."

After a pause, she added, "The same applies to Darcy I am sure."

This was too much. He was prepared to forgive Clarissa if it would make Nell happy, but Darcy?

He couldn't forget how Nell had cried in his arms the night of the ball. Perhaps she wasn't permanently injured by it, perhaps she had mistaken her heart, but Darcy hadn't known that when he'd shattered her dreams.

"You are too forgiving, Miss Ashley," he said bluntly. "Such faith in your fellow creatures will only bring you more grief."

"I had rather take that risk than go through life mistrusting and judging everyone I meet," she retorted.

Her words smote him like a fist in the gut, reminding him of how he had misjudged her. But surely Darcy was a different case.

"My brother has proven himself unworthy of trust," he replied.

"Unworthy at present perhaps, but I have been raised to believe everyone is capable of improvement."

James frowned. Why did she persist in discussing his brother? He'd managed to put Darcy out of his mind, at least most of the time. If only he could convince her to do the same, so he'd have a chance to build a future for them.

"It is too late," he said. "Darcy has been too much indulged and has had his way for far too long to be capable of change. My father . . . was not the best of examples, and I have failed to undo the damage."

"Perhaps Darcy needs to change of his own accord. Perhaps the pain he is enduring now will shake him up, make him consider his actions toward others."

"I would not count on it. Shall we speak of something else now? There are several details of the school we have not yet discussed."

She nodded, but looked disappointed. He tried to behave more cheerfully for the rest of the evening, but still their disagreement on this matter rankled. When would she realize how few people one could really trust? He couldn't bear for her to be hurt again.

On the other hand, he knew her well enough by now to understand that family bonds were important to her, that the rift between Darcy and him grieved her. On whose account, he was not sure. She hadn't said it directly, but he was sure she hoped he would reconcile with Darcy.

But how could he? To do so would be to condone everything he most despised.

Nineteen

Nell alighted from the Maylands' carriage and entered the vicarage. As usual, Hannah had waited up for her, but Nell sent her to bed. She could not even think about sleeping herself, not yet, so she went to her sitting room instead, carrying a candle with her.

She could not stop thinking of Lord Langdon's bitter expression when he'd spoken of Darcy and of their father. She'd had enough experience with troubled families in the parish to know the harm such resentment could cause. Perhaps it was too early to expect Lord Langdon to forgive Darcy, but if he didn't, the ill feeling between them could poison his life.

She saw, with newfound clarity, that the earl blamed himself for Darcy's behavior, however much he buried his guilt under anger. Then there had been that statement about his father . . .

She got up and went over to her writing desk. After opening up a crowded drawer, she pulled out several small books. She had never found the resolution to get rid of Mama's diaries, although in respect to her wishes, she'd never read them. She was sure Mama would forgive her curiosity now.

She soon found the book she wanted. Fortunately, her mother had written in a clear, elegant hand, so it was not too difficult to read even by the flickering candlelight. The first entry made her smile.

12 October, 1798. Nell helped me plant tulips yesterday. This morning she has been clamoring to go to the garden and see if they have come up yet. I suppose spring seems a long way away to a three-year-old child.

The next entry was made several days later. Nell noted its reference to Lord Langdon's mother and read it closely.

I visited poor Harriet today. She is no better. Daily, I pray for her recovery, but I have seen the look in her eyes, and I fear the worst. Were it not for her sons, I think I would pray for her deliverance from pain. I know she grieves for them more than for herself, and I wish there were some way I could ease her cares. I thank God we are all healthy and happy here at the vicarage.

Nell read quickly past a few more entries, descriptions of everyday joys and cares of life in the vicarage. Perhaps someday she would return to them, but now she had more important things to learn. She slowed down again at the first entry for November.

The end is near for my dear friend. Soon I shall mourn the death of one who has done much kindness to us and to the poor of this parish. The loss will be grievous to myself, to the parish; and most of all to her sons. Poor James is still at Eton. They have kept his Mama's illness from him, but now he has been sent for. I hope he will arrive in time to see her. Little Darcy does not quite understand what is happening. I grieve for them both and wish Lord Langdon were more worthy of being entrusted with their upbringing.

To his credit, he has remained at Charlwood throughout these final stages of Harriet's illness, reading to her and bringing hothouse flowers to brighten her room. 'Tis little enough after all that Harriet has borne from him, but since she does not complain, I suppose it is not for me to judge him.

When I think of my own husband, I know God has been very good to me.

20 November. A cold rain fell today. A dreary day, but somehow it seemed right for Harriet's funeral. What a comfort to return to the vicarage and sit before a cozy fire and read to Nell. Still I found myself weeping, not so much for Harriet, who must be happier now, but for her boys.

Little Darcy has been crying piteously, but I am more troubled about James. He has not shed a tear, nor has he said much since he was brought back from Eton. Alas, he was not in time to see Harriet. I fear that he blames himself somehow for what has happened. I tried to speak with him, but I could not reach him. I wish I had more time to try.

Lord Langdon intends to take the boys into Leicestershire for the holidays. Then James will return to Eton. Lord Langdon will take Darcy to London, I believe. I fear he intends to quit Charlwood entirely. I suppose it carries too many associations with his past guilt, but this will be a sad thing for the parish and his sons.

Nell felt tears start at the thought of Lord Langdon's loss, but she held them back. It was more important to understand what happened that autumn and confirm her growing suspicions about the previous earl.

Harriet gave me her diaries, asking me to burn them. I did so, except for the final one. I do not know what stopped me, why I could not complete the task. For some reason I felt it important to preserve her final thoughts, although I, who have been her friend and confidante for so many years, have no need to read it.

Nell quickly skipped through the rest of the book and found it contained little that related to the Maylands. She went back to the little pile of books on the desk and found the next one.

As she had expected, it was written in a hand different from her mother's.

The early entries closely resembled many of her own mother's: records of gardening, of the antics and achievements of Darcy and Lord Langdon as children.

Farther into the book, the handwriting deteriorated. It was clear the previous countess's health was beginning to fail and that, despite her physician's well-meant assurances, she knew her days were numbered. Nell felt tears start in her eyes again at Lady Langdon's fears and concerns for her sons.

> *I hope Langdon will be a good father to them. He has been an affectionate one thus far, always indulging their little whims, but leaving to me the more difficult task of correcting them. I pray I have left them with principles that will sustain them throughout their lives.*
>
> *I think I need have no fears for James. Perhaps only that he might take too much upon himself when I am gone. Already he has tried so hard to be a man, to support me during Langdon's long absences from Charlwood. It is too great a burden for a boy his age, but one he will not give up easily.*
>
> *Little Darcy is so sweet natured, perhaps I should not worry. He has not a shred of malice in his constitution. A more sunny child one could not imagine. Perhaps he will grow up a fine young man despite Langdon's petting.*
>
> *Langdon has assured me he will not just abandon the boys to the care of servants. I pray he may be relied upon in this case.*

The last entry was written in mid-November. Nell's hands trembled as she turned the pages.

> *The end is near. I know it. I feel less pain now, and but for the hope of seeing James one more time, I should have given up the struggle already. I hope he comes in time so I can hold him to my breast one more time. He*

seemed troubled when we left him at Eton, although stoic as always. Perhaps he had noticed the first signs of my failing health. Children have such fantasies. I must remember to tell him not to blame himself for leaving while I was sick, as if he could have done anything to prevent the onset of this illness.

Langdon seems concerned over James as well. He seems to rather dread his return, if that is possible, although he arranged to have him fetched here as soon as I decided it was time. Langdon really has been most kind these past few months. I find it is no longer time to harbor resentment. I have too little time to waste on recriminations.

We should never have married. We should never have allowed ourselves to be persuaded into this match by our parents. I was seventeen, and he was two and twenty, and they assured us we would learn to be happy together.

Perhaps some arranged matches do end that way. Ours did not. I see that love matches are becoming ever more popular, and although perhaps many of them fail as well, I am convinced they offer the greatest possibility of happiness.

I know my dear friend Elizabeth blames Langdon for the farce our marriage has become. I realize now that perhaps I must share some portion of the blame. I was not unfaithful. That was not my way, although it was his. However, I never gave him what he most needed. I gave him duty, loyalty, and sons, but I never loved him. I must always have known that, for much as his infidelities offended me, I always played the complaisant wife, content to occupy myself with my dear sons and my gardens. But Langdon yearned to be loved and needed, and so perhaps he came to resent my self-sufficiency. 'Tis strange how well we deal together now that I am no longer strong.

He means to do well by our sons. But his own parents were so inconstant, petting and indulging him, then ignoring him in favor of their own scandalous affairs, that he has had no proper example of how to be a father. He is weak perhaps, but not evil by nature. How very differ-

ently he might have turned out had they only known how to love him.

I can only hope and pray that my darling sons escape the legacy of anger and guilt, of passionless marriages and loveless passions that have plagued this family. I must place my trust in Langdon's good intentions and the goodness I know is in both my children. My life has held so much happiness because of them.

Nell read and reread the final entry, feeling a growing certainty that Lord Langdon's mother had understood only a part of her elder son's burdens.

Lord Langdon must have known about his father's faithlessness. It was easy to imagine him as a boy, tormented by the knowledge, punishing himself for having been unable to save his mother from the bleakness of her marriage or her final illness.

It was also terribly easy to imagine him in conflict with his father over Darcy's and his own upbringing. Then, in frustration, distancing himself from both of them, still burdened by a sense of failure.

Nell ached for him, yet she couldn't help but share his mother's hope for a better future for her children. The countess's last words echoed in her mind long after she had gone upstairs to seek her bed and blown out her candle.

The rose garden was the wrong place to come, James realized. Although the roses were well past their peak, it was still bright with various other flowers planted between the rosebushes. A spot so full of associations with soft, loving femininity was not conducive to forgetting last night's argument with Nell.

He could practically hear his mother calling for him to chase after Darcy and keep him from falling into the lake or into any of the hundred kinds of mischief the little scamp was susceptible to.

No, this was not the place to put Darcy out of his mind. When he remembered the cherubic little brother of his childhood, it became harder to associate him with the thoughtlessly cruel man who had sired them both.

James started up from the bench, only to see Nell coming swiftly toward him from the far entrance to the garden. Her cheeks were flushed, and she was out of breath as if she'd run the whole way from the vicarage.

"What is the matter, Miss Ashley?" he asked, hurrying to meet her.

"Nothing is the matter, Lord Langdon," she said, stopping as he reached her. "But there is something I must give you." She handed him a small book bound in blue leather.

He took it, but continued to look at her. He saw with relief that she seemed more embarrassed than distressed. She really looked quite fetching, her cheeks bright and her breath still coming quickly.

"It is your mother's diary," she said after a short pause. "I did not know until last night that my mother had kept it. I hope you will read it and will forgive me for having already done so. I promise you I shall not speak to anyone else about its contents."

He frowned. What could there be in his mother's diary that would change anything?

"Please, Lord Langdon. There are things written here which I believe your mother would have wished to tell you, had she had the chance."

He was helpless before that pleading, earnest look. "Very well then. I will read it," he said.

She smiled, curtsied, and fled the garden as quickly as she had come.

James sat back down, looking at the little book in his hand. He felt equal curiosity and reluctance at the thought of opening it. Why was Nell so insistent that he read this? Why did she want him to reopen past wounds?

Abruptly, he got back up. There were many things he'd planned to do today. There would be time enough to read the diary later.

Throughout the day, he kept busy, but still he could not stop pondering the significance of the little book now safely stored in his desk. After dinner, he told himself it would be rude to abandon his stepmother and Edward to their own devices.

Finally, he brought the diary with him to bed. After all, he'd promised Nell he would read it.

By the light of a single candle, he opened it and began to read, turning the old, fragile pages carefully. The earliest entries contained nothing unexpected. Except perhaps for the half-pleasant pang he felt at the memories they aroused of a happy childhood he'd half forgotten.

Soon he would reach less pleasant recollections. Why was Nell pushing him to this? Impatiently, he got out of bed and took several turns about the room. Then he forced himself to sit back down and continue reading.

Again his mother's words reached out to him like a caress. Words of love, of pride, of longing and forgiveness. Slow, un-accustomed tears rose in his eyes as he read the final entry. He let them fall with a feeling of peace he had not felt for sixteen years. Better than peace: a sense of absolution. The sense that a crushing burden of guilt and mistrust was finally dropping from his shoulders.

What a strange, rare gift Nell had given him. How could she have guessed his torment or how much he had needed to read these last thoughts of his mother? But he shouldn't be surprised anymore at Nell's wondrous acts of kindness. Even if his greatest hopes never bore fruit, at least he would always have this: that she had cared enough for him to look into his soul.

He knew what he needed to do next. He got back out of bed and, taking a candle with him, went to his study. There, he found some paper and sharpened his pen to write.

Dear Miss Ashley,

My deepest thanks for your great kindness. I would have wished to tell you so in person, but I intend to leave for

*Brighton early tomorrow morning. I think you will approve
of my purpose in going there.*

He stared thoughtfully down at the page for a few moments
before signing: *Yours ever, Langdon.*

Darcy's foppish, too long hair did have its uses. James held
on to it tightly as he plunged his brother's face alternately into
the basins of hot and cold water the servant had provided for
him.

It was just like the young fool to attempt to drown his sorrows
in Burgundy, brandy, and gin, as attested to by the various empty
and broken bottles that littered the Brighton apartments of
Darcy's friend. It was only amazing that Darcy and his cohorts
were still alive after repeated revels of this nature. At least,
James thought as he looked about the room, most of the bodies
sprawled randomly on sofas, chairs, and the floor seemed to be
still breathing.

"What in hell?" spluttered Darcy, coming back to consciousness.

"Never fear. It's only me," said James.

"You? What are you doing?" Darcy gasped and coughed,
from having inhaled some of the hot water. "Damn you, James.
Let go! My head hurts like the devil!"

Reluctantly, James let go. He'd positively enjoyed waking
his brother up from his drunken stupor.

Now, Darcy sagged against the table on which the basins
were set, listlessly letting the water drip off his hair.

"Time to change your clothes and eat something," James
ordered.

"No, please . . . later . . ." protested Darcy in a faint,
hoarse voice.

"Now. Will you dress yourself? Or shall I do it for you?"

Twenty minutes later, James propelled Darcy out of the apart-
ment and down into the street, having forced some bread into

him first. Although Darcy winced at the bright afternoon sun, James was sure the sea breezes would help with his headache.

Wordlessly, they strolled down the Marine Parade, stopping when they reached the end of the fashionable promenade, where the crowds thinned enough to make private conversation possible.

"James," Darcy began with a rather shaky smile. "Don't think I'm not happy to see you, but why have you come here?"

"I have several things I must say to you. First, I wanted to tell you that I am going to end the trust."

Darcy looked stunned. "You are? But . . . I don't understand. Why?"

"I've decided it's time you took control of your fortune. It's your choice whether you wish to squander it or save it or use it for some useful purpose. You may do whatever you wish."

"What I *wish* to do is to marry Clarissa, but that's impossible," said Darcy despairingly. He looked out at the sea and added in a low voice, "I'm sorry, James. I shouldn't have brought that up."

"I will survive."

"I really *am* sorry about how it all happened."

"I know. But why are you so quick to despair now?"

"You heard the Nettle. She'll never let me marry Clarissa."

"And you are accepting her edict so tamely?"

"What else can I do? She has Clarissa so thoroughly under her thumb that I'd never be able to convince the girl to elope. I would bet she's already looking for another lord for Clarissa to marry."

"As a matter of fact, she is."

"Damn her! She'll coerce her and play on her guilt and tell her she's her only hope in life until Clarissa will be obliged to give in. What shall I do, James? My life isn't worth anything without her."

James studied Darcy's face. He believed Darcy was sincere, but it was hard to tell whether this despairing mood was induced by true heartbreak or whether Darcy had merely whipped himself into dejection over what was very likely the first real obstacle to his wishes that he'd ever encountered.

"Have you given any thought to other possibilities?" he asked finally. "Surely if you love her so much you will exert yourself to think of a practicable solution. If you do, you may count on me to help you in any way I can."

"You will? That's dashed good of you!" Darcy looked back at James, eagerness lighting his bloodshot eyes. James could only wonder at how easily Darcy could plunge from gaiety to bleak despair and back again.

"I will think about it—that is, when I have the head for making plans," Darcy continued with a crooked smile. He turned, and they started to stroll back the way they had come.

"You said you had several things to tell me," said Darcy after a few moments. "What else did you have to say?"

"Only that you are welcome back at Charlwood if you wish to return. I hope you will."

"Kind of you, but won't it be awkward? I mean—what I should have said was—I don't want to upset Nell. I should have asked before—how is she?"

"Very well."

"I'm glad to hear it! I didn't think she was the sort to fall into a decline or any such foolishness."

"No, she is not."

"Do you mean she is still on terms with our stepmother?" James nodded.

Darcy smiled again and said, "I feared perhaps she wouldn't want to have anything to do with us anymore after what happened."

"Fortunately, that has not been the case."

Darcy slowed to a stop. He rubbed his temples and stared at James for a few minutes, then exclaimed, "You're in love with her yourself, aren't you? That's famous! The two of you should suit perfectly."

"I'll thank you not to spread that suspicion."

"You haven't told her yet? Very well, I'll keep mum. Y'know what? Maybe I won't come home just yet. One of my friends has invited me into the country—says he needs a repairing lease. I think I'll go with him."

"What? Do you think I have no chance with Miss Ashley in your charming presence?" asked James, laughing a little.

"No, you know I didn't mean *that*. I don't think she ever cared much for compliments and such flummery. Your sobersides style of courtship should suit her. Just don't wait too long to let her know how you feel!"

On his way home that evening, James kept reminding himself that Darcy's words sprang from youthful optimism. Not that he himself wasn't hopeful, but he could easily spoil things by rushing his courtship.

Still, the twenty miles that lay between Brighton and Charlwood seemed to crawl by, and he had to restrain himself from urging his horses to an unmerciful speed.

He chided himself for wanting to act like a callow lad. There was no reason to hurry and all the reason in the world to be patient. His heart told him to call on Nell tomorrow and tell her he loved her, but his mind told him the consequences of a premature declaration could be disastrous.

He knew the recent gossip linking their names had made her uncomfortable, although the fact that she was willing to continue their friendship despite the gossip was encouraging. Perhaps she was even starting to think about him as a potential suitor. But it was much too soon to expect anything more. If he moved too quickly, he might lose her entirely. He couldn't bear the thought.

Nor could he feel at all certain about Darcy's chances. He'd left his brother in a more cheerful state of mind, although still suffering the ill effects of the previous night. But they had been apart for too many years. He couldn't judge the strength of either Darcy's love or his resolution.

Perhaps his hopes and Darcy's were both doomed to failure.

But it was pleasant to crest the final hill and see Charlwood below, gleaming in the setting sun. It was good to come home and to be able to imagine a future homecoming when Nell and their children would be there to greet him.

Twenty

"Come along, Oddy. We're going for a walk."

Nell put on her bonnet and picked up her basket as Odysseus bounded eagerly up to the doorway. Clearly, he looked forward to this outing as much as she did.

She was bound to visit the Nuffields, tenants of Lord Langdon's living over the hill from Smallbourne who were presently rejoicing in the birth of their first son. Although they belonged to another parish, Mary Nuffield had come from Smallbourne originally and she and Nell were friends.

Nell had to admit to herself that she was not only eager to see Mary and her new baby, but she was also hoping the vigorous walk would ease her growing restlessness.

She'd practically driven Silas mad in the garden. They'd done everything that could be done at this season. But she couldn't bear the thought of sitting indoors and mending. The weather was too fine, and her mood too contrary.

Lord Langdon had only been absent two days, she reminded herself. Yet she longed to see him, to find out whether he had talked to his brother and how Darcy was feeling. Sternly she had restrained herself, not giving in to the shameless impulse to find a pretext to go to Charlwood to see if he had returned yet. She would enjoy her visit with Mary and try to keep her mind off Lord Langdon.

She did enjoy her visit. Mary was doing well, her husband Tom was ecstatic, and their two little daughters were fascinated by the new addition to their family. Everyone was pleased with the gifts she'd brought: caps for baby Joseph and some doll clothing she'd made out of scraps for Susan and Becky. After talking to her for a while, the girls ran outside to play with Oddy, and Nell was able to settle down to gossip with Mary and cuddle the baby.

However, when she started to climb the hill back out of their valley, Oddy frisking along beside her, the restless mood took hold of her again. The Nuffields' cheerful household reminded her too much of her own doubtful future. She should have married just such a hardworking farmer as Tom. Papa would not have objected; and she might even now be looking forward to the same marital bliss that her friends enjoyed.

But none of the respectable young farmers in the district had felt a fancy for her or she for them. No, she was foolish enough now to dream of an alliance with no less than the Earl of Langdon.

At least she knew in her heart that the gossipmongers were wrong. It was not his title or the power he wielded that made her love Lord Langdon. She wasn't sure exactly why she loved him. They had many tastes and concerns in common, but it was not just that. It was the kindness she saw in his blue eyes, which she had once thought so cold. The strength of his convictions that more than matched the strength of his powerful arms.

How she longed for him to take her into those arms again! She had been having such wanton thoughts recently it had been all she could do not to give him any disgraceful encouragement, which would have instantly destroyed his respect for her.

Still, she couldn't help thinking there was a special warmth in his eyes when he smiled at her. Last week, they'd gone walking with Lady Langdon and Colonel Huntley, and when Lord Langdon had helped her across a stile, surely he had held her hand a trifle longer than necessary.

She pushed herself to climb faster, chiding herself for air dreaming. Not that she felt herself to be unworthy of Lord Langdon. She knew society would say she was, but society's opinion was of little consequence after all. However, just because Lord Langdon considered her a friend and even an advisor didn't mean he cherished any warmer feeling for her.

Then she thought of the misunderstandings and troubles that lay between them. First she had made such a fool of herself over his brother. Even if he didn't think her a fortune hunter, Lord Langdon might not understand that she was wiser from the experience. And even if he didn't love Clarissa anymore, he still might find it difficult to trust another woman with his heart.

Nell pushed herself still harder, trying to ward off despondency. Finally, breathing heavily and perspiring from the effort, she reached the flat hilltop. After a few more minutes of walking, she came out of the woods that circled Bow Hill into the clearing where the barrows stood watch over the surrounding countryside.

Out in the open, the breeze was strong and delightfully cool, billowing against her light cotton dress and blowing her gypsy bonnet off her head. After putting it back several times, she gave up and let it hang down her back by its ribbons.

She took a few more turns on the hilltop and was about to make her way to the path that led down the other side toward Smallbourne when she heard hoofbeats behind her.

For a moment, her heart skipped a beat. Somehow she was convinced it would be Lord Langdon. But when she turned around, she saw Colonel Huntley riding out of the woods on a leggy young thoroughbred. Alone.

She hid her disappointment under a friendly smile.

"Good day, Miss Ashley!" he shouted. "Upon my soul, it's a pleasure to be meeting you up here! Splendid view, is it not?" he asked, while his horse danced about impatiently, looking eager to dash off across the soft turf.

"Yes, it is, Colonel," she answered. "This is my favorite place in all of Kingley Vale."

"I can see why. Quite lovely country, this is. I must apologize, Miss Ashley. I would dismount and walk with you, but this youngster I have just bought has not learned to stand still to be mounted, and I would hate to disgrace myself by having to chase him across the Downs or lead him home!"

"That is quite all right, sir."

He smiled and slowed his horse to walk with her. Nell called Oddy to her side so that he would not fret the young horse.

"I must tell you I have just had the greatest good luck," said Colonel Huntley. "A most attractive property has just become available just outside of Stoughton. Everything one could wish—lots of stabling, a fine house, elegant parlor and dining room—at least *I* think they are elegant. Perhaps you and Lady Langdon will do me the favor of looking at it and giving me your opinions. James and I were just inspecting it. He sent me on ahead, for he wanted to stop and visit some tenants of his."

"The Nuffields?"

"Why, yes, I think that was the name. Anyhow, I must be off before this silly greenhead dumps me off and destroys my reputation as a horseman!"

While they were speaking, a stronger wind had blown up. The colonel's mount fought to get his head, showing all the signs of pining for a good gallop. After a brief tussle, the colonel induced him to enter the woods at the other side of the hilltop at a civilized trot.

He was out of sight before Nell noticed that he had dropped his whip. She picked it up. Although the colonel would have little need for it with such a lively horse, she thought he might be glad to have it returned.

On impulse, she turned back for another stroll about the hilltop, even as she told herself it was silly to wait about in the hope of seeing Lord Langdon.

After a few more turns, she decided she'd waited long enough. She still had over an hour's walk to reach home. It was coming on to evening, but since it was not far past midsummer, the sun would not set for hours yet.

Once again, she heard hoofbeats behind her. This time when she turned around she saw it was Lord Langdon.

"Are you in a hurry, Miss Ashley?" he asked when he came closer. "Would you mind bearing me company here for a few minutes?"

"Not at all," she replied, smiling up at him.

She decided his errand in Brighton must have prospered. There was a bright, confident light in his eyes, and the breeze ruffled his fair hair. He looked happier and more carefree than she had ever seen him. She had to look away to hide the surge of longing that swept through her at the sight of him.

"I thought you might like to hear how I fared in Brighton," he said.

She nodded, and the earl dismounted and loosed his horse to crop the turf. Together, they walked along the slope facing the sea.

"Did you find Darcy?" she asked. "How is he?"

"As well as could be expected," said Lord Langdon with a wry smile. "Not in spirits, but he was pleased to see me."

"So you made it up between you?"

He nodded, and she smiled again. "I am so glad. Will he be coming home soon?"

"In a month or so. He is visiting with a friend in the countryside now."

She realized he was watching her closely, so she tried her best to look carefree. She had no intention to throw out lures to Lord Langdon, but she couldn't help feeling it was important to make it clear she cared for Darcy only as his brother.

"What do you think of his chances of marrying Clarissa?" she asked.

"I don't know," he replied. "I must admit I'm not at all certain this is not another infatuation on his part. If it isn't, if they both are steadfast in their commitment to each other, I may have to do something to help them."

"I am certain you have helped Darcy already, and I am so glad you have mended the rift between you. I feared it was causing you great pain."

She looked away when she saw his eyes darken. Did he think she was being presumptuous? Had she said too much?

James looked down at Nell. Interesting how in speaking of his reconciliation with Darcy she had emphasized her concern for *him*. Did he dare make anything of it? Or was she merely being kind? Still, it was a great relief to hear her speaking of Darcy in such a totally disinterested manner.

He continued to watch her, noting how the wind had pulled several locks of her hair out of their pins. He longed to reach out and finish the work the wind had begun, to run his fingers through those luxuriant chestnut tresses. The wind was also doing quite wicked things with her flimsy summer gown. The way it first billowed out and then pressed against her limbs was more than a man should have to bear.

She looked back at him and turned away again, blushing adorably. He felt an unexpected heat rise in his own face. She must have seen his expression. Still she hadn't looked annoyed, just enchantingly flustered. Perhaps he need not wait so long before declaring himself. He'd prepared himself to wait for months or even years, but suddenly happiness seemed a heartbeat away.

He reminded himself of the resolutions he'd made and composed his face as they turned back in the direction of Smallbourne. He wouldn't allow himself to agitate her any further, but he couldn't take leave of her, not yet.

He called Jack to him and continued to walk beside Nell, leading his horse. Her dog bounded back and forth around them. In a few minutes they entered the pleasant, shady woods that bordered the crown of the hill.

"I met Colonel Huntley on the hill," said Nell, her voice sounding a trifle nervous. "He told me he has found a property that might suit him."

"Yes," he said, hoping it would set her at ease to discuss a safer topic. "Actually rather a larger place than I would have expected. I was surprised to see him so interested in the dining room and the drawing room."

"Perhaps he is thinking of marrying one day."

"What, Edward? He vows he is a confirmed bachelor."

"Well, you must know him better than I do," she said. "He also said you were visiting the Nuffields. I am sure they were very happy to see you."

"I am sure they enjoyed *your* visit even more."

They talked some more of the Nuffields, and James was happy to see Nell lose her constraint in discussing his tenants and their family. Then he couldn't understand why she laughed. He'd merely expressed a mild concern over the odd shape of little Joseph Nuffield's head.

As she was laughing, she must have missed seeing a root lying across the path. She stumbled and would have fallen if he had not moved swiftly to catch her.

"How could I have been so clumsy? I must have walked this path a thousand times!" she said laughingly as he steadied her.

He should have released her then, but he couldn't will himself to do so. It was all he could do to hold her at arms length and not pull her in to his chest and cover her with kisses.

Her expression had changed from amusement to solemn inquiry, but she was *not* trying to evade his embrace.

For an endless instant he stood there trying to decide what to do next. The woods were blissfully serene, the only sound the wind in the treetops and the distant sound of sheep bells. He was alone with Nell. No one and nothing else mattered. All his resolutions to behave with rigid restraint and propriety—weren't they just unnatural barriers between two people who were clearly meant for each other?

He pulled her closer and looked into her face. Her eyes were wide and wondering, her lips slightly parted. He couldn't resist the innocent invitation. He lowered his head and slowly, gently pressed his lips to hers.

Abruptly she pulled away. Then he heard the sound of a horse and rider, coming their way.

In another instant Colonel Huntley came cantering around the bend toward them.

"Ah, Miss Ashley! You have my whip! Thank you. I can't believe I was such a cawker as to drop it!" he shouted cheerfully.

James silently cursed Edward. Looking back at Nell, he saw she was struggling to compose herself. Damn! He couldn't tell if she had pulled away of her own accord or because she had heard Edward's approach. It was small comfort to know Edward hadn't actually seen anything.

Nell wordlessly handed Edward the whip, smiling but still looking painfully embarrassed.

"Well, now that you have your whip, hadn't you better get

going before that silly gelding of yours takes matters into his own hands?" James asked.

"Very well, I will," Edward replied with an annoying grin. *Did* he suspect something then?

"Lord Langdon, please go with the colonel," said Nell, her cheeks still bright. "There is no need for you to escort me home."

Anxiety tore at him. Clearly he'd acted hastily in kissing her, and now he'd embarrassed her in front of Edward by too obviously wanting to stay with her. Did she realize how badly he needed to explain himself? That his kiss meant much more than an idle flirtation?

However, there was nothing he could do now. He would have to go along with her wishes.

"I will call on you tomorrow, Miss Ashley," he said in a low voice but with an emphasis he hoped she would understand. He could say no more within Edward's hearing.

As he mounted, he saw that Edward had already started down the path. Before he rode off, he looked anxiously back at Nell, standing there with her dog beside her.

She waved, and he nearly jumped off his horse to go back to her when he saw her expression. The tenderest smile he could ever have imagined, promising everything. So sweet, so loving, almost too good to be true.

Feeling light-headed, he rode on. There was nothing more he could do now, but at least she had understood him. *Tomorrow,* he told himself.

In a joyful daze, Nell watched Lord Langdon ride off.

Oddy barked at her, and she obligingly continued down the gentle slope through the woods. Soon she came to the hilly pastures that lay between the woods and the village. The late-afternoon sun shone brightly, lighting up the reddish and golden brown trunks of trees bordering the fields and casting deep shadows within their luxuriant midsummer foliage.

Somewhere very far overhead, almost out of sight, a lark trilled a glorious little tune, perfectly suiting her mood.

Tomorrow, she told herself.

Twenty-one

The following morning, Nell arose with the sun, feeling a vibrant expectancy, but beneath it all, a serene joy in the certainty that she was loved. She dressed quickly, choosing a favorite sprigged gown, and ran lightly down the stairs to the kitchen.

Hannah was already there. She had just paid off the butcher's boy, who was delivering their order for the week, and now gave Nell the news that old Matthew Cowden had taken a fall and was in a bad way.

Concern for her old friend temporarily pushed other plans aside; of course she must go to visit Matthew and do what she could for him. Lord Langdon, if he came to call, would surely understand her being away for such a purpose.

When she reached Matthew's cottage, she was relieved to find that village report had exaggerated his injuries. He had indeed taken a fall on the previous evening and sprained his ankle. However, since Mr. Olden had been to see him, wrapped the injured ankle, and given him something to help him rest, Matthew was looking quite himself that morning. He assured Nell that he lacked for nothing and demonstrated that he was perfectly able to hobble about with the aid of a stick. However, he was very glad of her company, so she indulged him by chatting with him and listening to his reminiscences for an hour or so.

When Nell returned to the vicarage, Hannah reported that the earl had called and had looked disappointed at having missed her. Nell consoled herself with the thought that he would certainly return in the afternoon and tried to occupy herself with a little gardening while she waited.

Finally, she felt she could wait no longer, so she set off to call on Lady Langdon. Perhaps it was shameless, but once she was at Charlwood, the earl would surely make an opportunity to speak to her privately.

Once again she was disappointed, for she learned that Lord Langdon, hearing of Matthew's injury at about noontime, had gone off to visit him. However, she happily accepted Lady Langdon's invitation to take a turn about the gardens, thinking that he would probably return to Charlwood before she left.

Lady Langdon was in the sunniest of moods that day. Nell suddenly realized that her friend no longer seemed to occasionally suffer from fits of melancholy as she had previously. Perhaps the countess was enjoying the increase in country entertainments that had followed the removal of the *ton* from London at the end of the Season. Whatever the reason, Nell was happy to see Lady Langdon in such high spirits.

She did not tell Lady Langdon of her own happiness. It was all too new, and although she was sure in her heart that Lord Langdon wished to marry her, he had not asked her yet. So she tried to occupy herself with talk of gardening. As they walked under a certain grove of trees growing by the lake, Nell observed idly that she thought a mass planting of spring bulbs would look particularly good there.

"But when you are mistress of Charlwood, you will be able to plant anything you like," said Lady Langdon. "Don't look so surprised, my dear! I have known for some weeks now that James wishes to marry you."

"What? Has he said anything to you?"

"No, but I am sure nevertheless. And you are too. You cannot hide your blushes from me! I will be so happy to have you in the family, dearest, even if things did not turn out with Darcy. Really, you and James are *much* better suited!"

"I must admit I have never thought of myself as a countess."

"I am convinced you will manage beautifully. You are much loved among the people here, and I have not lived in the country for these past months now without realizing how important that is. As for the silly gossip we've been enduring, it will die down soon enough."

Lady Langdon's next words puzzled Nell. "It is the highest piece of good fortune that your uncle has chosen to leave his fortune to you, for perhaps once you are married, James will be able to help poor Darcy and Clarissa."

"He will? But . . ." Nell stammered and stopped. How could Lady Langdon think her dowry would be sufficient to rebuild a house like Broadoaks? She couldn't think how else marrying her would enable Lord Langdon to help his brother.

"Oh!" exclaimed Lady Langdon. "Perhaps I should have told you this earlier, but Lytchett *did* ask some connections of his in London about the size of your uncle's fortune. But you must not think that that is James's reason for wishing to marry you. He has never said a word about your fortune, upon my honor!"

"No, of course not," she answered automatically, trying to gather her thoughts. It seemed Lytchett's informants were unaware of her eight cousins. That would account for the Maylands' misunderstanding the extent of her inheritance. Then she remembered some of the things Darcy had said when he had proposed to her and realized this must have been what happened.

The implications were chilling.

She needed to get away from here and think about them before she said anything more to any of them.

"I must go now," she said.

"Must you? My dear, you are looking ill."

"Not at all. I am perfectly well. That is, I think perhaps I have had a little too much sun."

"Shall I send someone with you?"

"No, please. Do not worry about me," she answered with a forced smile and left her friend.

Instead of heading directly home, she turned toward the cool green woods, hoping that under their shade she could think more clearly. As she walked, memories replayed themselves in her mind, combining to form a picture that she could not reject, however much she wished to.

It seemed clear enough now that Darcy must have pursued her with a view to her supposed fortune. Certainly he must have seen her as a means of escape from his brother's control. Perhaps later, he had thought to please Lord Langdon by marrying a supposed heiress.

She found she could forgive Darcy. He at least had turned away from her to Clarissa, and there could be no mercenary motive in that. But Lord Langdon?

Like a cold hand closing on her heart, the realization came that the earl had only begun to approve Darcy's courtship of her after Darcy had told him about her dowry. She remembered how she had been confused by his change of heart. Had she been wrong to think it was because he had come to know and understand her?

Was yesterday's show of affection calculated to lure her into another such loveless union?

Why not? He wouldn't be the first impoverished peer to repair his fortunes through an advantageous marriage. If she really were heiress to a large fortune, she would happily have used it to help him. If he loved her, she wouldn't have cared a bit. But now it seemed he didn't.

Blindly, she stumbled over a root and almost fell. Tears welled up in her eyes as she remembered how she had stumbled yesterday and how Lord Langdon had caught her. She remembered the look in his eyes then, the way they had glowed before he had kissed her. How could he have feigned such desire?

She steadied herself, trying to think clearly. Lord Langdon might be deceiving her; Darcy had certainly done the trick quite thoroughly. But then, why had the earl been so careless as not to verify the details Lytchett had given Darcy? Whatever else Lord Langdon was, he was no fool. It didn't seem likely he would trust the information provided by a bungler like Lytchett.

Her head was beginning to ache, but she continued walking, choosing paths that she knew to be less frequented than others. She could not return home until she knew what she should do next. Finally, the answer presented itself, and it was so simple that she wondered why she hadn't thought of it sooner.

She would inform Lord Langdon of the real size of her dowry. If he still wished to marry her, she would know he loved her. If not—and she felt the cold ache clutch at her heart again at the thought—she was better off without him.

She would know soon enough.

Twenty-two

Nell paced in her sitting room as Lord Langdon talked to her father. She'd passed a restless night, rehearsing what she planned to tell Lord Langdon and planning how she would comport herself depending on his response.

When she had returned home late yesterday, Hannah had told her the earl had called twice that afternoon and then she scolded her for showing so little enthusiasm. Idly, Nell wondered why Hannah approved the earl's suit when she had frowned on Darcy so severely. Hannah had probably been right all along. Perhaps not all men were to be distrusted, but those of the higher ranks of society now seemed painfully suspect.

Still, Nell clung to the hope that she was mistaken in her suspicions. She found herself standing by the window, praying that Lord Langdon would not disappoint her.

With a chill, she realized she hadn't prayed so fervently for anything since a bleak day four years ago when she'd been banished from her mother's sickbed. She'd trusted God then, and it had taken all of her grieving father's love and patience to help her regain her faith. Now she felt sick with doubt.

At last, the door opened. Papa, wearing a benevolent smile, escorted Lord Langdon into her room, and after a few polite words, he left them alone.

It didn't help that the earl had dressed with especial care for the occasion, in contrast to his customary casual country attire. She only risked a brief glance at his face, but the look of hopeful expectation on it was nearly her undoing.

She was determined not to play the fool this time. She would not betray her feelings until sure of his. She offered him a seat with an expressionless voice, but he continued to stand, looking down at her. She wondered if he was planning to kneel before her, as she had heard some gentlemen did. It was a relief when he did not.

"Miss Ashley, I was very sorry to have missed you yesterday," he began formally.

"Yes, I was visiting Matthew."

"So I heard. I saw him myself a little later and was glad to see him going on pretty well."

"So was I."

He paused, and she knew he was trying to catch her eye, but she looked steadfastly down at her hands. Finally, he spoke. "Perhaps you are aware of the purpose of my visit."

She realized that he was waiting for some sign of encouragement and that this was the moment to tell him about the size of her dowry. However, a sense of foreboding made her carefully prepared words stick in her throat. She could only nod.

"Then I beg you to do me the honor of accepting my hand in marriage," he said.

Her sense of foreboding grew at the continued formality of his words.

"First I must ask you something, my lord," she said carefully. "What is it that makes you believe I would be a suitable bride? You must know polite society considers me a very poor match for you."

He looked surprised and annoyed at her question.

"I hope you will not let malicious gossip affect your answer! You are all I could wish in a bride. You have the respect and affection of my people, and I know you will wish to continue to help me in running the estate. I also know you well enough to know that my earldom and Charlwood are of little consequence to you."

He paused, and she said nothing, still hoping he would continue and give her the one reason for which she was waiting. He cleared his throat before continuing.

"Although I suppose I should make sure you understand my circumstances before you accept. Perhaps you are already aware that the estate is encumbered. Matters are not desperate, however. I expect that, with your help, I will be in a position to redeem the mortgage within a reasonable period, without our having to forego any reasonable comforts."

She stood up and went to the window, suppressing an urge to press her hand to her heart, which felt as if he had just rent it in two. There was no need to tell him anything. He had given her answer. He wanted her fortune to pay off his debts.

She swallowed and said, "I understand."

"I assure you I will do everything in my power to make you happy."

She almost turned around at the warmth she heard in his voice. Then she remembered how Darcy had said something very similar to her once.

An unwonted anger possessed her, pushing aside her sorrow and disappointment. She turned around and gave him her answer, smoothly matching his conventional words. "I am sorry, my lord, but I am unable to accept your kind offer."

"May I ask why?" he asked, looking stunned.

What? Had he been so sure she would jump at his proposal? To hand over a fortune to his control so he could improve his family fortunes? The arrogant, cold-blooded, grasping scoundrel!

She wouldn't give him the satisfaction of admitting the truth. She wouldn't give him the chance to bless himself on his narrow escape.

"I wish to marry someone else," she improvised.

"You are not still pining for Darcy, are you?" he demanded.

"No, not at all."

"Who is it then?" he asked, taking an impatient step towards her.

The frustration in his voice fanned the flames of her own anger. He spoke as if he thought she was his for the taking!

"Someone in more affluent circumstances than yourself," she said coolly.

He stopped and froze in place. "What did you say?"

"I said I wish to marry someone who is in more affluent circumstances than yourself."

His face became rigid, almost masklike, but the look in his eyes was beyond any anger she'd seen there before. She held her ground, despite a strong impulse to take a step back. He would not hit a woman, after all, no matter how annoyed he was that she was obstructing his plans for Charlwood and his family.

"There is nothing more to say then. Good day, Miss Ashley." He bowed and left the room.

She paced about the room several times after he left, but her anger ebbed quickly. As did the bitter satisfaction of having maintained her composure and of having succeeded in striking him back.

All that was left was sorrow.

As soon as he left the village and reached open pastures, James spurred his horse into a gallop. Jack responded willingly, traveling at his top speed for several miles. But finally, the big chestnut began to slow and James settled him into a walk.

"I'm sorry, old friend," he said, patting the big horse on the shoulder.

Nell Ashley was not worth killing his horse over, he told himself. Unlike old Jack, she had proven wholly unworthy of the trust he'd placed in her.

How could he have allowed himself to be so deceived? How could he have let himself be cozened by her guileless demeanor and sweet looks? At their very first meeting, he'd recognized that she was using those very charms to snare his brother. When had he gone astray?

He remembered how she had struggled in his arms when he had kissed her in his study. Even then she was probably plotting to capture the greater prize, and damned clever she'd been to counter his suspicions with such a show of innocence.

His engagement to Clarissa must have frustrated Nell's plans for a time, but Darcy's defection had taken care of that problem quite neatly. She must be a consummate actress to have sobbed so convincingly in his arms that evening, playing on his chivalry. How could he have been so gullible as to believe her and to believe that she could transfer her affections so quickly from his brother to himself?

At the same time, she had skillfully played some other fool along. She must be pretty secure in the other man's regard to reject his own offer so freely.

James told himself he was lucky to have confided his true situation to her. His rival, whoever he was, would not be so fortunate as to escape her net. It was cold comfort, but at least he was seeing clearly again for the first time since returning home. It was time to bid farewell to fantasies and concentrate on his duties.

Almost a week later, Nell sat under the trees behind the garden, looking at the apples growing overhead. Her little orchard would bear abundant fruit this year, but she felt cold and barren. Tired. Tired of her chores, tired of gardening, tired of weeping.

She'd managed to hide most of her tears from Papa, who still couldn't believe Lord Langdon was as mercenary as she'd described. Papa still counseled her to speak to the earl, to make certain that she'd understood him correctly. But she knew it was useless. He had never loved her; she should have realized it, considering how reserved he had always been during all their dealings. She had built up all her hopes on one careless kiss.

It didn't matter anyway. Lord Langdon had left almost immediately after his rejection, to inspect his estates in Kent. Colonel Huntley was still in Smallbourne, arranging the purchase of the property he'd found nearby, but he'd removed to the inn, presumably to stave off any gossip that would have been caused by his remaining at Charlwood in the earl's absence.

So much Nell had learned through the usual village sources. She hadn't spoken with anyone from Charlwood for the past week. Lady Langdon had called several times, but each time Nell had instructed Hannah to say she was ill, and eventually the countess had given up her visits.

She looked up at the sound of children's voices. There at the gate, she saw several heads peeking over. The Wicke children. She'd forgotten she'd invited them to come over and gather some of her raspberries.

She put on a welcoming smile as she let them in, then sat back down to watch them fill their hats, baskets, and bellies with the ripe fruit.

Davey tired of the berries before his siblings and came over to sit with her. He climbed up on the bench and thanked her solemnly for the treat. Then he scrambled onto her lap, put his skinny arms around her neck, and gave her a sticky kiss.

Unexpectedly, she burst into tears.

"What's wrong, Miss Nell?" asked Davey.

"Nothing, dear. Nothing at all," she said, wiping her tears and hugging him closer in gratitude for the revelation he'd just given her.

She'd been going about things all the wrong way. She'd been so convinced that the only true happiness lay in the love of a husband and children of her own. She'd lost her judgment in pursuit of that dream, first with Darcy and now with Lord Langdon. Resolutely, she held back tears at the thought of her latter mistake. Soon, she told herself, this feeling she had called love would wither, now that she knew how little Lord Langdon deserved such a gift.

No more would she indulge in vain hopes, dependent on the actions of others. New plans formed in her mind, and the heavy gloom that lay over her heart began to lift just a little. Even if the greatest happiness was denied her, there would be love in her life. There would be consolations. In abundance, she realized, as she jumped up to mediate an argument amongst the children over who had picked the most berries.

When they were gone, she would write to Uncle Joshua.

Twenty-three

James was bone tired, but still he couldn't sleep. He paced about the best bedroom of the Dower House at Broadoaks a week after Nell Ashley had given him the lesson of his life.

In that time, he'd ridden over every inch of the property and talked at length with every tenant. Instead of taking his mind off his disillusionment, his travels only reminded him of her. At times he would forget what she'd done and would wonder what she would say about some tenant's family and what advice she would give.

He hated times like this, when there were no more duties to command his attention. He loathed going to bed. In that unguarded state between waking and sleeping, the sight, smell, and taste of her would invade his mind and heart, rekindling passions he was determined to extinguish.

He stopped by the window, staring out at the moonlight. Had only a month passed since that wretched night his brother and fiancée had duped him, thereby setting him up to be duped even further by the one woman he thought above all that?

Damn the little harpy! She cleverly used all her charms, her false compassion, even his own mother's diary to ensnare him. But even as he said the words to himself, he saw her again before his eyes, her shining hair tousled by the wind, her eyes dark and wide with emotion, and he felt longing for her tear at him. He told himself he would master it in time now that he knew her for the heartless schemer she was.

Pain racked him again, and he realized it was grief for the loss of the woman he'd thought she was. Loving, loyal, compassionate, tender. The worst of it was that part of him still believed in her, could not imagine the Nell he knew deliberately scheming to win a wealthy husband.

But that was just what she'd done, wasn't it? She had said so herself.

Nell brushed away an errant tear as she looked over some notes she was taking regarding plans for the village school. She couldn't help remembering how she had discussed some of these points with Lord Langdon. But it had all probably been a ruse to gain her favor; no doubt he would drop the project now.

All she could do was wait. Since Uncle Joshua lived in India, it would be some time before she knew whether he'd agreed to her request. She hoped he would not refuse to give her the money he'd set aside for her dowry to help set up a school instead.

She looked back at her notes, and again she remembered some comment Lord Langdon had made on her ideas. How seriously he had listened to all her suggestions, how interested he had seemed. No, she couldn't think it was all feigned. He was in earnest where the well-being of his dependents was concerned. Or else why would he have set so many improvements in motion?

Perhaps his motives for proposing to her were not entirely ignoble. Perhaps he'd seen it as a practical suggestion, a way for them to work together, as friends and companions, to achieve the goals they'd already agreed upon. The more she thought about it, the more it seemed likely. But how far from her ideal of marriage!

Still, for a moment, she pondered the thought. If she truly had a fortune, would she have been willing to enter such an arrangement? No. It would be a daily agony to be married to him, knowing she loved him, knowing that, if she told him, her only reward would be his pity.

Far better to face a future as a spinster schoolteacher.

The next morning, James set out from Broadoaks driving the phaeton. Alone, exactly as he wished to be. Farley and a groom were following in the coach. He'd been obliged to take this cavalcade into Kent since there were only a few elderly servants at the Dower House.

He couldn't decide whether he looked forward to or dreaded getting home. He would be bound to see Nell sooner or later. Perhaps she was already engaged to marry her next hapless victim.

He tried again to think who it could be. She'd certainly met some eligible gentlemen lately, but he could almost swear there was no one else he would have considered a rival. But what did it matter anyway? He had wasted enough time in this futile exercise.

Try as he would, however, he could not stop thinking about what she had said. Was it just wishful thinking on his part? Or was there something suspicious about her tale?

In fact, there was something strange about the whole affair. As they'd walked on Bow Hill, she had seemed shy, but open to his advances. But the next day, she'd avoided him, and on the following, she'd greeted him with a cold expression wholly unlike her usual smile. Had she received another offer or a hint that one would be forthcoming? Or was something or someone else responsible for the change in her manner?

He forced himself to relive the painful scene. When he'd come into her sitting room, he'd immediately noticed that she seemed nervous, unhappy even. What had happened next?

He'd asked her to marry him; then she'd asked him why.

Oh, Lord! He'd talked of the estate, of his debts, and of wanting her help, but like an insensitive oaf, he'd never said he loved her.

Didn't she know that already? If that was what troubled her, why hadn't she said so? There was no reason to wound him as she had. It didn't make any sense. He was probably wrong again, and he would be wise to put her out of his mind.

But the devil of it was that he didn't want to be wise. While a faint hope persisted in his heart, he would have to pursue it or drive himself mad with wondering. Whatever the risk, he would see Nell Ashley again and discover the truth.

At least it wasn't time to clean the henhouse yet, Nell thought as she fed the chickens that morning. Silas's back was paining him again, and it was Betty's day off, so the chore had fallen to her. Although she loved to garden, caring for the silly birds ranked low on her list of favorite tasks.

She looked down at the hens jerkily walking and pecking around her skirts, and she gave a wistful laugh. If she really wanted to escape such chores, she should have accepted the earl's proposal. As it was, she'd take the chickens.

When she looked up, she saw she had an unexpected visitor. Clarissa was standing at the gate to the vicarage yard, looking tired and dusty and carrying a bandbox in each hand.

"Clarissa? What is it? You look as if you have walked all the way from Southcott!" she said.

"I have. Please, you must help me!"

What could have made Clarissa walk a whole six miles from Southcott alone? Unlike Nell, Clarissa didn't care for long rambles. It must be something quite disturbing to make her undertake such an exertion.

Nell crossed the yard to Clarissa, who promptly backed away. Nell realized that the chickens were surrounding them and that Clarissa was watching them nervously.

"They are only chickens, Clarissa. They'll do you no harm," she said, turning to lead the hens to a far corner of the yard and tossing the rest of the feed there.

"But they are so dirty. Are you often obliged to care for them?"

"Why yes, I am. It is not my favorite task, I must admit," she said, returning to Clarissa.

"Well, I shall do the same, if I have to live in a cottage, which is what Mama says will happen if I marry Darcy. But I don't care, and I won't marry Lord Poxton!"

"I should hope not. Is that what happened to drive you from your home? Has he offered for you?"

"Yes—no. He has not offered yet, but Mama told me he is coming today to do so, and I had better prepare to accept and m-make myself pleasant to him."

"How horrid! Why couldn't you tell her you would not do so and put an end to it?"

"You don't understand, do you?" said Clarissa, wiping away a tear. "I thought you would after talking so kindly to me in the cathedral. I came here because I thought you would help me, and I could think of nowhere else to go!"

"Perhaps I will help, but you must calm down and explain it all to me," Nell said in a softer voice. "Why don't we go inside?"

"Yes, please," said Clarissa, looking back nervously over her shoulder as if expecting to see her mother in hot pursuit.

Having settled Clarissa in her sitting room, Nell went back to the kitchen to fetch her visitor some breakfast. She also swore Hannah to secrecy and made her promise not to answer the door. Nell thought it best to deal with any visitors herself.

Returning to the sitting room, she did her best to cheer Clarissa and coax her to eat while attempting to extract the full tale of her escape from Southcott.

Clarissa had shown more ingenuity than Nell would have expected. She'd recently begun carrying on a clandestine correspondence with Darcy with the help of her maid. The night before she made her escape, she'd arranged to send a message to Darcy.

Nell frowned as Clarissa unveiled the next step in her plan.

"I've asked Darcy to come here so your Papa can marry us as soon as he arrives," declared Clarissa proudly.

"I'm sorry, but he can't do that."

"Why not?"

Nell carefully explained the laws regarding marriage of minors, and Clarissa rewarded her by bursting into tears. It took ten minutes of soothing to calm her down, by which time Nell's patience began to wear thin.

However, Clarissa soon began to look a little more cheerful. But her next suggestion made Nell shudder. "Do you think perhaps Darcy and I should elope?"

"Only if you are prepared to deal with the scandal. You know you might be ostracized, at least for a while. Wouldn't it be easier just to go home and tell your mother you won't marry Lord Poxton? Perhaps you and Darcy could persuade her in time. In fact, Lord Langdon has said he might do something to help you both if you both prove steadfast in your affections."

"Oh, no. How could he? He must still be terribly angry with us both."

Nell fell silent. She'd spoken impulsively. Now she remembered how unsure she was of anything where Lord Langdon was concerned.

James urged his horses into a canter up the last hill. He saw another sporting carriage ahead going more slowly, but there looked to be enough room to pass it.

It was late afternoon. The bays were managing the last stage of the journey quite nicely, having been rested for several hours after the morning's drive. As if knowing their home stable lay over the crest, they rewarded him with a lively pace.

He hadn't been able to shake off his own newfound optimism or the growing conviction that there was some misunderstanding at the root of Nell's rejection of his suit. He was still trying to decide whether to call at the vicarage before returning to Charlwood when he drew abreast of the other carriage and cursed inwardly.

It was Lord Poxton's showy curricle, drawn by Lord Poxton's overfed, underexercised grays and driven by Lord Poxton himself. No wonder they were having difficulties climbing the hill.

No groom, just a lady passenger. Lady Nettlehurst, of all people, scolding in her shrill voice, asking Poxton why his slugs couldn't go any faster. The poor beasts looked quite blown. James hoped he could pass them with just a quick wave and a greeting.

It seemed he was out of luck. He drew abreast of the other carriage at the top of the hill, and immediately Lady Nettlehurst began to shriek at him instead of at Poxton.

"Lord Langdon! Are you aware that that rake shame of a brother of yours has run off with my daughter! Lord Poxton and I are most anxious to find her before he has ruined her. You must help us!"

Reluctantly, James stopped his horses alongside the other carriage. He would be quite annoyed with Darcy if he found this to be true; elopement was not what he'd had in mind when he counseled Darcy to think of other solutions.

"Are you quite certain of this?" he asked.

"Absolutely!" declared Lady Nettlehurst. "As soon as I discovered Clarissa was missing, I sent servants to search for her and make discreet inquiries. One of them brought back the reliable report of a curricle and four horses driven by a veritable Whip with a young lady beside him traveling at breakneck pace on the road north early this morning. Four famous chestnuts, which the observer instantly recognized as your brother's!"

"My brother has sold those horses," he said calmly even as horrid suspicions began to form in his mind.

"Whose are they then?" she demanded.

"That is no business of yours, ma'am. Good day!" he shouted and drove on.

He heard Lady Nettlehurst shouting behind him. Perhaps they would try to pursue him. They wouldn't catch him anyway, not with those exhausted beasts. And he didn't care. He didn't care for anything, except to make haste to the vicarage and discover the truth.

Edward? Was he the one?

No, Edward could never serve him such an ill turn. He'd

never confided in him, but surely Edward must have sensed how he felt about Nell. Or hadn't he?

Grimly, James recalled how Edward and Nell had always gotten on so well together, how he'd envied Edward's effortless ability to make her laugh. Edward was the possessor of a fine fortune with no encumbrances—circumstances at least temporarily much more attractive than his own. Then there was the matter of that house Edward was buying, with all its fine rooms designed for a lady's entertaining!

It was the only logical explanation. Besides himself, Edward was the only other man Nell had spent much time with since the ball. She must have managed to captivate Edward and convince him to run away with her before James could return and warn him of the trap into which he was falling.

Half blinded with rage, James drove on carelessly until one of his horses shied at a bird flying out of a hedge. He slowed to a walk and sternly tried to master himself.

How could Nell do something so wholly despicable? Like a damned fool, James had almost been convinced there was some other explanation behind her story of another suitor. He had best start believing it now. Torture though it was, he forced himself to think about it, to picture the false jade playing him against Edward, coldly assessing their relative merits.

And he couldn't do it.

All that came to mind were visions of her holding the Mullens' baby, helping Mr. Olden, talking to him about schools and gardens. Offering her advice, her warm sympathy, the revelation of his mother's diary.

No, he thought, asking his horses to trot again. He had thought he'd been reasoning clearly before, but suddenly he knew that he had allowed painful suspicions from his past to cloud his judgment. That Nell was indeed the forthright, caring woman he'd fallen in love with.

There had to be some other explanation for what she had said to him and for what was going on now. Perhaps Darcy had borrowed his horses back from Edward to elope with Clarissa. Or perhaps those weren't Edward's horses that had been sighted, after all.

He would reach Smallbourne soon. He could leave his horses at the inn and walk to the vicarage in five minutes. Three, if he ran. Nell *would* be there, or if not, he would learn that she was out on some errand in the vicinity. He would find her and open his heart to her as he should have done before. And then, maybe he'd reawaken the love he'd seen in her eyes in the woods below Bow Hill.

He urged his horses faster, driven by a mounting hope. But a demon of doubt still rode on his shoulders and whispered in his ear that he might be wrong.

Twenty-four

"Please, please promise you won't make me go home to Mama!"

Nell looked from Clarissa's face to Papa's. Her father was not happy about this situation. They were sitting in his study. Papa had just returned home, tired from a debate with some of the parish officials. She wished she hadn't been obliged to bring Clarissa's plight before him just yet.

"My dear, I am sure we will do everything we can to help you," he answered Clarissa. "But we cannot hide you from your mother. You would not wish to worry her so, would you?"

"But if I go back, she'll make me marry Lord Poxton!"

"I will speak to her, child. Perhaps I can convince her that that would not be in your best interests."

"Mama never changes her mind!" moaned Clarissa, bursting into tears again.

Papa looked quite harassed, so Nell poured him a small glass of sherry. Clearly, although he sympathized with Clarissa's plight, he also dreaded the possible repercussions of aiding her in thwarting Lady Nettlehurst's plans. It was really rather unfair of Clarissa to hope he would do something so scandalous as to hide her from her mother.

"There is always a first time for everything," Nell said to Clarissa in a bracing tone. "What you and Darcy must do is confront her together. Perhaps you will not win her over immediately, but if you stand firm, she'll be bound to relent rather than let you become an old maid."

Clarissa looked doubtfully at her and opened her mouth to protest, but she was interrupted by the sound of someone knocking on the front door.

"Darcy!" she exclaimed, jumping up from her seat.

"It could just as easily be your mother," warned Nell, and Clarissa cowered back into the chair. "Don't worry. We won't leave you alone with her until Darcy arrives, will we, Papa?"

"No, we won't, my dear," echoed her father faintly.

Nell hurried down the hall to the front door, sped on her way by the sound of another, louder knock. Whoever it was was getting impatient. She rather hoped it would be Darcy; she didn't look forward to dealing with Lady Nettlehurst.

She paused an instant, took a deep breath, and then opened the door. She blinked in the bright sunshine, and then she stared, stock-still, her heart leaping in her breast.

Standing on the step, his hand upraised as if he was about to knock again, every muscle in his face tense with worry, was Lord Langdon.

Abruptly, the anxiety in his face melted into a look of intense relief. "Nell!" he said, his voice rough with emotion. "You are still here! Thank God!"

Her heart pounded furiously at his unexpected presence and the strange passion in his voice, but somehow she managed to find her own voice. "Lord Langdon! I don't understand. Why are you here? And where else should I be?"

"I'll explain later. First I have something else I must tell you," he said and fell silent, still watching her hungrily but looking painfully unsure how to proceed.

An unlooked-for hope sprang up in her heart. "What is it?"

"I love you, Nell," he said simply. "I've been fighting it, but I think I've loved you since the day I came home. That's why I want to marry you. I know I should have said so before. I—I hope it is not too late to say it now. I love you," he repeated, raising his arms toward her. When she did not move, he dropped them again.

She longed to believe him more than anything. Looking into his eyes, she saw tender yearning there, and her last lingering doubt withered. The tiny slip of hope grew and blossomed, filling her with unexpected, but intense joy.

She came down onto the step and put her arms around him. "I love you too," she said, and with a deep sigh, she leaned her head on his shoulder.

"There is no one else?" he asked huskily, folding her in a strong embrace.

She looked up and replied, "No one else."

The unbridled joy in his face sent a responding shiver of happiness through her. He bent his face down and kissed her, a light, gentle kiss, over far too soon, like a sip of sweet nectar that only made her want to drink more deeply.

She raised her face up to his, and he answered with another tender, tantalizing little kiss. As he came down to meet her a third time, her lips parted and she closed her eyes, savoring the taste of him and the closeness of their embrace.

This time he was less gentle, more ardent, his tongue circling and caressing hers. Shyly, she tightened her arms around him. He sighed and delved deeper. Molding her against him, he lifted her up, kissing her all the while, until she was lost in a swirl of bright sunshine and deep rapture.

Gradually, the sound of high-pitched cheers penetrated her consciousness. Lord Langdon set her down, continuing to hold her as he turned his head to see the source of the racket. Dazed, she peered around his shoulder.

In the lane before the vicarage she saw a small group of the villagers' children, the little Wickes included, jumping up and down and clapping. They dispersed quickly on being seen, giggling as they ran.

"Perhaps we should go inside," she suggested breathlessly.

He nodded and went with her into the house, one arm still firmly around her waist. As they entered the hall, she remembered the confusion about her inheritance and the fact that Clarissa awaited them in Papa's study.

"There are some things I must tell you," she said, looking up at him. "I hope you will not find it all too annoying."

"I don't think anything could annoy me now," he said. "But I would like to know—"

He was interrupted by a little shriek and a dull thud. Nell turned her head. She saw Clarissa slumped in the doorway to the study, and Papa standing just inside the room, looking helpless.

"Oh, dear," he said. "I think Miss Nettlehurst has fainted."

"I suppose this is one of the things you were going to explain to me, my love," said the earl in a resigned voice. "Meanwhile what should we do for her?"

Nell hurried to Clarissa's side. Kneeling down, she examined Clarissa, finding her pulse to be normal and her color only a little pale.

"I think it is just nerves," she pronounced, getting back up. "Please carry her into the study and lay her down on the window seat. I will fetch some water and smelling salts."

She returned to the study to find Clarissa on the window seat and Papa giving Lord Langdon a brief account of Clarissa's escape from Southcott. She picked up the narrative, explaining Clarissa's further plans. She had just completed her tale when Clarissa's eyes fluttered a few times and opened. Clarissa glanced around and looked faint again on seeing Lord Langdon sitting in a nearby chair.

"My lord, please tell me you have not come to take me back to my mother!" she begged.

"My being here has nothing to do with you."

"No?" Clarissa asked. "You do not mind that I wish to marry Darcy? Truly?"

Nell was tempted to laugh at the shocked look on Clarissa's face.

"Not at all," answered Lord Langdon in the same calm voice. "Although I would prefer it if you did so without a scandal. I also must warn you I met your mother and Lord Poxton on the road. They are likely to be here shortly."

"Oh, no! What shall I do? Where is Darcy?" Clarissa asked, jumping up from the window seat. Nell saw her father nervously follow suit.

"Please sit down and calm yourselves," said Lord Langdon. "I have a plan." He paused, turning his head toward the door. Once again, Nell heard the sound of someone urgently rapping on the front door. She hurried out to answer, but this time, she felt no qualms. Surely she and Lord Langdon could deal with whatever happened next.

She opened the door to Darcy this time. Behind him, she saw his horse Demon, sweating profusely. Darcy himself was looking dusty, frantic, and unsure of his welcome.

"Hello, Nell. Is Clarissa here?"

"Yes, she is, and she will be very happy to see you."

"Thank you! So kind of you. You know I *am* sorry about . . . everything that's happened. We never meant to hurt you, you know."

"I don't blame you for having fallen in love with Clarissa," she said. "I only wish you had had the resolution to tell me sooner. And I know now you only wished to marry me for my dowry. That was *very* bad of you."

"I know that now. All I can say is I'm sorry," he answered, looking down at his feet like a schoolboy caught in mischief. How had she ever thought him more attractive than Lord Langdon? He was a mere boy. She couldn't even stay angry with him.

"Don't worry about it. You haven't broken my heart," she said cheerfully.

"I haven't?" he asked, looking surprised. Was he conceited enough to be disappointed? But no, he was looking relieved.

"Not at all," she answered. "Well, come in and see Clarissa. By the way, your brother is here as well."

When they entered the room, Clarissa jumped up and flung herself into Darcy's arms.

"Oh, thank God you've come! Reverend Ashley says he can't marry us, but you will think of something, won't you? You won't let anyone make me go back to Mama and force me to marry Lord Poxton?"

"Don't worry, my angel! Trust me—I'll think of something!" Darcy answered.

Nell looked away as they kissed. She saw that Papa was shuddering—no wonder, for he hated melodramatic scenes. She poured him another sherry and mutely offered one to Lord Langdon. He shook his head, looking torn between amusement and exasperation. But when he met her eyes, he smiled in a way that made her feel warm all over.

When Darcy and Clarissa stopped for air, James said, "You had best think quickly, brother, for if I am not mistaken Lady Nettlehurst and Lord Poxton are following me here as fast as his slugs can take them."

A look of panic crossed Darcy's face. "What shall we do?"

"We can elope to Gretna Green, can't we?" asked Clarissa.

"You would do that? Risk the scandal—just for me?"

"Anything for you, dearest Darcy! I'll even live in a cottage and raise chickens if I have to!"

Darcy and Clarissa kissed again, noisily. Nell tried to contemplate the image of them living in a cottage together and found herself struggling to keep from laughing. She nearly succumbed when she saw Lord Langdon rolling his eyes.

"I trust neither sacrifice will prove necessary," he said, with just a hint of laughter in his own voice.

"But what do you have in mind, James?" asked Darcy.

Before the earl could answer, Nell once again heard a strident knocking on the door, and she saw Papa wince at the sound.

"Oh no! It must be Mama!" cried Clarissa. Darcy sat down with her in the window-seat and put a comforting arm around her.

"Please stay calm. We won't allow her to browbeat you," said Lord Langdon. He smiled encouragingly at Nell as she got up to greet the newcomers.

Before she could reach the door, it was opened from the outside. Lady Nettlehurst stalked in, with Lord Poxton trailing behind her.

"Where is Lord Langdon?" she asked loudly. "They told us at the inn that he had come here. I insist on seeing him immediately—and my daughter too if she is here!"

"Of course. Please follow me," Nell answered, bobbing a curtsy. "Good afternoon, Lord Poxton," she added as Lord Poxton, who was clearly nervous and embarrassed by Lady Nettlehurst's rudeness, bowed and mumbled some polite words.

Lady Nettlehurst's eyes snapped with anger. Nell could see

Lady Nettlehurst was not used to her shrill demands being met so tranquilly.

Unhurriedly, she began to lead her visitors to the study. Lady Nettlehurst pushed past her and stopped at the threshold, taking in the whole scene before her.

Papa and Lord Langdon got up from their chairs, but Clarissa and Darcy were kissing again, apparently oblivious to the world.

"Clarissa, you wicked girl, stop that at once!" Lady Nettlehurst shrieked. "Do you forget you are promised to Lord Poxton?"

Clarissa started to get up, then settled herself back beside Darcy. "No, Mama. I'm not going to marry Lord Poxton, and I'm not going to go home with you either."

Lady Nettlehurst stood dead still for a moment, angry red splotches appearing on her cheeks. "What did I just hear?"

"She will not go with you, and I challenge anyone to try to force her!" Darcy said with a menacing look at Lord Poxton.

"Oh, no, if the lady's affections are otherwise engaged, I would be the last man in the world to force my suit on her, I assure you!" answered Lord Poxton, cravenly trying to edge out the door.

Lady Nettlehurst seized his arm and held on to it tightly, preventing his escape.

"You cannot run away like this, Lord Poxton! I assure you my daughter will come to her senses when I have her home."

"Madam, I will not allow Adam's sister to be so bullied," said Lord Langdon. "It would be useless, moreover, for all you will do is incite this foolish pair to elope. If you do not wish to court that scandal, you should listen to what I have to say."

Lady Nettlehurst glared at him and said, "Nothing you could say will convince me to give my consent to such a marriage. What? A girl of my Clarissa's beauty to be wasted on a paltry mister?"

"Who's a paltry mister?" boomed a hearty voice from the doorway.

Twenty-five

Nell turned around and saw Colonel Huntley and Lady Langdon standing behind her, both smiling, but dusty as if they had been traveling.

"We tried knocking, but no one answered," said Colonel Huntley. "Quite a party going on in here if I may say so."

"I am sorry. I didn't hear you. It been rather noisy in here," said Nell.

"We have just gotten back from London," explained Colonel Huntley. "The most amazing rumors are flying about the village, so we thought we'd come here to find out what's afoot."

"Oh, you must be tired and thirsty," said Nell. "Please sit down, Lady Langdon, and you too, Lady Nettlehurst. Can I bring you anything? Would you like some sherry?"

Nell bustled about, seating Lady Langdon and Lady Nettlehurst in the only chairs with which the room was furnished. Darcy and Clarissa looked comfortable in the window seat; and Nell hoped the other gentlemen would not mind standing while they untangled the rest of this coil. She perched on the desk as Papa poured sherry for himself and the latest arrivals. Lady Nettlehurst coldly declined any refreshment.

"First you must tell us what *you* have both been doing," said Lord Langdon to Lady Langdon and Colonel Huntley after everyone had settled themselves. "You say you have been to London? When did you set out?"

"The cockerels were all still asleep when we left. Lady Langdon was in quite a hurry, you see."

"You drove to London and back in one day?"

"Yes, we did. Darcy, those are some fine horses you sold me. They made it all the way to Billingshurst in under an hour and a half. Of course, we had to change horses then, but we made it to London in four-and-a-half hours! It took us a little longer to get back, for—"

"So it *was* you!" interrupted Lord Langdon, laughing. Nell watched him, bewildered. "My stepmother was the young lady you ran off with!"

"What are you talking about? Who did you think it was?" asked the colonel. "Lady Langdon had an urgent errand in London and I was happy to convey her there."

"Lady Nettlehurst was convinced it was Darcy running off with her daughter. But I can't understand why you had to go to London in such hurry. I hope he did not tire you out too much, ma'am?"

"Not at all! I never enjoyed anything so much!" said Lady Langdon, her eyes glowing.

"It is my belief it was all a plot to divert us from finding my daughter!" said Lady Nettlehurst.

"Oh, has Clarissa run away then?" asked Lady Langdon. "I can't say I blame her in the least, but I assure you, Lavinia, we had nothing to do with it!"

"However, we do ask your assistance, ma'am, in providing a refuge for Clarissa at Charlwood," said Lord Langdon.

"Of course! I shall be most happy to welcome you to Charlwood, my dear."

"This is most improper!" protested Lady Nettlehurst, looking daggers at Lady Langdon. "Before today I would never have believed that a lady of quality would lend herself to such an outrage, but now my eyes are opened indeed. I should not be surprised at such behavior in a lady capable of such hoydenish conduct as driving to London and back in one day without a female attendant in an open carriage—at her age, too! I cannot imagine why I ever wished my daughter to ally herself with such a depraved set of individuals. Understand, I will never permit her to marry Darcy. A fop, a gamester, a good for nothing without a title or an estate! Are you listening to me?"

Nell looked around. During Lady Nettlehurst's tirade, Clarissa and Darcy had gone back to kissing one another. Papa, flinching at the volume of Lady Nettlehurst's tirade, had poured himself another sherry. Colonel Huntley had beckoned to Lord Langdon, and the two gentlemen, together with Lady Langdon, had withdrawn to the doorway, where they held a whispered discussion. It seemed they held a brief debate, but quickly resolved it.

"Why, yes, ma'am, we do hear you," said the earl. "We can't help but hear you. I must tell you now that Darcy's circumstances are not so mean as you seem to believe. It is true he has no title, but he will be the owner of a very pretty estate in Kent called Broadoaks."

"Broadoaks! Yes, I know. A burned-out ruin. It will take a fortune to restore it to a decent state," she answered.

"Fortunately, we are now in a position to do so."

Nell started and wondered what he meant by that remark. Oh dear, was he thinking of using her supposed fortune to help Darcy and Clarissa? She couldn't help feeling hurt and irritated at the thought of his commandeering her nonexistent money without so much as a by-your-leave.

But he met her challenging look with a puzzled one, and she wondered if she was wrong. Perhaps he had another plan.

Meanwhile, Lady Langdon exclaimed, "Yes, Broadoaks would make the most handsome wedding present!" She smiled at Darcy and Clarissa. "What do you think, my dears?"

"It would be more wonderful than anything!" said Clarissa.

"That's famous, James. Thanks so much!" added Darcy. And they both embraced exuberantly.

"Not so fast," said Lord Langdon. "Darcy, I will give you Broadoaks on one condition. I found the estate there to be in a bad way. You must go there now to supervise both the repairs to the house and to start doing whatever needs to be done to make the estate profitable again. If I am satisfied with your progress after a year, Broadoaks is yours. If you succeed, and prove faithful to Clarissa for that time period, I trust that Lady Nettlehurst will withdraw her objections to your marriage."

He looked over at Lady Nettlehurst, who had been clenching

and unclenching her hands as she listened. Nell could see she was wavering, but still unhappy about the offered compromise.

"My dear Lady Nettlehurst," said Papa, "I truly believe you should listen to Lord Langdon. His plan has great merit."

"And what happens to Clarissa?" asked Lady Nettlehurst of Lord Langdon, rudely ignoring Nell's father. "You will not have her living at Charlwood with you for a whole year!"

"If need be, we will," answered Lord Langdon. "It is what Adam would have wished me to do."

"Pardon me, Lord Langdon, but I think I would prefer to go stay with my aunt Jane, in Tonbridge Wells," offered Clarissa unexpectedly. "She was ever so kind to me before she and Mama quarreled and stopped speaking to one another."

"Stay with your aunt Jane! How could you, after all I have tried to do for you?" shrilled Lady Nettlehurst.

"Aunt Jane it is then," said Lord Langdon agreeably.

Nell saw a defeated look finally begin to enter Lady Nettlehurst's eyes. At the same time, however, the color intensified in her cheeks. Nell hoped she wouldn't go into an apoplexy. Mercifully, she seemed to be at a loss for words, at least for the moment.

"Ahem!" Lord Poxton said and cleared his throat several times until Nell and everyone else looked at him. "I wish you both well," he continued, addressing himself to Darcy and Clarissa. "Of course I am most disappointed in not securing Miss Nettlehurst's affections. You will all be happy to hear, however, that I do not believe I am inconsolable. Perhaps, if I may say so, I made a mistake in seeking such a young albeit lovely bride. I am convinced now that instead I should seek an older lady, one whose elegance and refinement, whose social standing and talents as a hostess would make her a fitting companion for a man of my years and experience."

He concluded his speech with a meaningful look directed at Lady Langdon, who promptly succumbed to girlish giggles.

Colonel Huntley put an arm around Lady Langdon. Jovially, he said, "Sorry to disappoint you once again, Lord Poxton, but I must inform you that you are looking at my wife-to-be."

Nell smothered a chuckle as she saw the disappointment on

Lord Poxton's fat face. But he soon recovered his poise, joining the rest of the company, with the exception of Lady Nettlehurst, in offering congratulations.

Nell directed an eager, inquiring glance at Lady Langdon.

The countess nodded. "Yes, Nell. Edward is the suitor my parents sent away so many years ago. I know now I should have trusted him before, but he has forgiven me, and we are so happy! I expect you and James have some exciting news as well if what we heard in the village is correct?"

Nell looked at Lord Langdon and blushed, realizing the children must have spread word of their kiss. Smiling, he nodded in answer to Lady Langdon's question.

Nell saw her father smile. Everyone began to congratulate her and Lord Langdon, but their polite words were quickly drowned in Lady Nettlehurst's scream.

"Oh! You designing hussy!" she hissed, darting out of her chair toward Nell. "Pretending to be so innocent and convincing us all you were in love with Darcy when all the time you were scheming after his brother. So that is why you delayed in accepting Darcy's proposal, practically encouraging him to form another attachment. If it were not for you, you snake, my Clarissa would be a countess today!"

Bemused, Nell saw Lady Nettlehurst prepare to slap her. But before Lady Nettlehurst could do so, Lord Langdon caught her hand and forced it down. "One more word against Miss Ashley and I will throw you out on your ear! Edward, may I have your assistance please? I think Lady Nettlehurst would like to leave. And, Darcy, perhaps you can show Lord Poxton to the door."

Colonel Huntley stepped forward and seized Lady Nettlehurst's other arm. She gabbled furiously but incoherently as the two men half carried her out of the room, closely followed by Darcy, who looked pleased to be escorting Lord Poxton off the premises.

Nell saw that Papa was looking relieved but tired, so she urged him to sit back down in his favorite chair, the one Lady Nettlehurst had just vacated.

"I am so sorry, Nell," said Clarissa. "I wish Mama would not say such things."

"You needn't apologize. You are not to blame for what your mother said."

"No, and you won't have to blush for her rudeness any longer," said Lady Langdon with a twinkle. "You are with us now, although I hope you do not mind consorting with such a depraved group of individuals!"

"We've routed the enemy," said Colonel Huntley, reentering the room. "I don't mind saying those are two people I'm not sorry to see the back of."

"Thank you for fixing everything," said Darcy. "But I have to ask how you are going to—"

"I'll explain it all later," said Lord Langdon, looking back at Nell. His look plainly said he wanted to be alone with her again.

"Well, my dears," said Lady Langdon. "I think it is time for us all to go back to Charlwood. It has been a very exciting day, and we will all be better for our dinners."

"Yes, my love. An excellent idea. I'm famished—always was after a battle," said the colonel. "That is, if you two doves have finished billing and cooing over there."

This remark mobilized Darcy and Clarissa. Poor Papa got up one more time to bow as the party left. Nell urged him to sit back down and open a book while she and Lord Langdon saw the others out.

As they turned to go back into the house, Lord Langdon put his arm around Nell's waist again. "I think it is time we spoke to your father, don't you?" he asked as they walked back toward the study.

"Yes. But there is still something I must tell you."

He looked down at her, and a ghost of his earlier anxiety reappeared in his expression. "What is it, my love?"

The warmth in his voice reassured her. She paused to gather her thoughts, but then, the silence was broken by a gentle snore. Peering into the study, she saw Papa had fallen asleep in his chair.

"Poor Papa," she said with a chuckle. "He is quite worn out by the excitement. Shall we go to the garden to talk?"

Twenty-six

Nell led Lord Langdon through the kitchen past Hannah's curious eyes and into the garden. Once outside, she turned toward him.

"Lord Langdon—"

"Please call me James."

"James," she said and took a deep breath. "I hope you will not be too disappointed when I tell you this. I'm afraid you and Darcy have misunderstood the size of my dowry. I'm not my uncle Joshua's only heir. I will only have about two thousand pounds when I marry."

"I've always known that. What does it signify?" Then he turned, gripping her shoulders tightly. She didn't mind, for his words banished the final trace of doubt in her heart. "You didn't think I wanted to marry you for your uncle's fortune, did you? Was that why you refused me then?"

"Yes. I'm sorry," she said. "Please forgive me for misjudging you. I didn't want to believe it, but after what Lady Langdon said, and Darcy—"

"Darcy!" he said, frowning. "That explains everything. He paid court to you only to get out from under my control. The scoundrel! I'll flay him alive for this!"

"Perhaps he started that way, but later I think he did it to try to help you, because he knew you needed the money."

"Still worse!"

"Please don't be angry. It doesn't signify now, does it?" she said coaxingly.

He relaxed, taking her back into his arms. "No, it doesn't. We have more important things to discuss. Shall we sit down?"

They walked over to the bench, but when Nell tried to sit down beside the earl, he would have none of it, drawing her onto his lap instead. She blushed a little, but leaned against him willingly as he wrapped his arms around her. How could something feel so comfortable and yet at the same time so exhilarating?

Tempting as it was to lose herself in the delight of his embrace, she remembered she still had questions to ask him. "So why did you come here today then?" she asked, turning slightly so she could look into his eyes. "It wasn't to look for Darcy, was it?"

His face reddened, and she continued before he could answer. "You thought it was I who ran off with Edward, didn't you?"

He nodded. "I told myself that, at first. It seemed so likely, based on what you had said to me before. Edward's circumstances, so much more comfortable than my own! I hadn't thought anything could hurt so much. But then I found I couldn't believe it. I was convinced that there had to be another explanation. I was right, thank God!"

He tightened his embrace. Softly, he said, "Please forgive me for having misjudged you. Mistrust has ruled my life for many years, but I hope to do better with your help."

"I forgive you," she said, and smiled. "How could I not when I have been so very foolish myself? But at least I know my own heart now. I can't imagine how I ever thought myself in love with your brother. Which reminds me, there's one more thing I don't understand. If you were not expecting to use my fortune, how will you be able to rebuild Broadoaks?"

"My stepmother has taken care of that. That was why she and Edward ran off to London. She sold her jewelry and wanted to return in time to surprise me with the proceeds. I didn't want to take it, but she insisted, saying her debts had contributed to all our troubles and she wanted to make amends."

"I'm sure Colonel Huntley will buy her some more if she

wishes. But I don't think she needs jewelry to make her happy now."

"Now back to more important matters," he said and gave her a kiss. "Will you marry me?"

She kissed him back before answering, "Yes."

James tightened his hold on Nell again, pressing her up against his chest. He gave her another kiss. This time slowly, deeply, thoroughly, savoring the taste and fragrance of her, like mingled musk and honeysuckle. She twined her arms around him and lightly fluttered her tongue against his, and he groaned with the maddening pleasure of her sweet, tentative caresses.

She broke the kiss and looked at him with an adorably confused expression. "I'm sorry. Did I do something wrong?"

"No," he said, touching his forehead to hers. "You just don't know how much I've been longing to do this. I don't know how I shall be able to wait another month to make you mine."

"Papa knows the bishop at Chichester. We could get a special license," she offered.

"Don't tempt me!" he answered with a low laugh. "No, my love. We will marry in a month with sufficient pomp and celebration so that everyone will know how proud and happy I am to have you as my wife."

"You mean people will talk about us and even more so if we appear to be in a rush to marry," she said, nodding her understanding. "Perhaps you're right, but I would brave the gossip if you wanted me to."

He was about to show how much he appreciated her willingness when he heard the sound of a throat clearing. Nell turned in his lap, and beyond her, he saw the vicarage cook bobbing a curtsy. Nell made a slight move to slide off his lap, then settled when he maintained his hold on her.

"May it please your lordship, there's a roasted chicken, some peas, and some raspberry tarts if you were wishful to stay to dinner," announced the cook in the overloud voice of the deaf.

"That would be excellent," he replied. "Thank you."

"Has Papa woken up?" asked Nell, watching her cook as if she could not believe her eyes.

"Yes, but he's gone off to bed now. I've laid two places in

the dining parlor. Your dinner will be ready in two shakes of a lamb's tail." The cook bobbed another curtsy and walked back into the vicarage.

Nell watched until she was almost into the house, then turned back and said, "I've never seen Hannah behave this way before. After all her lectures on the depravity of men and the proper way of dealing with them—"

"It is perfectly proper to sit on the lap of one's future husband."

"It is, is it?" she asked, laughing. "Shall we go in? Are you hungry?"

"Famished," he admitted. "But just one more kiss before we go in."

But one led to another, and so they sat a little longer in the evening glow, under the apple trees laden with ripening fruit, before they rose and, their arms still entwined around each other, walked into the vicarage.

Epilogue

"We do employ several gardeners, you know."

Nell looked up from her kneeling position to see James standing a few feet away, a mixture of laughter and concern on his face.

"But where would be the pleasure in gardening if I couldn't get my own hands dirty sometimes?" she said, setting the last seedling into its place and firmly pressing the earth around it.

"I just hope you are not overexerting yourself."

He helped her as she rose unsteadily to her feet.

"It's not the gardening. It's the getting up afterward that is tiring," she answered with a chuckle.

He hugged her from behind as she surveyed her work. She'd been so excited this past winter when she'd found the plans for this new border among some of his mother's gardening books. She'd eagerly anticipated the spring when she'd be able to bring to life what the earlier countess had died before completing.

"It is not much to look at yet, but I assure you in a few months this will be very beautiful."

"Mmmm . . . yes, very beautiful," he said, moving to one side of her, the corners of his eyes crinkled in a smile. He was not looking at the flower bed at all.

She smiled back. If he thought she was beautiful now, just two months from the birth of their child, why should she tell him any differently?

He moved a hand up to caress her breast. She gasped and

leaned back against him. Her breasts were exquisitely sensitive these days, and he took a wicked delight in fondling them and enjoying her breathless reaction.

"Perhaps I do need to lie down for a while," she said.

Instantly he stopped.

"Only if you will join me," she added with a deliberately provocative glance.

"You are certain?" he asked, those beloved blue eyes of his darkening with anticipation. He always asked now, but thank heaven, she'd managed to convince him it would do no harm to her or the baby.

She nodded, then let out a little shriek as he swept her up in his arms. Soon she stopped protesting, delighting in the feel of his strong arms bearing her swiftly up the terrace and into the house. In the joy and love that shone in his eyes. The love that had started this child and the anticipation of more loving still to come.

ABOUT THE AUTHOR

Elena Greene lives with her family in New York. *Lord Langdon's Kiss* is her first Regency romance and she is currently working on her second. She loves to hear from readers and you may write to her c/o Zebra Books. Please include a self-addressed envelope if you wish a response.